DARK PLACES

ANTHONY GIANGREGORIO

DARK PLACES

Table of Contents

LAST STOP

The Boston subway system is one of the oldest underground train systems in the world. In the past two hundred years, the tunnels have slowly grown into hundreds of miles of twisting, turning shafts of darkness; cut into the earth like jagged cylinders, like crystals constantly growing until they threaten to consume their entire surroundings.

Tunnels have been closed and others added. Sometimes in the interest of progress, new tunnels are built under old ones, the subway system constantly burrowing deeper and deeper into the earth like a bunch of manic moles.

Sometimes, man goes too far.

Sometimes things better left undisturbed can be awakened.

And once awakened, it's possible these things may never rest again.

*   *   *

Jonathan Ramsey sighed and shifted the weight of his young son onto his other hip. His son was going on five and was starting to get heavy. Either that or Jonathan was getting older and just couldn't manage to carry his growing son like he had when he was first born.

Walking into Government Center, he slid his T pass into the slot and pushed through the turnstile.

He glanced into the ticket booth where there would normally be a ticket agent for the subway, but true to form, it was empty. He checked his watch one more time to make sure he wouldn't be late for the last train out of Boston for the night.

It was 12:45 am.

Good, he still had fifteen minutes.

Walking down the wide stairwell with a metal railing in the middle, he headed down to the platform that would take him home; to his house and empty bed.

But first he would have to reach his waiting car, parked at Wellington Station in Medford, and then drive home another twenty minutes that would see him pulling into his driveway.

This was supposed to have been his day off, and so he had given the babysitter some much needed time off as well. He had been called in to work to fix some problem with the server. Though he hadn't wanted to, he really had no choice in the matter, and so had brought his son with him, letting the boy play with a few action figures he kept in his desk drawer for just such an occurrence.

He was a widower, his wife dying in a fatal car accident over a year ago.

Now it was just him and his son, Billy. He looked down at the angelic face of his sleeping son, the boy's head resting on his shoulder, while he walked onto the train platform and sighed.

Even at his son's young age, Jonathan could see so much of his wife in the boy's face.

Billy was all he had left of the love of his life. Billy had been the only thing keeping him grounded when he had found out that fateful night a year ago that his wife was dead. He had been so overcome with loss, he had reached the point he may have actually eaten his gun, the one he kept in a lockbox under his bed, but then Billy had come into the bedroom and asked what was wrong.

Realizing he had to stay strong for his son, he had placed the revolver back into his bureau draw and had never looked back.

He had a son, dammit!

He couldn't afford to be so selfish, to kill himself, even if it would end his pain.

Then what would happen to Billy?

He had hugged his son and had delicately tried to explain the nuances of his mother never coming back. That Billy would never see her alive again, but would see her in Heaven some day, that she was waiting for them both.

Billy had, of course, cried, and the two of them had sat on her side of the bed and cried together long into the night until both of them had finally succumbed to exhaustion and had fallen into a restless slumber.

Now, almost a year later, he had learned to manage his grief, only now the loss would sneak up on him at odd times, usually in the middle of the night when he would get up to use the bathroom. He would return from the bathroom and sometimes see her hump of a sleeping body on her side of the bed, but then he would blink and the mirage would disappear like a light snow falling on warm asphalt.

The sound of the train approaching pulled him from his reverie and he took a step toward the painted red line that lined the edge of the platform. It was two feet away from the edge, actually, and he had learned long ago not to cross it. A regular denizen of the city, he had heard countless horror stories about men and women getting struck by the train or just plain falling off the platform, sometimes pushed, to be ground into putty by the train's metal wheels.

And then there were all those stories about the third rail.

Checking around to make sure no one was near him, he waited as the train slowed and came to a halt. The platform was far from empty and he studied the few other people waiting for the train with him. There was a young woman, around his age waiting near the tunnel that would lead to the other side of the station. She had brown hair and a pretty face. She was covered by a heavy jacket and so he couldn't see if she was trim or fat, not that it mattered really, but he was still a male and would admire beauty when he came across it.

On his opposite side was a man in his late forties. He wore a three-piece suit and a gray overcoat over his outfit. In his right hand was a briefcase and in his left was a cell phone, which the man was actively using, his voice echoing off the dirty tile walls. The man had his hand to his ear, and Jonathan couldn't help but admire the handsome timepiece he wore on his wrist. That was how you got mugged on the subway, flashing that kind of bling around. Jonathan couldn't help but wonder who the man could be talking to so late at night.

Perhaps a girlfriend or wife maybe?

The train came to a stop on the platform, the wind of its arrival ruffling Billy's hair. Jonathan brushed the few errant blonde hairs that fell over his son's eyes and prepared to enter the car.

The doors opened with a lilting, *cling, clang,* and then he was inside.

The operator of the train, a few cars up in his stall, mumbled the next stop into the speaker and then the train was off once more. Jonathan sat near one of the doors, gazing out the tinted, tempered glass windows. As the train rocked back and forth gently, like a sea-going vessel, he couldn't help but read the advertisements spread out overhead on the curved corners of where the ceiling met the walls.

He was a captive audience after all, just as the advertisers knew he would be. He saw an ad for Night College. Earn a degree in his spare time, it read in bold letters. Another one told all who read it of equality, no matter what the color of their skin or ethnic background; reminding him of Sesame Street for some strange reason. Maybe it was because he watched the show so often with his son. He didn't mind it actually, remembering it from when he was a kid. But Barney was another story. That show made him want to shoot himself in the head all over again but for very different reasons.

Looking back up at the ads, he saw another one was for some cleaning solution that did everything but make you dinner.

He closed his eyes and stopped reading, though the pictures still seemed to spin around inside his head.

Deciding he wouldn't be resting anytime soon, he opened his eyes and decided to people-watch a little. Across from him, five seats up, was an older man in his late seventies. He was wearing a plaid coat and his nose was buried in a newspaper. Despite the man's advanced age, he looked fit, the hands holding the newspaper strong, not looking frail and thin like many other men of his similar age. He had a long face like a Bassett hound and his hair was brown with a few streaks of gray that only made him look more mature, or scholarly.

Jonathan looked to his right to gaze at the two remaining passengers in his particular car. The first was a young business woman in a gray power suit, her hair tied up in a bun. She sat with an open folder in her lap. If Jonathan was right, she looked like a lawyer or perhaps a legal aide. She had on a pair of slim wire glasses and despite the professional getup, she was beautiful.

The second passenger was very obviously a bum or homeless person. He was stretched out at the front of the car, his body covering five seats, and he was snoring contently, his back to anyone who was watching him.

The woman in the power suit crossed her legs, one of the pant legs riding up to show a large amount of well-toned skin. Jonathan stared at the shapely leg, admiring the contours. If her leg was that attractive, then what would the rest of her look like unclothed?

For just a moment, Jonathan felt something in his loins he hadn't felt in almost a year. Feeling dirty for even thinking such a thing, still too much in love with his late wife to even consider dating, he turned away to gaze back out the dark windows; nothing on the other sides of them but stone as the train shot through the miles of tunnels.

The train slowed at its next stop and the doors swung open with the expected *cling, clang.*

No one entered his car, but when he glanced through the windows at the rear of the car and into the next one, he saw two teenagers wearing black leather coats step aboard. One carried a guitar case and the other a paper bag with the writing, *Newbury Comics* on it. He knew there was one near State Street and figured the boys must have shopped there earlier in the night.

As the train pulled away from the platform, the two boys laughed and sat down; talking together about God knew what. The train operator muffled the next stop into the speaker.

Jonathan looked away then, remembering what it was like to be seventeen with the world in front of him, all the potentials of life like fruit from a tree just waiting to be plucked.

He looked down at the face of his sleeping son and decided things weren't so bad. Sure, he had lost his wife, but at least he still had his son.

The door separating one car from another opened with a loud thump and a man in a Transit Policeman's uniform stepped through. He was tall, slightly over six feet, definitely, and his wide shoulders and muscular forearms—easily discernable under his leather jacket—only added to the picture of masculinity and confidence.

His heavy black work boots echoed in the empty car as he moved down the center aisle. As the man moved closer, Jonathan's eyes went like a magnet to the handgun holstered to his belt. The cop had a radio on his belt and frivolous chatter could be heard coming from it; though hard to make out clearly with the noise of the rolling train.

When the cop reached Jonathan, he nodded politely, actually smiling slightly at the sight of the sleeping boy in Jonathan's arms. Now that he was closer, Jonathan looked again at the man's handgun and the picture of a steer that was embossed on the holster.

Then the cop was at the next door for the following car. He stopped and glared down at the bum, but did nothing, leaving the sleeping man alone. Then he opened the door and slid through.

Jonathan watched him talk to the two teenagers in the next car for a few seconds and then move on. One of the boys gave the cop the finger when the large man's back was to him and despite himself, Jonathan found himself chuckling at the sight.

The older man across from him looked up from his newspaper, wondering what was so amusing, but when Jonathan smiled at him and controlled himself, quieting his snickering, the man went back to his paper, digging his nose into the folds of pulp like a dog seeking warmth in the creases of a blanket.

With nothing much to hold his attention, Jonathan closed his eyes and tried to rest again. The gentle rocking of the train lulled him into a false sense of security, and only the weight of his son on top of him kept him from sleeping.

The train pulled into the next stop and the doors opened wide. Seconds ticked by, but no one boarded. Then, just as the doors began to close, Jonathan heard voices on the platform and looked up to see three more passengers step into the car behind him. The one with the two teenagers in it.

The doors closed and the train began rolling again. As the train left the station, Jonathan looked up at the map on the wall. They had just left the last stop in the city, Aquarium station now behind them. The next stop would be six miles away, the tunnel actually going deep underground as it made its way to the suburbs.

Jonathan studied the three new passengers. Two were male and one was female, all different ages ranging from twenty to forty. They were all Spanish, and if Jonathan had to guess, he would have figured they were a few of the thousands of workers that went into Boston every night as part of the hundreds of cleaning crews that would clean the buildings after the office workers had gone home for the night.

In his building alone, there were more than twenty cleaners, all happy people who seemed to work hard and enjoyed their jobs.

He smiled as he watched them in the next car. They were all talking together, but due to the divider of the car doors, all he could see was their mouths moving and sometimes their hands waving as they tried to make a point with one another.

The teenage boys were quiet now, as they too, watched the three newcomers in their car.

Jonathan leaned back and tried to relax. It would be fifteen or twenty minutes before the train reached Wellington station.

He closed his eyes and tried to get comfortable when he began to feel a rumbling.

At first he just assumed it was the car rolling along, but he soon realized it was something else. As he looked around the car, he saw the pretty woman in the power suit and the old man also looking around, trying to discern the cause of the rumbling.

As for the bum, he still slept, blissfully unaware of his surroundings.

Jonathan was sitting upright in his seat now, but all there was to see was the blackness outside the glass windows. They were now a mile or so from the station they had departed and at least a few hundred feet underground, the train still rolling along.

Then a mighty roar filled the inside of the car, sounding like an earthquake or a bomb had gone off, and the car seemed to jump off the tracks. Jonathan reached out, grabbing a nearby pole—put there for just such an occurrence—when a loud screeching sound filled the car, tearing apart the white noise of the train's wheels rolling on the tracks.

The train lurched forward, throwing Jonathan and the other passengers across the car like feathers in the wind. Something heavy fell on top of the car in front of the one he was in, and the entire world seemed to explode with light and sound.

Petrified, not understanding what was happening, he cradled Billy to his chest and rolled across the floor, his back coming up hard against the door at the front of the car. Glass shattered in some of the small, five inch upper windows as the car twisted on its frame.

Yelling filled his ears and he wondered if it was his voice or one of the other passengers in the car with him. Billy woke up then, screaming in fright as he saw there was something terribly wrong with his world.

Another body struck him, slamming into him hard and Jonathan wondered which of his other passengers it could have been. The lights in the car had flicked off and there was only darkness.

At first he thought there was nothing but silence surrounding him, but then he realized it wasn't that there was no noise, it was just that the amount of noise had decreased exponentially.

There was still a slight rumbling coming from both sides of the car he was in.

Not knowing what could possibly be happening, he lay still, holding his son, squeezing the small body tightly, trying to soothe him.

His shoulder ached from where he struck the door and he gritted his teeth, sucking up the pain. He needed to be strong for his son; at least until he knew what was happening.

The only thing he could think of that could have happened, was that the train had somehow become derailed, the entire train, cars and all, actually jumping the tracks to fall onto the rocks and stone of the tunnel floor.

There were moans of pain surrounding him, but with no lights, he could see nothing. But then small lights on the ceiling, and a few scattered near the floor, flickered on. Small emergency lights filled the car with a diffuse yellow glow. Dust clouds filled the car, smoke swirling in the circumference of the emergency lights' glow, and he had his first look at who had slid into him.

It was the old man.

The man had a small bruise on his forehead, but other than that appeared to be unharmed. With his free right hand, Jonathan gently pushed the man off him and to the side, letting the man's head slump onto his shoulder.

With the lights on, though dim, he was able to see that the car was still upright, though at a slight angle. Billy was still crying in his arms and he patted his head, telling him everything would be fine. Though he said this, he honestly prayed it would be so.

Another loud crashing sound came from somewhere outside the car and he felt the train rumble and vibrate from the shock. Vivid images of thousands of tons of earth falling through the roof to bury the train and all who were in it flooded into his mind, but he tried to keep those frightening images at bay. Billy stirred in his arms again, burying his head deeper into his chest.

Not knowing what else to do, he hugged his son tighter, wishing by his will alone he could make sure Billy stayed safe. Next to him, the old man was stirring, groaning, as he came back to the world of consciousness.

"Oh my God, what the hell happened?" he asked in a daze as he looked around the cockeyed train car.

"Don't know," Jonathan said. "I was just thinking the same thing myself."

From across the car, lying on the seats, was the woman in the power suit. She sat up, brushing her hair from her forehead as she tried to fix her suit, as if at a time like this how she looked mattered.

"It doesn't matter what happened," she stated briskly. "All we need to do is wait here for help to arrive. And let me tell you, someone's in for a lawsuit."

The old man chuckled at the first part of the woman's comment.

"Oh, you think so, do you? Listen to me, young lady, it's one o' clock in the morning. It's gonna take time for them to get to us. And while we're waiting, the whole damn tunnel could fall down on top of us. Thanks, but I think I'll see to myself. If I can make it through WW2, I think I can get out of here in one piece."

The woman pursed her lips in distaste, the inflection aimed at the old man. "You can do whatever the hell you want, mister, but I'm staying here."

Jonathan decided to try and keep the peace. "Look, please, both of you. Why don't we at least see what's happening before we go off half-cocked," he pleaded.

The old man frowned at him, but otherwise stayed quiet, deciding to inventory his body for damage.

As for the woman, she went back to fussing with her suit; brushing dust off her clothing like it would turn into acid and eat through to her skin if she didn't remove it quickly.

Jonathan tried to see through the glass windows of the car, hoping to see what had happened to them, but the black tint made it all but impossible. Every few seconds, a few sparks could be seen as a torn wire flashed and flickered in the darkness of the tunnel.

Billy was stirring in his arms and he looked down at his son's small face.

"Hey, how you doin'? Better I hope?" he asked his son.

Sniffling with bouts of hitched breaths, Billy nodded yes.

"I'm okay, Daddy. What happened? Did we crash? I thought there wasn't stuff down here that could hit us like when we drive in the car. You said so."

Jonathan smiled down at his son, wiping a tear off Billy's cheek with his sleeve.

"Yeah, son, I know I did. We just need to wait for help to arrive and then we'll be fine, you'll see."

"Yeah, right, you hope so. What if everyone has gone home or snuck out early and no one knows we're down here?" the old man asked accusingly.

Jonathan shot the old man an angry look, trying to stop him from talking. "Look, mister, will you please not talk like that around my son?"

The old man seemed to hesitate for a moment and then understanding flooded his face and his countenance softened. "Oh, gees, you're right, I'm sorry, I don't know what I was thinking." Then he looked over at Billy. "Don't worry, there, sonny, your father's right. We'll be fine; you just wait and see."

Jonathan shifted his weight, climbing to his knees. "Listen, Billy, I need to put you down so I can see what happened, okay?"

Billy squeezed him tighter, not wanting to be let go.

"It's all right, I promise. I just want to see if I can get one of the doors open, maybe see if there are other people that need our help."

Billy hesitated for a second, but then he relaxed his arms.

"You're sure you're not gonna leave me?" Billy asked in his tiny voice.

Jonathan nodded. "Uh-huh, I'm not going anywhere."

Billy let him go and sat back on one of the canted seats. "Okay, Daddy, but be careful."

Jonathan grinned at his son. "You bet I will," he said and then turned to look at the old man. "Hey, if you're all right, want to help me with the doors?"

The man dusted off his lap and stood up with a grin. "Happy to help, whatever will get us out of here sooner rather than later, I'm all for it."

"You're both wasting your time," the woman said. "Just stay put until help arrives."

Slightly annoyed, Jonathan turned to look at her. The woman's face was barely discernable in the wan light of the emergency lamps. "Yes, well, thank you for your opinion again, but I think we'll be fine," Jonathan told her brusquely.

The woman only shrugged her shoulders and began digging into her purse, taking out a cell phone and trying to use it. What a shock when she found no signal. In frustration, she tossed it back into the purse and dropped the bag onto the seat next to her, then she sat back and crossed her arms, deciding she would watch the show. As for the bum, he merely sat on the seat he had climbed onto after hitting the floor and he watched everyone silently. No one talked to him.

Jonathan and the old man moved to the doors on the left side of the car and tried to open them, but the doors were sealed tight. Jonathan put all of his muscle into opening it, his hands wrapped around the rubber gasket that lined the edge of each door, but nothing would budge.

After a full five minutes, he waved for them to stop. "Shit, they won't budge," he said to the old man.

"Told ya," the woman said briskly. Jonathan turned his head to glare at her, then decided what was the point.

That was when he heard something banging. "Hey, you hear that?" he asked the old man.

The man nodded, cocking his ear to the side.

"Yeah, I do. That's not mechanical. You can tell by the rhythm. That's got to be people."

"Come on, it's coming from the car in front of us," Jonathan said while moving back to the door he had slammed up against when the train had lurched to a halt.

The old man followed, and just before Jonathan reached the door, he took a moment to tussle his son's hair. Billy smiled up at him and giggled at the attention.

Jonathan got his hands on the door and yanked it open. The door opened with ease, sliding to the side, like a pocket door in a modern home.

Stepping over the small open area that separated the two cars from one another—only a small platform with large rubber walls that looked like the inside of an accordion on both sides—he opened the next door that would lead into the car in front of him.

Opening the door, he was shocked to see nothing but darkness, dust, and crushed metal.

"What the?" was all he could say. The emergency lights behind him weren't strong enough to penetrate into the next car, so he squinted his eyes a bit, trying to peer into the gloom.

Then the old man was next to him with a small Zippo lighter in his hand. Shoving the small flame forward, the lighter cast flickering shadows over the inside of the car, and they could see it was buried in rubble. The roof of the car had collapsed under the weight of the tunnel ceiling and tons of rock and dirt had fallen inside the car, in all likelihood killing anyone who had been unfortunate enough to pick that car to ride in.

"Oh my Lord, there must have been a cave-in. That's what we felt before, and it looks like the front of the train is buried under a shitload of rocks and dirt," the old man said in shock.

"Then that means..." Jonathan said in a hushed voice.

The old man nodded. "Yeah, that everyone on the train in front of us is probably dead."

But then the banging sounded again and both men looked at one another.

"Daddy, are you okay?" Billy called from a few feet behind him.

"Yes, son, I'm fine, just stay there. I'll be back in a minute," Jonathan called.

"'Kay," Billy replied.

Turning back to the car in front of him, the old man had already entered it, climbing over some of the large boulders. He had only reached a few feet into the car when he called out to Jonathan.

"Over here, I've found someone!" he called out frantically. "Help me with this thing, will ya?"

Jonathan climbed over the rubble and helped the old man move the four foot piece of sheet metal that had fallen in from the roof. The work was hard and the air was growing stale, filled with dust. The old man had jammed his lighter into a small outcropping of torn metal, and by the flickering light, the two men worked.

It was hot, sweaty work, but in ten minutes they managed to dislodge the piece of metal, shoving it off to the side. Jonathan looked down into a small hole to see a woman's dirty and frightened face looking up at him.

With eyes wide with terror, she reached out one shaking hand.

"Oh my God, thank God, I thought I was going to die under here. Please, help me," she said in a voice fraught with controlled panic.

Jonathan quickly scanned the area around her and made an educated guess. There didn't seem to be anything stopping the woman from just climbing up and out of the hole now that the roof piece was gone. She had been lucky, when the train had derailed, she had been tossed off her seat and had ended up rolling under the seats opposite her. When the roof had fallen in, she had been saved by the seats above her, all hard plastic and metal with steel pipes running the length for support.

Jonathan reached down with his hand. "Here, take my hand and I'll pull you up," he told her.

"I don't know; there's something holding my leg. I can move it, but I don't know if it's free."

Jonathan smiled the same reassuring smile he had just used on his son at the woman and kept his voice as calm as he could, trying to sound confident. "Well, we'll just have to see then, won't we?"

She smiled back, though it wasn't heartfelt, her terror still in full force. Jonathan found himself impressed with this woman though he knew nothing about her. She seemed strong and able to maintain a sense of calmness even though she was petrified inside.

With his hand dangling over her head, the woman reached up and wrapped her hand around his.

"You got her?" the old man asked from his side.

"Yeah, I got her, you just keep the light on so I can see," Jonathan told him.

"You got it, chief," the old man replied.

Jonathan began pulling her up and out of the hole, his eyes locked on hers, waiting for her to cry out that her leg was in pain from whatever had grasped it, but she only nodded that she was fine.

"Your leg?" he asked, not happy with the fact that she was halfway out of the hole and doing fine when she said there was something holding her. He had heard stories of people in earthquakes and other tragedies that had thought their lower parts were all right until they were removed from the rubble to find the limb was missing altogether.

"It's okay. There's still something on it, but it's not holding me back. There was a slight tug when you pulled me the first time, but now it's fine."

"Okay, good, let me know if there's a problem," Jonathan said.

She only nodded, the gesture barely seen in the flickering light of the Zippo.

Another minute of gentle pulling found him leaning backward as she scrambled out of the hole of wreckage. By luck alone, the debris had landed in such a way that she had been spared the total impact of the crushed roof. Overhead, where the ceiling of the car once was, the darkness of the tunnel couldn't be seen. The Zippo wasn't strong enough to penetrate it, but a few sparks shot out every few seconds, the severed wires making themselves known.

When the woman was entirely out of the hole, Jonathan stepped out of the way so she could stand up. There was almost no room from the wreckage to the door leading back to his car and he had to scurry back into the doorframe so she could fully stand up.

The old man had the Zippo in his hand again and he was moving it over the woman's body, checking for signs of wounds.

"I'm fine, really. I think I'd know if I was bleeding," she told him.

The old man shook his head. "Now, not so fast, there, missy, sometimes you can get some shrapnel in you and not even know it's there until infection sets in. Just hold still and let me check." He moved the lighter up and down her body and when he was inspecting her legs, he stopped and leaned back in surprise.

"What the hell...?" was all he said. "Hey, kiddo, come over here and see this," he told Jonathan.

Jonathan stepped over the rubble and leaned forward to see what was so interesting on the woman's leg. As he leaned in, the Zippo illuminated something long attached to her right ankle. As the old man placed the Zippo on top of the object, the object became clear as day, and Jonathan let out a small gasp and leaped back, afraid it would grab him. Which was totally irrational. He just guessed he'd watched far too many zombie movies.

The old man chuckled at him and then told the woman to hold still.

She did as she was told and the old man fidgeted on her ankle for a second, then he stood back up with the object in his hand. "Here's what had a hold of you, young missy," he said with a slight sadness to his voice.

The woman turned to see what was attached to her and she gasped in shock, her right hand covering her mouth.

In the old man's left hand was a severed arm, the end that connected to the shoulder torn skin and material from the suit sleeve it was in and nothing but thin bits of gristle hanging from the edge. As he held it in his hand, small drops of blood seeped from the end of the arm, and after he was sure everyone had seen it, he gently set it on top of the rubble.

"Holy shit, that's an arm. A human arm," Jonathan said in awe, his stomach rolling inside him.

The old man nodded. "Afraid so, must have been another rider who wasn't as lucky as you, miss," he said to the woman and made the sign of the cross. "Poor bastard, hope he's dead already."

"You mean he might not be?" Jonathan asked.

The old man shrugged, picking the arm up again and inspecting the end where it had been separated from its owner. "Depends; if the arm got pinched off when it came off then it's possible the wound might be sealed by the pressure of what's on top of the body. But chances are the guy bled out a few minutes after it happened; probably less." He sighed. "This is nothing. In the war I saw more body parts and dead bodies to last a hundred lifetimes. After you've been in the middle of that, well, this seems like a day at summer camp."

Jonathan stared at the severed arm and that was when he noticed the timepiece on the wrist. Though covered in blood, it was unmistakable. The arm had belonged to the man he had seen on the platform talking on his cell phone.

The old man shrugged and set the arm back down on top of the rubble.

"Why'd you do that? Seems a bit callous to just leave it there, doesn't it?" Jonathan asked.

"Why, did you need it?" the old man asked.

"Uh, well, I..." Jonathan stammered, not really having an answer. It just seemed like they should have held onto it--for evidence maybe.

"Do any of you know what happened to us?" the woman asked.

Jonathan and the old man stared at one another and then the woman.

"No, no idea, but hopefully help will be here soon to get us," Jonathan stated.

"Well, thanks for helping me. I don't know what I would have done if you hadn't come to my aid," she said to Jonathan and the old man, respectively.

Jonathan was struck by just how pretty she was. Even with her face and clothing covered in dust and dirt, she was very beautiful in a girl next door kind of way. As he helped her closer to the doorway, he realized he had seen her on the platform. And now he, her, and the rest of them were trapped in a cave-in.

In a less than a half hour, all their perspectives on life had shifted.

The old man waited while the man and woman gazed at each other and then he cleared his throat.

When both pairs of eyes were looking at him, he gestured to the demolished car.

"It looks like we can try to climb out through the torn roof, but I think at this point that's a risky proposition."

"Why?" the woman asked.

The old man pointed to the exposed wires hanging down from the ceiling, most of them sparking fitfully.

"Because if one of us tries to get through there and something shifts, they're likely to end up getting electrocuted, that's why."

Jonathan stared up at the wires, contemplating what would happen if he tried to slide through one of the two small holes in the ceiling. The rest of the roof was gone, crushed by falling rocks and debris. There would be no escaping that way anytime soon. Perhaps if the power was cut off, and even then, would the debris be stable enough to crawl over? Or would it all shift and swallow the climber whole.

The old man waved for them to head back to their former car.

"Come on; let's get back to our car. At least there we can breathe easier," he said and stepped through the doorway. It was true, once they had passed through the door and had closed it behind them, the air was infinitely better, though a little murkier now thanks to the dust that had seeped through the open door.

The woman stepped into the car and immediately sat down on a seat. Billy was only three seats away from her and he watched her intently, almost like he was studying her. The woman noticed after a few seconds that she was being watched and smiled at Billy. "Hello, there, what's your name?"

"I'm Billy," he said in a soft voice. His dad had always told him not to talk to strangers, but he had been scared waiting for his dad, and the other lady in the car and the dirty man who were with him had said nothing to him.

Jonathan sat down next to his son and hugged him. "This is my son, Billy, and I'm Jonathan, by the way."

"Oh, of course. You two saved me and I haven't even introduced myself.

She pointed to her chest with a dirty hand. "I'm Trudy, Trudy Harcourt."

Jonathan grinned her way. "Nice to meet you, Trudy." Then he looked over to the old man who had taken a seat across from him.

"How 'bout you, sir, what's your name?" Jonathan asked him.

The old man shrugged slightly, but in the pallid light from the emergency lights, it was hard to see the gesture.

"You can call me Eddie," he said flatly.

"All right, nice to meet you, Eddie," Jonathan said in return.

"Listen, if you guys are through with the introductions, then how 'bout we figure out what to do next." the woman in the power suit exclaimed from the opposite end of the car, now changing her tune and wanting to be part of the group. "Surely someone should have come by now," she finished.

Just then the door behind her was pushed open and people began flooding into the car with them along with small bits of rocks and debris.

Jonathan stood up, telling Billy to stay in his seat.

From the rear of the car, Jonathan saw the faces of the people he had seen boarding the train when they had pulled into the last stop before departing the station. Covered in dirt and dust, he saw the two teenagers stumble into the car, and behind them were the three Spanish people, the man and the two women. He noticed now that they were closer to him, that each wore a blue jacket with their company's logo on it. He recognized the SSC as one of the many cleaning company's in the city. He had been right, they were building cleaners.

But it was the last man who entered that had Jonathan hoping for the best.

In the wan light, the T cop strode into the car. He was standing tall and his jaw was set tight. He was in total control of the situation, whatever the situation might be.

Holding his hands up in front of him, he tried to regain some order inside the car.

"All right, people, please stay calm. We had to come in here and join you because our car has collapsed in on itself. Luckily, we were all able to get to the front before it came down on our heads. It took us some time to clear the door, but here we are."

"Do you know what's going on, Officer?" Jonathan asked in a concerned voice, hoping the man did.

The cop moved through the aisle, gently shifting people to the side so he could pass. When he reached Jonathan, he looked down at him.

"I'm not really sure, sir, my radio's out, but it looks like there's been a cave-in."

"A cave-in? How the hell did that happen? For Christ's sake, this is Boston, not California," Power Suit Woman yelled at him.

The cop took the abuse in stride, a professional to the end. He knew to keep everyone as calm as possible for as long as possible. At least until help arrived.

"Now, miss, just try to stay calm and everything will be fine. We just have to wait for a rescue crew to come dig us out. This has only happened one other time here and that was in the early 1900's; and I believe everyone got out of there alive."

"Well, sorry to break your record there, sonny, but there's at least one dead already," Eddie said while he gestured to the front of the car.

"Are you sure about that, sir? Maybe they just need help," the cop said, moving towards the doorway that would lead to the next car.

"No, sorry to say it, but we're pretty sure the guy's dead. But it's not like we know for sure. All we found was his severed arm," Jonathan told the cop.

The cop's right eyebrow went up in curiosity, but he said nothing, only grunting. Though he did stop moving towards the door.

"I'm sorry to hear that, but other than that I believe we're it. Can we get out through the next car?"

"No, the whole thing's caved in. There's a few small holes in the ceiling through the rubble, but they're surrounded by sparking wires," Jonathan told him.

"Hmm, what about this door, can we get it open?" the cop asked, moving to the double doors that would be used for passengers to exit the train onto the platforms at the stations. There was another set of double doors on the opposite side of the car, as well, but both doors were connected to the same hydraulics.

"Be my guest, sonny, but we already tried and the damn thing's closed tighter than a straight man's ass in prison. Must have frozen when the power cut off," Eddie told him.

The cop ignored the old man's warning and began trying to force the doors apart single-handedly. He did manage to pry the doors open two inches or so, but then they snapped shut again, only the rubber molding keeping him from losing some fingers. "Dammit," he spit, angrily.

"See, I told you so," Eddie said, sitting back in his seat. "Though I hate to admit it, the lady over there is probably right and we'll just have to wait for a rescue."

The cop was about to reply when a scraping sound filtered in from outside the car. It sounded like someone had an axe in their hands and was drawing it across the base of the train.

"Wait, did you hear that?" Jonathan asked excitedly.

For a moment no one heard him, everyone talking to themselves. The two teenagers were arguing with Power Suit Woman and the three cleaners were speaking Spanish to one another, arguing about something, or so Jonathan thought by the way they were waving their hands in the air at one another.

"Dammit, listen to me, there's someone outside on the tracks!" Jonathan yelled, and this time voices stopped, as everyone listened intently, looking at the walls of the car.

"Just listen, I know I heard something, it sounded like scraping," he said again, and pulled Billy closer to him.

Now all were silent, only the steady sound of each person's breathing filling the air. With everyone quiet, the sounds of rubble shifting and metal creaking could now be heard as the wrecked train settled under the weight of the collapsed tunnel.

At first there were no other sounds outside the car, the noise stopping. Power Suit Woman was about to speak when the scraping began again. Every single person in the car held their breath, listening to the scraping. The sound felt like someone was scratching their fingernails over a chalkboard, causing Jonathan's insides to tighten up.

His throat moved slightly as he swallowed, his Adam's apple bobbing up and down. Then the cop went into action, banging on the door, and trying to get the rescuer's attention.

"Hey! We're in here! Hello, we're in here!" the cop called out and soon other voices joined his. As for Jonathan, he sat in his seat, hugging Billy. Next to him, Trudy slid closer to him and he reached out his hand to her; which she took. Something wasn't right, though he had no idea what it could be.

If there were rescuers out on the tracks, then why didn't any of them inside the car hear the work crews as they shifted the rubble to enter the tunnel? And why weren't there any lights shining into the tunnel, as the work crews illuminated the danger zone.

But all these questions were in the back of his mind, nothing tangible he could put his finger on.

Soon, other passengers were banging on the dark windows of the train, hoping to get the attention of the work crews coming to save them. The cop stood by the double doors, banging on them for help. In the middle of each door was a two foot long window, about a foot wide. These were made of the same material as the windows lining the walls of the train and were just there so passengers could see the feet of other people when the train would pull up at a brightly lit platform.

Jonathan sat in his seat, watching the cop bang on the door. The cop turned around then, as if he was going to say something to Jonathan, and right before Jonathan's eyes, like the flash of a camera going off, the left window on the door shattered, sending black crystals of tempered glass flying everywhere.

Jonathan looked away for a moment, protecting his eyes on instinct, his other hand covering Billy's face, and when he looked up again, the cop was screaming.

Like trying to shove a square peg into a round hole, the cop was being pulled through the small window by his waist.

In the shadows of the emergency lights, Jonathan could only see the briefest glimpse of claw-like hands wrapped around the cop's torso. The hands were yanking him backward, through the small hole, and the cop was far too large to fit.

With his mouth hanging open in shock, Jonathan watched the cop bend at the waist, like he was being folded, and then his ass was pulled into the broken window.

Screaming for help, blood shooting out of the cop's mouth like a geyser as his internal organs ruptured and compacted, his body was slowly pulled through the window inch by agonizing inch. The man was bent over, his head in-between his knees as he was yanked through the hole bit by bit.

That was when Jonathan broke free of his stupor, handed Billy to Trudy roughly, and lunged across the car, his right hand out to grab the cop's left hand. At the same time, one of the cleaners, the older man with a mustache, did the same thing, grabbing the cop's right hand.

With Jonathan and the cleaner holding on, they each tried to pull the cop back through the window. A scarlet jet of blood shot out of the cop's mouth again, bathing the cleaner in gore, and the man's grasp slipped as he shied away.

"Please...don't let...go..." the cop choked through blood, his face so red it looked like it was about to explode like a massive red pimple.

Even with the other passengers screaming and yelling from the sight of the man being yanked through the window, Jonathan could hear the popping and snapping of the cop's bones as he was slowly pulled further and further out of the train.

Jonathan struggled to hold on, but even as he was slowly pulled toward the window, he watched the light go out of the man's eyes. The cop's head slumped down as the massive trauma to his chest and heart finally reached its conclusion and he died.

Jonathan let go, and just as he did, there was one more mighty tug at the body and the cop slid through the window to be lost in the darkness. Running to the broken window, Jonathan looked out into the tunnel. It was almost pitch black, but the sparking wires would flash every so often, resembling lightning on a storm-tossed night.

He saw the cop's feet being dragged across the ground and he tried to see what had a hold of him, but all he could see were black shapes that seemed to blend into the darkness like chameleons.

Then the cop was gone from view and there was nothing to see. But there were sounds to hear. Cocking his head to the side, Jonathan could hear the sounds of feeding, of bones snapping and flesh being torn, though it was hard to know for sure, as the other passengers inside the car were freaking out, his son included.

Stepping away from the window, he ran to Billy, scooping him up in his arms and hugging him close; Trudy passing the boy to him easily.

"What the hell just happened, man? What the hell just happened?" the cleaner covered in blood asked, his accent heavy but easy to understand. "What the hell could do that to a man?"

Eddie was up as well, staring out the broken window.

"Jesus Christ, what the hell just happened here?" he whispered, his eyes never leaving the broken window. Around the edge of the window, blood dripped, vermilion rivulets that slid down the door to pool on the silver molding where the door met the floor.

"There's nothing alive that I know of that could do that, especially down here in the tunnels," Eddie said, taking a step back from the window. "This can't be real, it just can't."

"Oh my God, we're all gonna die down here. We're all gonna die!" Power Suit Woman yelled, wringing her hands in front of her in terror as she stared at the broken window.

It was Trudy who dealt with Power Suit Woman, walking over to her and slapping her across the face, the resounding slap echoing inside the car. Power Suit Woman looked up at Trudy, eyes wide with fear, but she stopped screaming, bringing her hand up to her face to touch where she'd been slapped. In the dull light of the car, a small red mark could be seen on her cheek. After that, a few of the others quieted down, also.

"Dammit, listen to me," Trudy said. "We have to stay calm. I don't know what's happening here, either, but whatever it is, we're not going to do anything about it by freaking out!"

Jonathan stood up then, Billy still in his arms.

"She's right," he said. "We need to stay focused. Find a way out of here and then escape the tunnel."

"But what about the cop, man? What about the fucking cop? Whatever just did that to him is out there? It could be waiting for us," the cleaner ranted while wiping blood from his face with a wrinkled handkerchief.

"That's true," Eddie said, now joining the conversation. The entire time the cop had been yanked through the door, he had merely stared, open-mouthed. "But it's probably just some crazy homeless guy that lives in the tunnel. After the cave-in, he must have freaked out and attacked the cop."

Jonathan gave that idea some thought for a moment. He decided not to say anything about the claws he'd seen, or thought he'd seen. To tell the truth, now that it was all over, he wondered if maybe he had just imagined it all and Eddie was right.

Hell, it would sure make a lot more sense, he reasoned. After all, what would be the alternative? Some kind of C.H.U.D.-like creatures running around the subway tunnels of Boston?

Ridiculous.

"Are you insane, old man? Whatever pulled that cop through the door sure as hell wasn't human. No way could a human being do that," the cleaner said, his voice filled with panic. "Unless the guy was high on PCP or smack or something."

Jonathan watched him talk, and as the man stepped under one of the emergency lights, he saw the name **Carlos** stitched on the left breast of his jacket.

"Look, Carlos," Jonathan said, trying to reason with the man. "Whatever we saw, it had to be a man. This is Boston for Christ's sake, not the Twilight Zone.

Carlos turned to stare at Jonathan. "Look, man, I don't really care what any of you people say. I know what I just saw. Ever hear of El Chupacabra? Well, I guess you got them here too. You just don't want to believe it."

Trudy turned to Jonathan. "El Chupacabra? What's that? It does sound familiar."

Eddie spoke up then. "It's a folk tale about monsters on the countryside. Mexican or Spanish I think. There's supposed to be this vampire-like creature that kills cows and sucks their blood. It's all a story to scare children into being good."

Carlos was talking to the other two people that were with him, the man and the woman. Jonathan figured out pretty quick that these two people didn't know English very well as Carlos was filling them in using Spanish on the topic of conversation presently being discussed. The woman answered back and Jonathan definitely heard El Chupacabra in her words, though he didn't understand much else.

Finally Carlos turned back to the others, his face set. "There, you see? Roselle agrees with me."

"What about the other guy? What does he say?" Eddie asked.

Carlos asked a few questions to the other man, and after a minute, Carlos turned back to Eddie. "Caesar doesn't have an opinion. He says it can't be true, but then what the hell just happened? He's willing to go with whatever decision the rest of us make. He's like that, easy going to the point it gets ridiculous."

At the sound of his name, Caesar nodded happily, as if he knew what Carlos was saying about him and agreed with all of it.

There was the sound of someone clearing his throat, followed by the sound of someone hawking up phlegm, followed by a spitting sound.

All eyes turned to see the man sitting by the rear door of the car. It was the bum. The entire time he had said nothing, just watching what everyone did and said. Now he spoke up, and as Jonathan stared at him, he saw a man that didn't look like he was all there.

"You people are all full of shit, you know that? I've been listening to you all talking back and forth and I can't take it anymore. Listen to me, all of you. I've lived in and around the subway for over ten years and I've seen some strange shit. The shit you won't hear about on the evening news. Some of the other guys I used to know went down into the lowest tunnels to stay warm in the winter, and come spring, no one ever saw them again. Sometimes there's been stories about people seeing these *things*. They look like us, but they're off, you know? They got long fingers like claws and their skin is all dark, so they can blend into the darkness. That's what happened to the cop. When the roof collapsed, it must have woke some of them up. It happens sometimes, but not too often."

For a few heartbeats, no one said a word, but merely stared at the bum.

Then Eddie barked laughter and sat down. "Are you serious, buddy? Monsters living in the tunnels? Come on, that's crazy. If there was such a thing, then wouldn't we have heard about it by now?"

The bum took two steps toward Eddie, his index finger pointing at him accusingly. "Why the hell would you? It's not like anyone listens to me or my kind. And the transit cops and workers never go down that deep. Even if they do, they have lights and shit with them which gives the things more than enough time to hide."

Eddie crossed his legs and leaned back, checking his wristwatch like he had a date. "I don't care what you say, it's all crazy and I won't hear anymore of it. It was just some bum, like you, probably. And now you're trying to cover it up for the bastard. Look, I changed my mind about what I said before. Let's just wait here until help arrives. I don't want to be running around out there if there's some crazy homeless people waiting for us to come out so they can rob us and God knows what else."

The bum was about to refute the accusation when Jonathan decided it was time to step in. "All right, listen, enough, please," Jonathan pleaded. "You're scaring my son. Whatever happened will all get sorted out when help arrives. Until then, I think we should all just sit down and stay put."

"But what about if that man who took the policeman comes back? What do we do then?" Power Suit Woman asked with fear in her eyes.

Eddie was the one to answer. "Listen up, everybody, just stay away from the doors and sit down. Jonathan, let's see if we can get some pipes or something to use as weapons...just in case."

Jonathan nodded and handed Billy to Trudy. "Will you hold him for me while I go with Eddie?" he asked her.

"Sure, Jonathan, no problem," Trudy said with a warm smile. "Come here, honey, and sit with me. I need someone to keep me company."

Billy consented and Jonathan moved away from his son, Eddie already up and ready to go into the front car where they had found Trudy. As soon as the two men stepped through the doorway into the next car, the sounds of discontent floated to their ears behind them.

Jonathan took note of this with Eddie. "You know, Eddie, we've got a lot of different people with different ideas on what's right and wrong. You know that, right? We'll never get them to agree with one another," he said as he began poking around in the rubble for some kind of a weapon. "It's like the damn United Nations in there."

Next to him, his hands digging and tossing wreckage aside, Eddie chuckled. "Yeah, or they're like Congress. They need to discuss something for days when all someone needs is to just say yes or no. What we need is someone to take charge, like that cop was doing before he got taken."

"That's not a bad idea, actually, Eddie. And I think it should be you."

Eddie stopped digging and looked up, trying to see Jonathan in the dark.

"Me? You want me to lead? I'm just an old man. No one listens to me anymore."

"Well, I would. Look, obviously you've seen some shit that the rest of us can only imagine. The closest I've ever come to a war is what I see on CNN. You're perfect for the job. So what do you say?"

Eddie began rooting through the wreckage again, and a moment later he yanked a pipe from a large pile near the edge of the car. If Eddie was going to answer Jonathan, the answer would have to wait, because when Eddie removed the pipe, the entire pile shifted and some rubble and bits of stone fell to roll away onto the floor.

Both men shifted to the side, not wanting to get their feet crushed, and that was when the rest of the business man's body was found. At first, the dead man was nothing but a shadow amidst other shadows, but then Eddie pulled out his Zippo and flicked the small wheel, igniting the flame. Holding the lighter down to the floor, both men gazed down at what had, less than an hour ago, been a living breathing human being, with hopes and dreams and emotions and all the other wonderful things that made each one of God's creations beautiful.

But now all that lay on the floor, buried under hundreds of pounds of rubble, was a husk, an empty shell, surrounded by congealing blood.

Eddie moved the lighter closer, the flame flickering gently.

"Do you think he's dead?" Jonathan asked.

"Well, shit, yeah, he's dead," Eddie said, moving the Zippo to the right side of the corpse's head. When the light illuminated the man's head, it was blatantly apparent he was most definitely deceased. The right side of his head had been pulverized by the pressure and weight of the rubble that had landed on him, not to mention all the blood. The man was only visible from the shoulders down and it was now easy to see where the man's arm had been severed from his torso.

It was a gruesome sight, made even more horrifying in the shadows of the flickering Zippo, as the blood reflected the light like a dull mirror.

"Poor bastard," Eddie said, reaching out and closing the man's remaining eye.

Jonathan crossed himself, old habits hard to break, and then he reached out, picked up a small piece of sheet metal and laid it over the dead man's face.

"Rest in piece, fella," he said quietly.

"Amen," Eddie said softly.

Just before the two men turned away, Jonathan heard a soft beeping. "Hey, Eddie, wait a second. You hear something?"

Eddie shook his head no and pointed to his ears. "A grenade went off too close to me in the war. Don't hear much if it ain't right in front of my face. Why, you hear somethin'?"

Jonathan nodded and went to one knee, cocking his head to listen. It was hard, trying to focus while the passengers in the next car continued arguing.

"Hey, Eddie, close that door, will ya? I can't hear too well."

Deciding to humor the young man, Eddie did as he was asked, sliding the door closed with a soft click. The moment the door closed, Jonathan's ears picked up the beeping better, now able to zero in on it. Moving around slowly, he ended up over the corpse again.

Removing the sheet metal, feeling like he was desecrating a grave, he put his head as close as he could to the man's crushed skull. As he leaned over him, the odors of after shave, blood and dirt came to his nose, making him want to sneeze, or throw-up, or both simultaneously.

He heard the soft beeping again, he reached down, and shifted the man's body. As soon as he did this, the beeping grew louder. There was a small light showing now and Jonathan stretched out and retrieved the cell phone that had become trapped under the man's body when he had fallen to the floor, and been subsequently crushed.

The man's body had protected the phone from being destroyed and Jonathan stood up with the prize in his hand, waving it back and forth so Eddie could see it.

"Hot damn, a phone," Eddie said happily. "Great job, son. Call someone and get us the hell out of here."

Jonathan held the phone to his eyes and immediately saw there was no signal, no bars. Holding the phone over his head and waving it around like a bad cell phone commercial, he was still rewarded with nothing.

"Dammit, there's no signal down here. There's probably thousands of tons of rock and earth over our heads. This damn thing is useless."

He was going to toss it back onto the pile, but realized the small screen was a paltry light but still better than nothing, so he put it into his pocket for safe keeping.

Dejected but still optimistic, Eddie patted him on the shoulder. "That's okay, son, it was worth a try."

Eddie bent over and handed Jonathan a two-foot piece of rebar, keeping the pipe he'd found for himself. "Here, take this, it'll do the job if one of those tunnel bastards tries to get in here again."

Jonathan took the rebar in silence and turned to leave the car, Eddie right behind him. Just before Eddie was going to walk into the car, he paused and stepped back to the corpse. Picking up the severed arm, he rested it on the man's back, picked up the piece of sheet metal, holding it carefully in his hands so as not to become cut from the serrated edges, and placed it back over the man's head and shoulders. Then he followed Jonathan back into the main car.

When Eddie had stepped through the doorway, and had pulled it closed behind him, the soft click of the latch was the only sound in the destroyed car. But soon the sounds of scurrying and scratching could be heard coming from around the body.

A second later, rubble began to shift and the sheet metal over the corpse's head shifted and fell to the floor with a muffled *clang* as the body began to be pulled backward into the rubble, one inch at a time. A bloody trail of bone and brain matter was left on the floor as the body was slowly pulled into the wreckage.

Then, with one quick yank, the body slid from view, the remaining arm and hand trailing after the corpse like it was reaching out for help.

The severed arm fell off the body to tumble to the floor, where it remained for a second or two, until a black claw reached out and grabbed it, so fast that if someone was watching and blinked, they would have missed the action.

When the scuttling had stopped and the body had completely disappeared from under the rubble, the hole that had been formed around the body fell in on itself, filling the area the dead man's husk had been in only moments before.

The sound of a trap door, a service door, actually, that each car had in the floors that led to the underside of each car, slammed shut again, and the sounds of scratching and scuttling could be heard outside on the gravel of the tunnel floor.

Then silence regained its foothold inside the demolished car, the only other sounds now coming from the final car that still had living humans inside.

* * *

Jonathan stepped into the car and frowned as he watched the passengers arguing with one another. Caesar and Roselle were going at it in Spanish, the bum was arguing with Carlos, and Power Suit Woman was arguing with the two teenagers who seemed to have gotten their voices back.

It was loud and annoying and finally, Jonathan couldn't take it anymore. "Enough!" he screamed, smacking his piece of rebar against the wall of the train, the loud *whack* causing everyone to look his way and stop talking like a switch had been flicked. "What the hell is wrong with you people? Look, I don't know what's going on anymore than you do, but arguing about it isn't going to accomplish a damn thing. Listen up, I'm making a rule right now. Anyone who wants to work together and deal with this crazy situation come over here and stand with me and Eddie. The rest of you can stay over there and shut the fuck up. Well, what's it gonna be?"

No one moved, paralyzed by the rage in Jonathan's voice and the piece of rebar he held in his hand, which he had been waving around menacingly, not realizing it.

Trudy stood up, and though she was only a few feet away from him, she moved the few feet so she was standing next to him. As she did this, she handed Billy to him, who hugged his father with tears in his eyes. Jonathan could feel his son's heart beating in his small chest as his body pressed against his and it made him want to cry. He never wanted his son to have to experience the fear and confusion he was feeling right now.

"I'm with you, Jonathan, just say what we should do," Trudy said with a smile.

Jonathan nodded to her, smiling as well. Looking into her eyes, he felt something he hadn't felt since his wife had died.

Was it hope? Hope that he could care for another woman again?

Eddie clapped his hands together as he glared at the other passengers.

"Well? What's it gonna be, folks? Are you with us or against us?"

Carlos held up a finger for him to wait and then he spoke rapidly in Spanish, filling in Caesar and Roselle on what had just occurred. Both replied and then began talking to themselves, the entire conversation taking less than a minute. Then, with Caesar going first, the three of them crossed the car to join Jonathan and the others.

"Good, that's great, glad to have you with us," Jonathan said to Carlos, shaking the man's hand.

"No problema, amigo" Carlos said and then realized Jonathan might not understand. "Oh, sorry, I said no problem, we're with you. It is as good as anything else and better than fighting amongst ourselves."

Caesar nodded, smiling widely, as if he was part of the conversation.

"That's great," Jonathan said, then turned to look at the others. "How 'bout the rest of you? You in or out?"

The two teenagers looked at one another and then the first one shrugged and said, "Yeah, man, it's cool, we're with you. We just want to get out of here in one piece."

The second teenager agreed with his friend and the two crossed the car, standing next to the three cleaners.

"That's great, guys. Say, you two got names?" Jonathan asked.

"Yeah, man, I'm Glen and he's Chris," the first teenager said.

"Okay, good, Glen and Chris, good to know you," Jonathan said, shifting Billy on his arm. God how heavy he was getting.

There were only two more people left at the end of the car: the bum and Power Suit Woman.

"Well, what about you two?" Jonathan asked them as amiably as he could muster under the circumstances.

The bum made a sound, like a raspberry, and he shot his middle finger at Jonathan and the others. "Fuck you, I don't need any of you, I've been surviving in these tunnels for years and I'll be around years after you're all worm food."

Jonathan frowned, not exactly happy with being cursed at and insulted, but instead of replying, he turned to look at Power Suit Woman.

"Well, miss, what about you?" he asked.

All eyes in the car turned and stared at the woman. She sat in her seat, high-heels and pant suit that showed off her shapely legs. Her suit was dusty, but she had done her best to wipe it clean.

She was staring back at everyone as they waited for her answer, when the floor seemed to explode upwards under her feet. She screamed and jumped onto her seat, like she had seen a mouse, and that simple act saved her life.

As the service door in the floor popped open, claw-like hands reached out from under the train; searching for prey. In the emergency lights of the car, it was difficult to see anything clearly, and as soon as the hatch popped open, everyone began screaming and trying to do something, anything, whether it was to escape or attack the threat.

But it was the bum who had the unfortunate luck of standing directly next to the hatch. Before he could so much as shriek, scream or curse, he was yanked off his feet by the ankles and pulled into the hatch.

In less than five seconds, the hatch had popped open, the bum had been pulled into the dark hole, and the hatch was closed again.

Though everyone tried to help the bum, by the time Jonathan had given Billy to Trudy, and Eddie and him had tried to fight their way through the other passengers—though Carlos did join in the battle with what was in the hatch—the entire episode was over, leaving everyone within the train filled with a sense of hollowness. Adrenalin was pumping and there was nothing to fight.

Jonathan ran to the double doors where the cop had been pulled through, and just as he gazed out into the darkness through the broken window, he saw the bum's face. The man appeared to be floating about four feet above the ground, though the sense of dark shadows under him was prevalent.

His face was one of surprise, and his mouth was hanging open, his lips moving up and down as if he was trying to say something. From Jonathan's vantage point inside the train, he couldn't see that the bum's throat had been slashed by a razor-like claw and all Jonathan could hear was the man's death rattle.

Then the bum was lost in the darkness and all was peaceful outside the train.

Inside the car, it was chaos as everyone tried to talk at once and Power Suit Woman cried steadily. Billy had begun crying as well. Though he didn't know why, he could sense the dread inside the car and for him it was nothing but fear.

Trudy consoled him, standing against the front door of the car, watching the floor with wide eyes of terror, expecting it to burst open again at any second.

Jonathan turned back to the others. Eddie was at the closed hatch and said, "It's some kind of service opening. For the maintenance crew probably."

"How are we going to stop it from opening again? And what the hell grabbed that guy? I saw *something* and it sure didn't look like any hands I ever saw before," Carlos ranted, his face a mask of panic.

Jonathan let out a heavy breath and tried to slow his beating heart. Whatever had just happened, it was over now, and for the moment, they were safe again, though for how long that might be was anyone's guess.

"Look, we need to have people stand on the hatch. That way, they, whatever they are, can't push it open. And we need to make sure there aren't any other hatches in this car. If there are, they could just go through those later and pick us off one by one."

"Good idea, Jonathan," Eddie said, and began inspecting the rest of the floor. "Carlos, have Caesar or Roselle stand on the hatch so it doesn't open again," Jonathan told him.

"Si, Senor," Carlos said, speaking to Caesar and Roselle quickly, telling them what needed to be done. As soon as he had explained it, both man and woman did as asked, crossing the car and stomping down hard on the hatch with their feet, where they remained.

Next to them, Power Suit Woman cried into her blouse, her eyes staring at nothing.

A minute later, Eddie returned to Jonathan's side.

"The place looks okay. If there are anymore hatches in here, I can't find them.

"Good, that's good," Jonathan said.

Eddie was grinning, and for the life of him, Jonathan had no idea why the old man would be doing that, as they were all in mortal danger.

"Why the hell are you smiling?" Jonathan asked, curiously.

"Because we found our leader, guess you didn't know you had it in you, huh?"

Jonathan shrugged. "No, I guess not, well okay then, if I'm in charge, here's what we need to do." He held up his hand and began ticking off fingers as he counted. "One, we need to post a watch on that broken window as well as the other doorways. Two, we need to figure out what our next move is going to be. Is it, A, wait here for help to arrive, or B, try to get out into the tunnel and try to dig our way out. For all we know, there's a way out and all we have to do is get to it."

"I'll do whatever you think is best, Jonathan, just say the word," Trudy said from the seat next to him. Though she tried to look courageous, it was clear in her eyes she was petrified.

Carlos walked back to the middle of the car and turned to look at Jonathan.

"My vote is for getting out of here. Those things are picking us off one at a time. We need to just make a run for it. If we all fight, then we should make it."

"Easy for you to say, dude, but what if it's not you that freak out there goes for next?" Glen asked by the rear door. He kept looking back into the car he had come from, as if he was looking for something.

Carlos turned to face the teenager. "Well, if we stay here, what happens then? We've been here for almost an hour already and nobody's come to rescue us. Why the hell not? Surely someone knows there was a cave-in."

Eddie frowned. "Yeah, I've been thinking about that and I don't think you'll like what I've come up with. The T has been doing cutbacks big time. It's very possible there was no one in the switching room at the time the tunnel collapsed. It's possible everyone has already gone home. Chances are they left a half hour before the tunnel fell in. Once the driver got back to the yard, he probably just went home. It's very possible no one will know we're down here until five, maybe six in the morning."

"But that means it could be over four hours before anyone knows we're down here," Jonathan said, "and after that it's still gonna take time to get a rescue crew together and dig us out. That could add even more hours; two or three at least."

"Yeah, I know. That doesn't bode too well for us, I'm afraid," Eddie stated.

"Daddy, when are we gonna go home? I'm tired and hungry and I want to go to bed," Billy said from the seat next to Trudy as he rubbed his eyes.

Jonathan smiled down at his son, trying to be strong. "I know, buddy, but I think we're gonna be here for a little while longer. I'm sorry."

Trudy's eyes lit up and she reached into her pocket and pulled out half a candy bar. "Hey, Billy, do you want to finish this for me?" she asked with a smile.

Billy looked to Jonathan, who nodded yes. "Sure, go ahead and take it."

Billy did, and a second later was chewing happily.

Trudy wiped Billy's hair off his forehead and watched him eating. "And when you're done with that, you can stretch out on the seats and use my lap for a pillow. How's that sound?" she asked.

Billy only nodded, concentrating on his candy bar.

Jonathan smiled at Trudy and whispered a thank you. She returned the smile and reached out her hand for him. He took it and squeezed her hand once, then she took it away. For just a brief flash of clarity, he realized in the midst of all the craziness and death he was falling for this woman who had taken to his son like a mother bear to her cubs. Then he had to focus on the here and now as Carlos was speaking.

"So I think we should try and make a run for it," Carlos finished, Jonathan missing the first half, though he knew what he missed was just a repeat of what Carlos had said before.

"Look, Carlos, you might be right," Jonathan said. "But what if you're not? We should hold up here for a while and see what happens. Tell you what; if nothing happens in two hours, then we'll try it your way. By then we won't have a choice."

Carlos bit his lip as he mulled it over and then nodded and said, "Okay, Jonathan, fine, we'll do it your way. For now."

Jonathan nodded as well. "For now," he repeated. "Now, why don't we all just rest up and try to relax. Who's gonna watch the broken window?"

Eddie spoke up. "Yeah, I've been thinking about that. Why don't we see if we can get a piece of metal or something from one of the other cars and use it as a cover for the window. That way someone can just lean against it."

"That's a good idea, Eddie," Jonathan said. "Any volunteers to go on a hunt?"

Chris held up his hand. "We'll go, I need to see if I can find my guitar in all that shit back there," he gestured to the caved in car he had vacated.

"Okay, here, take this with you," Jonathan said, passing the rebar he'd been holding. "It's better than nothing."

Chris took the bar and nodded thanks. "Cool, thanks. Okay, we'll be right back."

"Good luck, son," Eddie said to the teenager.

Chris waved a thank you and then the two boys were opening the door and stepping out of the emergency lights. As for the rest of the weary passengers, they all sat down to rest. Caesar and Roselle merely sat on the floor, their butts on the hatch, while Power Suit Woman cried softly. She had totally lost it. A child of the twentieth century, she wasn't able to handle hardship or discomfort.

Jonathan sat next to Billy; Trudy on his son's other side.

With the boy sandwiched between them, he stretched out and tried to sleep.

Eddie sat across from the broken window, the pipe in his hands. His jaw was set and his eyes clear. Like in the war, he took his post as a guard very seriously. Nothing would get past him without having to deal with him first.

The two teenagers could be heard digging around in the next car and Jonathan was wondering if he should go and keep an eye on them, but the truth was, he was exhausted. Though only an hour had passed since the tunnel had collapsed, it felt like he had been inside the train for more than a day. He was hungry, also, not to mention thirsty, and he wasn't looking forward to the next few hours where the thirst would only grow. Not to mention his son. He was young and didn't understand he would have to wait. In his pampered life, when he was hungry or thirsty, he got what he wanted, immediate gratification for his needs. Now, inside the train, trapped by a cave-in and something that surely had to be human, though crazy, he would not be getting what he wanted, and perhaps, what he needed. All he could do was try to make his son's discomfort less, and hope for the best, though it broke his heart to do so.

And it would be a lot longer than a few hours before the situation became dire, in the food and water category anyway. He still couldn't wrap his head around everything that had happened so far. He'd been to busy acting to actually think about the truly ridiculous situation he and the other passengers now found themselves in.

The tunnel collapse was bad enough, but crazy homeless people that were attacking them like animals? It was ridiculous. It was fodder for some cheesy B movie with a bad plot and even worse actors.

But if that were true, then how could he explain away what had happened to the T cop? That man had been yanked through that small window like he was made of clay. The sheer amount of strength to do that would surely surpass a human male, even more than one. And what about the blur that had taken the bum? That occurred so fast he still couldn't believe it actually happened.

No, whatever was going on outside in the tunnel, he doubted it would be a pleasant explanation when it was all over and they were rescued.

A cheer rang out from the next car, as one of the teenagers called out that he found his guitar. But then he cursed when he yelled that it was destroyed, the case not strong enough to protect the instrument inside.

There was some more rummaging and shifting of rocks from the car, but Jonathan ignored it, truly beginning to relax. His heart was finally slowing as he tried to make sense of everything he'd experienced thus far.

Trudy smiled wanly at him as she rubbed Billy's shoulder soothingly. "He really is a special boy, you know that?"

"Yeah, I know. When my wife died, he was the only thing keeping me going," Jonathan told her sadly.

She appeared embarrassed and she looked away from him, her eyes studying one of the posters on the wall, though in the dim light, she was probably just looking for an excuse to look away from him.

"Oh, I didn't know, I'm so sorry for you...and Billy," she said softly.

He forced a smile at her, though it wasn't real this time. It was just something he did when someone told him how sorry they were for his loss. It was a way to put them at ease so they didn't feel pity for him.

"That's all right. It's been almost a year now and I think I'm finally coming to grips with it."

She nodded. "Oh, that's good. I'm glad."

"What about you? Married? Boyfriend?" he asked, trying to change the subject.

"Me? Oh God, no. I mean, I've dated, but I never seem to find the right guy...at least not yet."

He smiled at her again, and this time it was genuine. "Don't worry, I'm sure you'll find someone, it just takes time," he said out loud, but inside he wanted to say, *And maybe that guy is me.*

She smiled back, and for the first time since he had met her, he didn't need to talk to keep the silence at bay. He looked into her eyes and she into his. And with Billy laying between them with his head on her lap, for some reason, everything seemed right. Just for that one brief instant.

Then the moment was shattered by screams of pain coming from the two teenagers in the next car.

Jonathan looked up, prepared to go see what was wrong when a black shape appeared in the open doorway that separated the two cars from one another.

The creature hissed at the passengers and held up its right claw. Hanging from the claw was the severed head of Glen, the face still frozen in shock at the moment his head was separated from his shoulders. But it was the eyes that were the most appalling; or lack thereof. The eyes were missing, the empty, bloody sockets dripping blood onto the head's cheeks in small rivulets, like scarlet tears. But the eyes weren't exactly missing. They were in the creature's other hand, and like it was holding a pair of hardboiled eggs, the creature popped the eyes into its mouth, chewing heartily.

Before anyone could react, the creature tossed the head into the main car, blood droplets spraying from the jagged neck, the head rolling across the floor like a warped bowling ball until it stopped at Eddie's left foot, who was gazing down at it in shock.

Jonathan stared at the black shape in absolute terror, not knowing what to do for a precious second. He was like a deer caught in the headlights of an oncoming vehicle on a lonely road in the country.

Then, as if things couldn't get any worse, the emergency lights flicked off inside the car, plunging the train into utter darkness.

With everyone screaming and trying to figure out what to do next, the black creature charged out of the doorway, directly into the group of passengers.

Then total chaos ruled the darkness as each person fought for their life.

* * *

Jonathan jumped up from his seat but was immediately knocked back down by someone, though who it might have been was unknown in the utter darkness of the car.

"Trudy, get on the floor and under the seats with Billy!" Jonathan yelled at her, feeling for her shoulder and shoving her to the floor. He didn't know if she did as instructed, because an instant later, he was hit hard by a body, his face becoming squashed in the folds of its clothing.

He smelled Old Spice and sweat as the body fell on top of him and he struggled to keep his face from getting buried under the body's clothing, worried he might not be able to breathe. He shoved as hard as he could with his arms, and then he was breathing freely again; the body falling away from him with flailing arms and legs.

His ears were filled with screaming and shrieking as everyone tried to get away from the creature now in their midst.

Another body struck him, causing him to fall, and his head hit the floor hard, his vision showing white flashes of light like small stars. Shaking his head, he thought he heard his son crying and tried to reach out and find him, but in the darkness he could see nothing. Then a foot landed on his right hand and he cried out, yanking the hurt hand to his chest and crawling away from what he perceived as danger.

Another scream and a squeal came to his ears as someone else was hurt. In the darkness of the car, it was impossible to know who it was. Then he could hear Eddie's voice yelling over the chaos. "Everyone, get to the front of the car! Now!" the old man yelled, though why he wanted everyone to do this was unknown. Jonathan was already at the front of the car, and a second later he felt a few more bodies surrounding him.

He could hear people speaking Spanish above him and he knew it must be Roselle, Carlos and Caesar. Then he heard a woman cry out and he was pretty sure it was Power Suit Woman. That was when he realized he had never learned the woman's name.

He could hear Eddie grunting and the sound of metal striking metal. Glass shattered and the tinkling sound filtered into the car and over the yelling people as they all tried to get to the front of the car and away from danger.

Jonathan tried to get off the floor, managing to pull himself onto a seat. He was petrified. He had no weapon and it was pitch black. Just how the hell was he, or anyone else, supposed to fight the thing that had entered the car with them?

Eddie grunted again and there was the sound of metal striking meat, a dull thump that was felt more than heard.

Then there was the scratching of claws, or long toenails, on the floor of the car, followed by a high-pitched scream that squelched all other sound. It was so high and loud that Jonathan was pretty sure it didn't come from one of the passengers.

Suddenly, all the noise around him seemed to quiet down, only the frightened whimpers and crying of the other passengers filling the train car.

"Eddie? Are you there?" Jonathan called out.

In heavy gasping breaths, Eddie answered, "Yeah, I'm still here, Jonathan. And I think I scared the bastard off. Here, wait a second. Just let me get my..."

There was a spark and a small light lit up the middle of the car. Eddie stood there, the metal pipe he had found in his left hand and his Zippo in his right. God, how Jonathan loved that Zippo. If it wasn't for that lighter, what would any of them have done?

Jonathan moved off his seat, his eyes already searching for his son. He was praying in his head that Billy was all right, and a moment later, he saw him, wrapped in Trudy's arms under a row of seats, both of them curled up tight. There was a foot and a half of space from the floor to the bottom of the seats and Trudy and Billy had fit inside easily.

Reaching down, he took Billy from her arms and helped her out.

"Is it safe? Are we okay?" Trudy asked, her eyes wide with fright.

"Yeah, honey, I think we're okay," Eddie said to her. The car wasn't that large and he heard her question easily. "I'm pretty sure I got a few good licks in. I think I scared it off."

Jonathan held Billy with his right arm and pulled Trudy next to him with his left.

"Hey, kiddo, how you doin'?" Jonathan asked Billy.

His son was in tears again, his face drawn and tired and frightened and a dozen other emotions, all crossing his face at the same time. "I'm scared, Daddy, I don't want to be here anymore. Can we leave now, please?" he begged, his head going against Jonathan's chest as he tried to burrow under his father's arm for safety.

"I know, Billy, God I know. You just have to hang in there a little longer."

Jonathan rubbed Billy's back, trying to comfort him. He truly believed he would give his life up right now, at this exact second, if it would see his son safely out of the Hell he'd been thrown into.

Then he looked over to Eddie. "What the hell was that thing?" he asked, his shaking voice evident to all, not that any of the others noticed or cared. They all felt the exact same way.

Eddie shook his head. "I don't know, but whatever it was, it bleeds." He pointed to the floor, where there were bright red patches of blood, like someone had dipped a paintbrush into a can of paint and to then flick the brush at the floor.

In the wavering light of the Zippo, Jonathan spotted a body slumped on the floor near the doorway leading to the rear car and once again he handed Billy to Trudy.

Eddie spotted the body at the same time and both men worked their way to the rear of the car and leaned over the prone form.

"Oh God, it's Carlos," Jonathan said, staring down at the man's open, yet glazed-over eyes. Then he noticed the heavy dent in the man's forehead, the size and shape of the pipe Eddie held in his hand. "Eddie, look at this, this doesn't look like it was from claw marks or a fist," he said, pointing to the wound.

Eddie moved the Zippo closer and then cursed under his breath. "Shit, goddammit!" he screamed, standing up and walking away.

Jonathan stood up, too, and walked the three feet until he was back with Eddie. "What? What's wrong! You're acting pretty broken up over a guy you didn't even know," he said.

"No, you don't understand," Eddie snapped back. "I did that to him...in the dark. He must have gotten in my way. I was swinging blindly in the dark where I thought that thing was. He got in my way and I killed him. Shit!" he screamed, punching the wall.

"It's not your fault, Eddie, it's not. No one blames you," Trudy told him.

Eddie turned on her, his face wild with anger and frustration, his eyes reflecting the light of the Zippo like they were reflecting the fires of Hell. "Well, I blame me! I just killed a man in cold blood. Do you know how that makes me feel? Huh? Do you?"

Trudy shrank back and Billy let out a cry, scared. He had been doing better after Jonathan talked to him, the boy really not un-

derstanding what was really happening. Now, with Eddie screaming at him and Trudy, he began to cry again.

Jonathan grabbed Eddie's arm and spun him around. "Dammit, Eddie, get a hold of yourself. Whether you want to believe it or
not, it's not your damn fault. It's that fuckin' thing that did it,
whether it struck Carlos or you did. Now, pull it together, we need
you. I need you...sane!"

Eddie blinked twice and he seemed to come back to himself,
though there was still a light twitch to the side of his mouth. His
throat moved a few times as he swallowed and then closed his eyes.
One, two, three, four, five heartbeats went by until Eddie opened
his eyes and seemed more like his old self. He reached out a hand
and patted Jonathan on the shoulder. "Okay, Johnny, okay. I'll get
it together. You're right, there's no time for screwing around."

He looked over Jonathan's shoulder at the rear of the car, the
door still open.

"Oh my God, those boys, those boys were in there. We need to
see what happened to them," Eddie said and was off, running to
the rear of the car, taking the only light source with him.

"Eddie, wait..." Jonathan called, but Eddie wasn't listening, the
pipe leading the way as he walked through the doorway.

Jonathan shook his head. He had to give the old guy credit; he
was one tough old man. He looked at Trudy, or where she should
be in the now darkened car. "Trudy, you stay here, I'll be right
back," he told her.

"Okay, but you be careful," she replied.

"Oh, yeah, you better believe it," he said and then moved to the
rear doorway, the light of the Zippo bouncing ahead of him as
Eddie walked into the next car. The others were talking together,
no one wanting to move.

Upon stepping into the rear car, Jonathan moved over to Eddie.
Only half the car was useable space, the other half nothing but
large rocks and caved-in ceiling. In the light of the Zippo, Eddie
illuminated the decapitated body of Glen.

A large pool of blood surrounded the supine body, the spilled
blood now contaminated with dirt and rocks. As for Chris, he was
nowhere in sight.

Jonathan leaned over the body as he stared at the jagged neck wound. "Jesus Christ, Eddie, look at this. It's like a giant razor blade just sliced his head off. What the hell is out there? What the fuck is going on here?" he asked, trying to hold it together though he was really wondering if he would just break out with the shakes and just curl up into a ball and die.

Eddie played the light over the wound. "Yeah, I see what you mean. It's like a razor just went *swipe* and took his head clean off." He frowned, shaking his head. "Poor kid, he had the rest of his life ahead of him, now it's nothing."

"What do you think happened to the other one? Chris was his name, right?" Jonathan asked.

"Don't know. Either he ran away or he was taken. Either way, he's out of our reach," Eddie said in a practical tone. It sucked but it was the truth.

Eddie stood up again, moving his hand around with the Zippo, trying to chase the shadows away. It was when he was pointing the lighter at the left side of the car that he saw an opening in the rubble.

Handing Jonathan the pipe, he moved closer. "Jonathan, look, that's how they got in. There's a hole up there. You know, we could get out that way too...if we wanted to."

"With those things out there? They'll slaughter us," Jonathan replied. "We don't even have any weapons."

Eddie turned and glared at Jonathan. "And what do you think is gonna happen if we all stay in here? Jesus, man, think of your son, for God's sake! They're picking us off one by one. We either take a chance and run for it or we're all just gonna end up dead; slaughtered like cattle waiting for the farmer to send us to the butcher!"

Anger flared in Jonathan's eyes. "I am thinking of my son, goddammit, that's the only thing I have been thinking of since all this shit happened!" he snapped at Eddie, but then realized getting angry was a bad thing to do right now and he tried to calm down, trying to take his own advice. Only level heads would win the day. "But what about getting rescued?" Jonathan asked in a more steady tone. "Surely help is on the way by now."

"Help...help?" Eddie asked in a questioning tone. "Are you serious? Wake up, man. Even if help comes, I sure don't think it's gonna get here in time. Not by the way those things are getting the courage to come in here. By the time a rescue party arrives all they're gonna find is a few body parts and a lot of empty train cars." He lowered his voice, and tried to be more reasoning. "Look, Jonathan, I'm an old man. Even if I die tonight I've lived a good life. But you, and Trudy, your son and the others, you've all got full lives ahead of you. I don't know what's out there, but I know it's trying to kill us and has already done so on at least three occasions so far. So we need to make a decision and take it back to the others. Do we stay here and wait for the next assault? Or do we try to make a run for it?"

Jonathan bit his lip and closed his eyes, thinking, his mind filled with ideas and images. Flashes of the creature as it entered the car, all black and shiny, flew into his mind. He remembered how it had thrown the severed head into the car as if it was playing with its food, then gulped down Glen's eyeballs like they were candy. And Eddie was right. What about Billy? He couldn't let those things get a hold of his son. He knew he'd die first before he let that happen.

Opening his eyes, he gazed back at Eddie. "All right, Eddie, I'm with you. Let's get the hell out of here."

Eddie nodded and slapped him on the left arm. "All right, that's what I'm talkin' about. Finally we're gonna do something and not just wait for it to happen. Come on, let's go back and tell the others," Eddie said happily.

Both men departed the destroyed car, closing the door as they left. They left Glen's body where they had found it. There was no material to use as a shroud and the time it would take to cover the body was better spent getting ready to leave.

Upon entering the car, all eyes looked at them, everyone glad to have some light back inside the car with them thanks to Eddie's Zippo. Power Suit Woman was curled up into a tight ball on a seat, her arms wrapped around her legs, and the two cleaners, Roselle and Caesar were leaning over Carlos' dead body.

Roselle was crying as she looked up at Jonathan. He nodded to her, trying to show his support for the loss of her friend. He hadn't known Carlos too well, but he seemed to be a good man. Trudy went over to him and Jonathan pulled her to him. Billy hugged him, too, and the three stayed that way for a brief moment, secure in each other's arms.

After a few seconds, Jonathan gently separated them from him and looked into their eyes, then turned to face the others.

"There's no sign of Chris and we already know what happened to Glen. I'm sorry, guys," he told Trudy and the others.

He remained silent as he studied the other faces around him, and then said, "Look, Eddie and I have been talking and we've decided it's for the best if we try to make a run for it. Hopefully, there's an access tunnel we can use or the cave-in isn't that bad once we get out into the tunnel. Truth is; we won't know unless we try. For all we know, there's a wide open path and all we have to do is walk through it."

"But what about staying here? Didn't you say that was the best thing to do?" Trudy asked.

Jonathan nodded. "Yeah, I did, but things have changed. Whatever's out there is coming in here to get us. We're sitting ducks in here. We've got no weapons to speak of and we're trapped with nowhere to run. The best chance for us is to try and make a run for it. Escape or die, those are our options."

Caesar and Roselle looked at Jonathan, not understanding what he was saying. He moved closer to them and pointed to each of them, then he mimicked running with his fingers, pointing outside the train. It took a second or two, but finally they understood.

"Si, Si, okay, okay," Caesar said as Roselle nodded, too. Both were smiling, trying to be strong, though Roselle still had tears on her cheeks after saying goodbye to Carlos. She was now without her jacket, and had used it to cover Carlos' body.

Jonathan smiled back and then turned to Eddie. "Okay then, now that that's decided, what's next?"

"Next we need to get some more weapons," Eddie said. "Pipes like this are good and maybe we can use some of the sheet metal in the front car as shields. After that we go."

Jonathan deferred to the older man's experience, and the two men, with Caesar now included, went into the front car to search for weapons for their desperate escape. The first thing Eddie did upon entering the car was to find some flammable material. He wrapped the material around the end of the pipe and then lit it, an oily flame sprouting up.

"There, my lighter was getting to hot to hold," Eddie said. "We need to make some more like this, too. If those things live down here then maybe they don't like the light. I know I wouldn't."

"Good idea," Jonathan said and the three men got to work. It wasn't that hard to show Caesar what they wanted and soon the man was pulling rebar and sheet metal out of the debris, carrying it back into the main car that had become their base of operations.

Billy and Trudy stood in the doorway, watching, and Jonathan tried to send good thoughts their way, telling Billy that everything would be okay.

Twenty minutes went by, and by the time they were done, they were all hot and tired. Thirsty was another discomfort to add to the list, but there was nothing to drink.

With everyone back in the main car once again, Jonathan talked to Eddie quietly while he poked holes in sheet metal to use as handholds for the makeshift shields.

"Man, when we get out of here, I'm gonna get the biggest pitcher of beer and down it in one swallow," Jonathan said.

Eddie chuckled at that. "Yeah, I hear that. Wow, I can almost taste it now. I can't remember the last time I was this thirsty."

"I can," Jonathan said. "I was stuck on Route 93 in the middle of the summer a few years ago and there was an accident in the Sumner Tunnel. I sat there for three hours until traffic began to move. I had no water with me and my a/c was broken. After that, I always carried water in the car, just in case. Of course, something like that never happened to me again."

"Yeah, until now," Eddie said.

"Yeah, until now, thanks for pointing that out to me," Jonathan frowned.

"Happy to help," the older man quipped.

They looked at one another for a second and each man smiled, the two of them sharing a chuckle. They continued working, making weapons, with Caesar by their side, while the three women and Billy waited and watched with fear and trepidation in their eyes.

* * *

When they were finished with the weapons and shields, each man sat back and wiped their brows. Perspiration covered each of their faces, the car becoming warm as time went by.

Only the missing window on the door and a few of the smaller, broken glass squares near the ceiling let in any fresh air, and though the cool air was nice, the window was a constant threat of danger from attack.

Trudy was sitting on a seat just in front of Jonathan and they had talked a little while he worked. Eddie had listened to them, smiling now and then and sometimes had entered the conversation, giving his opinion. The one thing that Jonathan had learned in the time he had known Eddie was that the man was very opinionated, though not so much that he became overbearing. He had known many a man that only their opinion mattered and if you were foolish enough to ask for their opinion, well, you better take their advice or you'd never hear the end of it. Not to mention when they would just force their opinion on you whether you wanted it or not.

But Eddie was an easy going man, and once they were free of this ordeal and were safe once more, he hoped the older man would want to stay in touch with him. Jonathan looked up at Trudy, Billy in her arms once again, and he definitely hoped she would want to stay in touch, too. He had only known her for a short time, but the feelings were there, just like they had been with his wife when he first met her.

Trudy noticed him smiling at her and she returned it with one of her own. "What?" she asked, curious what the smile was for.

He shrugged, blushing, thankful for the dim light of the torches they had set up in the car. "I was just thinking, that's all."

"Oh, and about what may I ask?"

He swallowed hard, his pulse beating in his temple like a drum, but he forced himself to say what he was thinking. "I was just wondering if maybe, once this is all over, we could, uhm, you know, like, get a cup of coffee or something."

Her smile grew wider and she gazed down at his dirty face. "Jonathan, are you asking me out on a date?"

Scratching his head, he nodded; the butterflies in his stomach making him want to vomit. "Yeah, I guess I am."

Eddie spoke up then, true to form. "So, what do you say, honey? You gonna give the poor guy a break and say yes?"

Jonathan flashed Eddie a withering stare, but the man acted like he didn't notice it. Trudy closed her eyes, as if she was considering his proposal, and when she opened them, she gazed down on Billy's sleeping face. The boy had fallen into a restless slumber ten minutes ago, though he was constantly fidgeting in her arms.

"Well, considering I have your child in my arms, I guess I should give you a chance. Even if it's just so I can see this little guy again," she said, looking at Billy again and grinning.

"Sure, of course. That sounds great. Maybe we could go to the Museum of Science or the Aquarium or something. Billy loves those places."

Trudy nodded again. "Sure, okay, sounds fun."

"Okay then," Eddie butted in, "if you're done playing the Dating Game, what do you say we get this show on the road?"

Jonathan sighed, pulled his eyes away from Trudy's, and stood up, scrunching up his face from his frozen leg muscles. He had stayed in the same position for too long and now he had a Charlie horse.

"Okay, Eddie, let's get this done," he said as he gathered up the shields from where they lay on the floor. He was about to set the shields down onto one of the seats when one of the windows at the rear of the car exploded inward. The window was on the same side as the double doors with the already broken window.

Power Suit Woman was sitting in front of this window, her legs curled up under her as she mumbled to herself in fear, and when the window shattered, she slumped down as low as she could go, but still remained in her seat.

Though Jonathan and Caesar acted fast, running to the woman's aid as soon as the window imploded; they were still far too slow to save her.

As the window exploded inward, a large stone crashed to the floor of the car, obviously from the attacker. With lightning speed, claw-like hands reached into the car and grabbed the terrified woman by the shoulders. She let out a squeal of anguished pain and her eyes went wide as the claws bit deep into her flesh. Then, like she was on a bungee cord that had reached its extension, she was ripped out of her seat and pulled through the window. The last thing anyone saw was her legs, kicking erratically, one of her shoes flying off to land onto the seat she had been occupying only seconds ago.

Though she was gone, her tortured screams continued to echo in the darkness of the tunnel. But then they ceased, like someone had flicked that fateful light switch once again. One second she was screaming in pain, and then nothing, only silence.

By then Jonathan and Caesar had reached the shattered window, Eddie right behind, and all were staring out into the darkness of the tunnel. Eddie grabbed a torch, holding it just out of the window, trying to penetrate the darkness.

"Do you see her? Does anyone see her? Jesus Christ, it just took her; there was nothing we could do! It was so damn fast!" Jonathan screamed, staring out into the obsidian darkness.

Suddenly, something flew out of the darkness. It struck the train just below the broken window and fell to the tunnel floor with a meaty *thump*, before rolling away.

Eddie looked at the other two men with fear written on his features, each man gazing back with the same look. "What the hell was that?" he asked.

"Don't know. Here, give me the torch, Eddie, I want to check for myself," Jonathan said, and took the torch from the older man. Swallowing hard, with a piece of rebar in his right hand and the torch in his left, he stuck his head through the window, careful not to cut himself on the safety glass. As his head popped out of the train, he breathed in the cool, moist air, his eyes peering intently around him as he searched for movement.

Nothing moved, though he imagined monsters and demons just on the edge of where the light penetrated, just waiting to reach out and pull him from the car, to then drag him to their lair where God knew what would happen to him.

He leaned out the window and held the torch as far out as he could. Swinging it back and forth, he scanned the tunnel floor for what had struck the train. As the torch went by the train's metal wheels, he spotted something at the edge of the light. Leaning out just a little more, he stretched his arm as far as it would go, and as he did this, the empty eye sockets of Power Suit Woman's severed head flashed back at him, the open and blood-filled sockets reflecting the light of the torch.

"Jesus Christ!" Jonathan screamed, jumping back into the car. His face was as white as a ghost's as Eddie moved next to him.

"What did you see, what did you see?" Eddie asked, almost shaking Jonathan's shoulders for an answer.

Jonathan swallowed hard, his throat dry. And when he was sure he could talk, he looked Eddie straight in the eyes. "It was her head. Jesus Christ, they cut off her fucking head, gouged out her eyes and threw it at us like it was a basketball!"

Eddie's jaw dropped. "Good God. What the hell are we dealing with out there?" he whispered.

"Did you see her? Jonathan, what happened? Is that woman all right?" Trudy asked. Billy was awake again, his eyes wide with fear. The only reason he wasn't crying was that even a small boy could get used to a situation given enough time, and as there was no apparent danger—he was sleeping when the woman was pulled through the window—he didn't feel the need to cry.

Jonathan shook his head no. "No, Trudy, she's not all right. I did see her, well, part of her anyway and I can say with an absolute certainty that she's dead."

Trudy leaned back against one of the poles lining the car for passengers to hold on to when the train was in motion.

"Oh my Lord, not her, too." She turned to look at Eddie and Jonathan. "We're all gonna die down here, aren't we." It was more of a statement than a question.

Eddie moved over to her, taking her hands in his, Billy now in the middle of them.

"Hey, now you listen to me. We're gonna get out of here. I promise. Just stay calm and be positive." Eddie turned to look at Jonathan and Caesar. "You guys ready to go? I don't think we should stay any longer than we have to. Hell, maybe they'll be busy with that woman and we can get away free and clear."

Jonathan moved next to Billy and took him back, Trudy giving him his son without protest. He hugged his son to him, almost making him cry out in pain.

"Hey, kiddo, how you doin'?" Jonathan asked Billy.

He sniffed a few times and then tried to stop crying. "I'm okay, Daddy. I'm scared though. I don't want those monsters to get me."

Jonathan rubbed his son's back, trying his best to sound strong and confident.

"And they won't. Because they have to go through me first and you know I won't let that happen. Right?"

Billy nodded slowly, then wiped his eyes with the back of his hand.

"Okay, good. Now listen. I need to give you back to Trudy so she can take care of you, okay?"

"But I want to stay with you," Billy pleaded.

"I know, sport, but I need to have my hands free in case any of those bad ol' monsters come near us. Then I'll hit them hard and make them leave us alone. How 'bout that?"

Billy thought about it for a second and then he nodded okay.

"That's a good boy," Jonathan said, handing him back to Trudy.

She took him with a smile and Jonathan gazed down at her. "I don't know what I would have done if you weren't here to help me," he said.

She shrugged. "Hey, just glad to help, now let's get out of here so you can take me on that date."

He smiled and nodded at her and then turned to face Eddie and Caesar. Eddie was looking impatient; wanting to get the show on the road. Caesar didn't quite understand what was going on, but he saw Jonathan talking to his son and he got the idea, and so was waiting patiently for him to finish. When Jonathan nodded to him and tapped his shoulder, the man began picking up the shields and pipes.

He quickly handed one out to Eddie and Jonathan, then took one for himself.

Trudy didn't carry anything as she had her hands full holding Billy.

"You know, we never even knew that woman's name," Jonathan said to Eddie.

"Huh, really? Wow, you're right, we didn't. Shit, to die without a name, that's terrible." He grabbed a torch and handed one to Jonathan and one to Roselle, then the small group moved to the newly shattered window. "At least they made it easier for us to get out of the train," Eddie said almost cheerfully. The torch in his hands sputtered and sparked. There wasn't much to burn so they had taken Roselle's jacket off of Carlos as well as the dead man's shirt. Then each of the surviving passengers had donated something from their own clothing. Jonathan and Eddie had lost their socks, and Trudy had given up the sweater she had worn under her jacket. Caesar had donated his shirt; his jacket wasn't the same brand as Carlos' and Roselle's was, and if it wasn't flammable, it was useless for the cause.

Eddie stuck the torch out the broken window and peered into the darkness. He counted to ten before sticking his head back into the car. "Looks clear," he said, "I'll go out first and then you guys can follow me."

"Okay, but be careful," Jonathan told the old man. Eddie nodded and slipped a leg through the window, then dropped the torch onto the tunnel floor. He waited again for signs of movement, but when nothing stirred, he swung the other leg over the sill and dropped to the tunnel floor with a soft crunching of rocks under his feet.

Crouching in the light of the torch, he swallowed hard, anticipating being discovered at any second, but saying a silent thanks when he wasn't. "Okay, come on down, the coast is clear," he whispered up to the others.

Caesar was next, followed by Roselle. They each slid out of the window effortlessly. Billy was dropped down to the tunnel floor next, Roselle taking him for a moment. Jonathan followed and he handed his torch out the window to Caesar and then slid out one leg at a time, careful of the glass. Once he was out, he waved up to Trudy who was standing in the window, her face a mask of apprehension.

"Come on, hurry up. So far so good," Jonathan called to her.

She nodded and quickly did as the rest had done, with the exception her skirt caught on a piece of the safety glass still in the window frame and it was ripped. Ignoring it, she dropped to the tunnel floor, Jonathan there to catch her. Once down, she took Billy from Roselle, thanking the woman for her help.

When the group was all together once more, they began to move off to the rear of the train.

Eddie's torch began to flicker, and then it went out, the material totally consumed by the fire. He pulled out one last sock from a pocket and wrapped it around the end of the pipe. He pulled his Zippo out of his pocket and tried to light the torch again. The Zippo sparked a few times but didn't light. "Shit, the damn things out of fluid," he said in the dark.

Jonathan moved next to him and held his torch under Eddie's.

"Here, let me light it, we should be fine as long as at least one torch is always lit."

Once Eddie's torch was lit again, they began moving down the tunnel. They had only reached the end of the second car behind the one they had used as their base when it was apparent they wouldn't be going any further.

The entire car was buried under rubble, large boulders, piping and wiring from the overhead ceiling of the tunnel covering everything on both sides of the train.

"Dammit. Well, we knew it might be blocked. Let's try the front of the train. Maybe it's better up there," Eddie said, taking the lead.

The five survivors, and Billy, trudged back the way they had come, passing the car they'd holed up in, and then continued onward to the front of the train.

Just as they passed the second car, Jonathan raised his hand for them to stop. "Wait, I see something in the wall over there," he said, pointing ten feet away to the right.

"What did you see? Was it them?" Eddie hissed.

Jonathan shook his head. "No, it's something else, come on, I want to check it out. Maybe it's a way out."

They followed Jonathan away from the train until he was standing at the tunnel wall. Where the wall had once been smooth, with no openings, now there was a large crack in its facade, the crack no more than a foot wide.

There were large splatters of blood covering the edges of the wide crack, like something human had been forced in there without its consent and the flesh had been caught on the sharp edges of the stones.

Jonathan leaned closer and then pulled his nose back, the charnel house smell coming from the crack overwhelming. As the others noticed the odor of decay, everyone began gagging, trying not to throw up.

"Oh my Lord, what is that awful smell?" Trudy asked, covering her nose. Billy buried his face into her jacket, trying to stop the smell from penetrating his sinus cavity.

Eddie was the one who answered. "I know what that smell is. That's the smell of death. I've smelled that odor before in the war. It's when corpses and pieces of corpses would lie out in the sun for days on end, that's what that smell's like."

Jonathan was already backing up, deciding this wasn't a way out, when he spotted something on the ground, reflecting the torchlight.

Leaning over, his eyes went wide when he saw it was a pistol, the holster it had been in lying next to it. On the holster was the picture of a steer and he knew who the weapon belonged to.

The Transit cop.

Jonathan quickly reasoned out what must have happened. When the cop had been taken from the train, he must have been dragged this way and had lost his weapon. Evidently, the creatures didn't know what they had left behind. Picking up the gun, he showed it to the others.

"Well, well, look at what I found?"

Eddie moved up next to him and whistled softly. "Outstanding, great job. But let me ask you something. Do you know how to use that?"

Jonathan realized that, no, he didn't. He had fired a few handguns at the gun range a few times with friend's years ago, but he was far from proficient with firearms. In fact, the handgun he had at the house had never been fired. When he was going to kill himself with it a year ago, that would have been its first time being used.

Eddie saw the look on Jonathan's face and he nodded, clicking his teeth. "Uh-huh, that's what I thought. Why don't you let me handle that and you take the torch so I can see."

Jonathan reluctantly gave the pistol to Eddie, who upon taking it, quickly popped out the clip and checked the chamber, then slapped the clip back in, cocked the weapon, and then gazed back at Jonathan.

At that moment Jonathan saw the young man Eddie had once been. The man who had gone to war and had seen things Jonathan could only imagine.

"This is a Glock 9mm," Eddie said. "It has seventeen rounds in the clip and has good stopping power. When you get hit by this, you don't usually get up and dance the jig, if you know what I mean. It should do the job nicely." He grinned widely, his teeth reflecting the torchlight. "I'll tell you one thing, I sure as hell feel a lot better. Just let those bastards try something now."

As if something in the dark was answering his challenge, running footsteps could be heard moving across the gravel.

Caesar yelled something in Spanish, and a second later, everyone was looking around in fear, trying to peer past the glare of the torches.

"Oh my God, it's them! Jonathan, what do we do?" Trudy asked in a panic.

Roselle and Caesar stood next to her, holding one another, though Caesar had his right hand held in front of him, the torch waving back and forth, the left holding a shield. He moved away from Roselle and pulled the piece of rusted rebar from the belt of his pants. Waving the rebar in front of him menacingly, he called out to the darkness in Spanish.

Though Jonathan didn't know what the man was saying, he had a pretty good idea. He was saying, "Come on you bastards, I'm ready for you!"

Eddie waved the gun around, searching for a target, but all he found were shifting shadows that seemed to appear at the edge of the light and then dart backwards to vanish again. They were so fast he wondered if he was imagining them.

"Dammit, I can't see shit, they're so damn fast! They could be anywhere!" Eddie yelled. "Everyone, get over here by me and let's get to the front of the train. Maybe we can find an opening in the cave-in up there."

Jonathan patted Caesar's shoulder, pointing to Eddie and motioning with his hand that they were going to go over to the front of the train. The man nodded, and ever so slowly, the group began moving again with Eddie trying to cover all vulnerable positions at the same time.

The noises surrounding them began to grow. A tapping began, as if long nails were impatiently rapping on a piece of sheet metal. But there had to be at least half a dozen hands doing the tapping, and in less than a minute, the entire tunnel was filled with the noise.

Like smaller scale African drums, the tapping continued and Eddie lost a small piece of his nerve and shot the gun into the darkness. One, two, three, four times he fired, the gunshots echoing like a cannon had gone off. If he hit anything, there was no sign.

Trudy moved next to Jonathan, Billy cowering in her arms. "Oh my God, Jonathan, what's going on? Maybe we should get back inside the train."

"No!" Eddie snapped. "That would be a mistake. We're in this for the long haul, people. It's now or never, now stop talking and get moving. Jonathan, stay with Caesar and cover our backs. And give Roselle one of the torches so I can see up here."

Jonathan did as ordered, the tone of Eddie's voice making him do it without thinking. Eddie was in battle mode now, like he was back in the war against the Germans. Only this time the enemy was an unknown force, and if they were taken prisoner, there would be no mercy, only a terrible, suffering death.

Roselle moved up next to Eddie as they all slid their feet across the gravel of the tunnel floor. Shadows danced just out of sight of the perimeter of the torches and Eddie fired off another two shots, though once again, nothing was hit.

"Dammit, where are they?" he asked, sweat beading on his forehead.

Roselle moved to his side, and without realizing it, she began moving out and away from the rest of the group. She became like a baby goat in a herd, the wolf spotting the lone animal wandering away from the pack, the perfect target.

Eddie noticed she was almost five feet away from him and he was just about to call out to her, wanting to tell her to get back next to him, when a flash of something obsidian charged into Roselle, knocking the torch from her hand.

She let out a screech of surprise and then she was gone, carried off into the darkness.

"Roselle!" Eddie screamed and began firing in the direction he thought she had been taken, each gunshot lighting up the tunnel like a flash of lightning.

"No, stop, Eddie, you'll hit her, too!" Jonathan yelled out.

Eddie stopped firing and turned to Jonathan. "Well, what the hell am I supposed to do? Wave goodbye to her and leave it at that!"

"No, of course not, but what if you shoot her in the dark?"

"Jonathan, if we can't get her back, she's dead anyway," he snapped back, the fear clear on his face in the flickering torchlight.

From somewhere in the darkness, there was a high-pitched scream and Caesar called out to Roselle. There was no return answer.

Seconds passed and each of them stood perfectly still. The torchlight was like a small island in the ocean of darkness with sharks all around them, prepared to pounce at any second. The tension was maddening, and finally, after three minutes of nothing happening, a round object flew out of the darkness to land on the tunnel floor in front of the group. It rolled a few feet until it stopped in front of Jonathan. Moving the torch closer to the object, he had a feeling he knew what it was before the actual image was fully inside his mind.

It was Roselle's head, her long hair draped messily over her face. Her mouth was open, turned up in a last scream, frozen forever in time, but it was her eye sockets, the eyes missing once more, that was the most chilling sight to behold.

She had been decapitated, de-eyed, and then the head had been tossed back to the others like a toy, used to taunt and terrorize.

Whatever these creatures were, they were now playing with Jonathan and the others. Caesar gazed down at the severed head of Roselle and he fell to his knees, his hands hovering over the head, as if he was afraid to touch it.

Tears fell down his cheeks and he pulled a gold cross from under his shirt, kissing it softly. When he stood back up, his face went from one of sorrow to one of anger. He glared at Jonathan in the gloom, his face a mask of loss, and handed his torch to Jonathan, who took it, not understanding what the other man wanted to do.

Caesar raised the piece of rebar he was holding over his head with both hands, and with a snarl of sorrow and frustration, he charged out of the circle of torchlight, and into the tunnel before any of the others could even think of stopping him. He was screaming long and loud at the top of his lungs, the Spanish unintelligible, but the tone of his voice clear to his meaning.

"For Roselle!" he yelled, wanting vengeance for his fallen friend, swinging the metal rebar like a warrior going into battle, and at that moment, Jonathan wondered if perhaps the two cleaners had been lovers.

Thirty seconds went by, Caesar's voice echoing off the tunnel walls and the sound of the rebar clanking on rocks and sometimes something fleshier, meatier. Then it stopped, like that ill-fated light switch had been flicked yet again.

There were sounds of scrabbling and scuffling in the darkness, the entire group remaining motionless, too scared to move.

"Caesar! You all right?" Jonathan called out, not really expecting an answer.

Trudy moved next to him, trying to get into his arms, but with the two torches and the piece of rebar in his hands, Jonathan couldn't hold her. He looked down at Billy and his heart broke.

How was he going to get his son out of this impossible situation?

There was the sound of a meaty *thwack*, and a second later, another object flew out of the darkness. This time the object was thrown too hard and Jonathan had to be the one to dodge out of the way or risk being struck. The object just missed his head and bounced off the wall of the tunnel. When it came to rest on the floor, he held the torch over it. It was Caesar's severed, bloody head, minus the eyes, and the tongue was hanging out at an odd angle.

"Oh my God, oh no!" Trudy cried out and tried to get behind Jonathan.

"You bastards!" Eddie screamed into the blackness. "You bastards!" he repeated and then fired three more shots into the dark. With the exception of the ricocheting bullets echoing through the tunnel, there was no outcry that he had hit anything.

Silently, a large rock flew past Eddie's head and he ducked instinctually. Another, smaller rock flew out of the darkness and struck Jonathan on the shoulder. He cried out and tried to shrink away, but there was nowhere to go so he just made sure Billy and Trudy were behind him, safe from the onslaught.

In the circle of light, they were like fish in a barrel to their hunters. They were helpless.

"Come on, we have to make a run for the front of the train!" Eddie yelled out, firing two quick shots over his shoulder.

The three remaining adults ran for it, the torches in Jonathan's hands flickering from the wind of his running, threatening to go out and plunge them all into perpetual darkness. In Trudy's arms, Billy screamed in fear, his voice filled with the terror they were all feeling. Jonathan wanted to console his son, but there was no time. Now they needed to run.

More rocks landed around them as they tried to escape, and Trudy cried out when one struck her right leg, blood seeping from the wound. But there was no time to check how bad it was. All they could do was run and hope for the best.

Eddie fired one more round over their heads, hoping to keep the creatures at bay, and then they were at the front of the train, and once again there was nothing but rubble blocking the tunnel on both sides. To their left, the train was a flattened mess of metal and steel, and if there was an opening somewhere, it would take hours of excavating to try and find it.

"Dammit, no!" Eddie screamed, slapping the rubble with his hand. "There's no way out. The entire tunnel has collapsed in on itself. Good God, how the hell did this happen?"

Scratching and scraping from behind made them turn around, their backs to the rubble as they gazed out into the darkness. Jonathan handed Eddie one of the torches and the older man took it, waving it back and forth in his left hand, the gun in his right and aimed into the abyss.

Jonathan made Trudy and Billy hide behind him, as if his body alone could shield them from danger.

Then they waited, one second at a time. A few sounds could be heard in the darkness and Eddie fired a round or two in the estimated direction. One time he was greeted with a high-pitched scream and he laughed out loud. "Ha, there ya go, ya bastards. How do you like it! Try to get us and you'll get some more of that!" He fired again at the shadows in his enthusiasm, but hit nothing for his trouble.

But after that one incident, there was only silence. Whether it was because they now respected the three survivors with the weapon that shot liquid fire or not, was unknown, but for whatever reason, there were no more rocks thrown and nothing tried to attack them.

The three frightened adults and one child waited with their backs to the rubble, shivering in fear and the dampness of the tunnel. In the train they had been relatively warm, but inside the tunnel it was moist and cool and the darkness only made it seem worse.

"What are they waiting for, Jonathan?" Trudy whispered, sniffing from crying. "Why don't they just get it over with?"

Billy was curled up in Jonathan's arms. The small boy had passed out from exhaustion a few minutes ago, not able to keep up the state of alertness required by the others.

"I don't know, Eddie said. "Maybe they're scared of us." He waved the gun back and forth. His arm was killing him and he didn't know how much longer he could keep it up. It was almost a half hour since they reached the front of the tunnel and he was all out of ideas as to what they could do to escape.

Jonathan stared at his torch, watching the small flame dance in the darkness. It was going to go out soon, so he carefully took off his coat, took out anything in his pockets that mattered, and wrapped it around the end of the torch, careful not to extinguish the flame by accident. A second later and the torch was burning brightly again, casting a wider circle of illumination out in front of them. As the circle of light grew larger, all three adults gasped when they saw they were completely surrounded by the creatures.

Just before the torchlight pushed the creatures backwards, Jonathan got a quick glimpse of the beings that were hunting him.

He saw that creatures were the same size as him and Eddie, but some were larger and some smaller. Their skin appeared to be covered with oil or some other dark viscous fluid, giving them their obsidian look. They had heads the same size as he did and their arms and legs were proportioned to an average human being.

Though hard to believe it, what he saw was essentially a human being, or what had once been one at some time in the past. But now this tribe of tunnel dwellers was nothing more than beasts hunting for food. How they had arrived here and why no one had ever seen them before was a mystery, but not one he cared to contemplate at the moment.

For now, all he wanted to do was get past them.

"Jesus Christ, did you see their eyes?" Eddie whispered as he waved the gun before him.

Jonathan nodded. Yes he had, but there had been too much to take in at once. Their eyes had been very odd. They had been all white, and had almost glowed when the torchlight touched them. He could only assume it was from living in perpetual darkness their entire lives, never seeing the sun or perhaps light of any kind.

At least, until now.

"Jonathan, my torch is dying, I need something to keep it going," Eddie said worriedly.

"Here, take this," Trudy whispered, sliding out of her coat. Billy stirred in her arms, but thankfully remained asleep.

Thank heaven for small blessings, Jonathan thought. At least his son was oblivious to what was happening.

Taking the coat from Trudy, Eddie inspected the material to make sure it would burn. It was some kind of cotton blend and should burn well when added to the torch. He wrapped it around the torch slowly, and a second later it flared higher, pushing the darkness back another four feet.

At the ring of the circle of light, the creatures reared up and hissed, this time flashing their sharpened teeth, each one filed to wicked points. In the light and shadows, Jonathan thought they looked like vampires, though of course that was entirely ridiculous.

One of the creatures tried to swipe at the torch Eddie was holding and the old man shot it in the face. The creature flew backwards into its brethren and a loud hiss filled the tunnel as the others glared at the offending humans.

"I don't think they liked that," Jonathan told Eddie, his voice a fraction away from cracking into madness.

"Ya think?" Eddie snapped back.

Without warning, lightning fast, a blur came out of the darkness on Eddie's left side, the movement so quick that even in full daylight the motion would have been difficult to see.

Eddie's out-stretched gun arm wavered in the torchlight for another second, before it was sliced off just above the elbow, the severed limb falling to the tunnel floor.

Eddie screamed in mortal pain, blood shooting out of the stump like a geyser. Turning to Jonathan, he dropped the torch in his other hand and sprayed the younger man's face with blood like he was holding a fire hose, and Jonathan felt the warm sticky blood fill his mouth and nose.

Sputtering the blood out of his mouth, Jonathan tried to figure out what just happened to his friend. Eddie's face was absolute insanity incarnate, his eyes so wide his eyes balls were ready to just pop out of his head. There was a large vein on the side of his forehead that was thumping steadily in rhythm to his pulse. Jonathan saw the stump where the man's arm used to be and he screamed as well, totally losing it for a moment in the terror of the situation.

Trudy screamed behind him. Not quite understanding what was happening, but knowing it was bad.

Eddie was lost in a world of pain without reason. He took one look at Jonathan, his eyes not actually seeing him, and he ran off and out of the torchlight. He didn't make it more than five steps before he was pounced on by the creatures like a lion would a wounded zebra.

In the edges of the flickering torchlight, Jonathan stared in utter horror as Eddie was ripped into and gutted like a fish. His head was pulled from his shoulders after a neat slice across the jugular. Blood shot outward for a second, and then one of the creatures leaned over and began to drink, slopping up the scarlet fluid like it was rare wine.

Jonathan's voice was gone as he stood utterly helpless. If the creatures had wanted him, Billy and Trudy at that moment, they could have easily taken them. But they didn't. It seemed that at the present time, they were pleased to play with Eddie, feeding on his desecrated corpse.

Jonathan watched as one of the creatures picked up Eddie's head, and with one long nail that was trimmed like a dagger, plucked out each of the old man's eyes. With a low moan of pleasure, and just like they were candy, it popped the orbs into its mouth, leaning back its head as it enjoyed the delicacy. Bits of white goop slid out of the corner of its lips to drip onto the tunnel floor.

When it was finished eating, it chucked the head away like a discarded shell, finished with its meal.

"Oh my God," Jonathan said as he stared at the creature. "Oh my God."

He fell to his butt, his back leaning against the rubble, and Trudy crawled next to him for comfort, Billy thankfully still asleep.

The torch Eddie had been holding sputtered on the ground, and then slowly, it died. Now only the torch in Jonathan's shaking hand seemed to be keeping the creatures at bay, and after the way they had attacked Eddie, he wasn't too confident that the light was really working that well as a deterrent.

Trudy nuzzled her face next to Jonathan's cheek and he wrapped his arm around her. In the circle of light, he began counting the creatures as they swayed back and forth at the perimeter of the torch's glow He stopped counting at twelve. After that, what would be the point? Whether there was five or five hundred, there was no way he could stop them all.

Even if he had a fully loaded gun there were just too damn many to fight.

Wait, the gun!

His eyes went to the ground, searching for it, and there it was, still in Eddie's hand, the severed arm lying on the tunnel floor. Swallowing hard, he reached out the three feet separating him from the gun, expecting to see a blur in the darkness and then his own arm would become separated from his body. But for whatever reason, he reached the arm and gently slid it across the gravel unmolested. When he had it in his grip, he pried the gun from Eddie's hand, the fingers locked around the trigger in a death grip.

Tears appeared on Jonathan's face and he tried to fight them off. He needed to focus on what he was doing. Prying one finger at a time, he finally managed to get the gun out of the dead hand and he tossed the arm at the creatures angrily. They jumped out of the way, but once they realized what it was, they jumped on it, devouring it like it was a turkey leg at Thanksgiving dinner.

He felt only slightly more secure with the gun in his hand, as it was almost useless against such odds.

"What are they waiting for?" Trudy sniffed, hugging Billy tightly. "Why don't they just finish it?"

"I don't know, honey, I truly don't know," he whispered, his voice cracking. "We just have to wait."

* * *

They sat for thirty more minutes and no attack came, and despite himself, he began to feel sleepy. No one could maintain the constant state of alertness he needed to keep up; it was physically impossible. Next to him, Billy was awake and crying again. He took his son from Trudy and handed her the torch.

"Daddy, why are we still here? What happened to Eddie? Did those monsters eat him? I don't want to be eaten, Daddy, I just don't," he cried.

Tears welled up within Jonathan's eyes as he gazed at his son's dirty face in the flickering shadows of the remaining torch.

It was almost ready to go out.

Everything worthy of burning had been burned in the past half hour, all three of them now clothed in nothing but their underwear. And he knew what would happen when that torch finally went out.

Trying to hold back the sobs filling his chest, he shook his head back and forth.

"And you won't be, Billy. Didn't I say that wouldn't happen to you? Huh, didn't I?"

Billy nodded, his nose running and his eyes red from crying almost non-stop.

"Now listen to me, son. I need you to be brave for me, okay? I promise I'll see you safe, I promise."

Trudy was crying next to him and he wrapped his arm around her, placing the Glock on the ground. It was useless anyway, there were far too many of them to stop. Plus, Eddie had fired so many times he had no way of even knowing how many bullets were left; couldn't be that many, anyway.

Trudy looked up and into his eyes, the shadows deepening as the torch began to flicker and fade. "I don't think we're gonna be going on that date after all, huh," she said to him in a shaky voice.

He hugged her closer. "No, I don't think we are. Tell you what," he grinned slightly. "What do you say we call this our first date and leave it at that?"

She nodded, the motion making her face rub against his cheek. He turned to face her, and their lips were no more than an inch apart.

Right now, at this moment, all his inhibitions were gone. There was nothing to save them for.

"I could have loved you, you know," he whispered. "I didn't think there would ever be anyone after my wife died, but now, I know I could have loved you."

He cried some more, the tears falling onto his shoulder and she nodded, as well.

"I could have loved you, too. Both of you," she said, nuzzling Billy's hair.

The torchlight began to flicker some more, and as it did, the creatures moved a step closer, slowly surrounding them until they were only a few feet away.

They were all crying now that they knew what was to come and Jonathan's hand reached out for the Glock on the tunnel floor. Picking it up, he brought it close to Trudy's eyes so she could see it.

She stared at the gun for a full five seconds.

And then she nodded.

Jonathan took Billy off his lap and he set him on the ground next to him.

"Billy, would you do me a favor?" he asked in a sweet voice, though he was shaking so hard he could barely maintain the tone, tears filling his eyes like they would never end.

"Sure, Daddy, okay. Hey, Daddy, what are those monsters doing over there? You go away monsters. You leave me and my Daddy alone!" Billy yelled at the creatures. He looked up at Jonathan. "There, Daddy, I'll make sure they don't hurt us," he said, his voice high and sweet with youth and wonder. "Don't cry Daddy, it'll be all right, I'll protect you, too."

"Thank you, Billy, that was great," Jonathan smiled, the tears pouring out of his eyes. "Now do me that favor. Turn around and close your eyes for me and think of Mommy, okay. Would you like that? Would you like to see Mommy again?"

He nodded, the back of his head moving up and down. "Yes, Daddy, I would. Can we go see Mommy now?"

Jonathan slowly raised the Glock to the back of his son's head and then had to use the other hand, as well; his right arm and hand were shaking so hard.

"Yes, honey, just close your eyes and think of Mommy and you'll be with her soon." He let out a slight sob that wanted to be a roar of anguish, and he squeezed the trigger on the handgun as he screamed at the ceiling of the tunnel.

He had to look away, not able to see the results of the bullet penetrating his son's head, and still without looking, he turned to Trudy. She caressed his cheek with her hand, tears flooding down her face in rivers, and she kissed him once more, softly and tenderly.

It was a kiss that would last a lifetime...and an eternity.

"See you soon?" she asked, her shoulders shaking as she cried.

He nodded, crying so hard he could barely see straight, and the tears filled his eyes to the point that everything was just a blur. "You bet, see you soon," he said in a whisper.

She turned around so the back of her head was facing him, and in the shadows of the dying torch, her shoulders shook as she sobbed softly.

She crossed herself and mumbled an Amen and then she whispered to him. "Whenever you're ready," she said, but the second she had uttered the word *ready*, he squeezed the trigger. Her head shot forward and she fell to the tunnel floor, her fingers spasming as her nerves shut down.

He screamed once more, long and loud, his heart actually breaking in half inside his chest. He reached out for Billy's limp body and pulled him to his lap, cradling his son's dead body in his arms, rocking him back and forth as blood seeped from the jagged hole in his son's head and soaked into his underwear and coated his legs.

"There, son, now you're with Mommy," he said in gasps of strangled breaths, crying so hard he couldn't breathe.

The torch flickered briefly and finally, with one last sputter, it died, and he heard the sounds of clawed feet scratching on the rocks in front of him.

They were coming for him.

Though he thought he could do it, just close his eyes and let them take him in the darkness, he realized he still couldn't let go of his life in the inky blackness and he remembered the cell phone he had found in the front car of the train earlier; the phone now sitting under his left butt cheek. When he had burned his jacket, he had slid the phone into his pants pocket and had then placed it on the ground when his pants had needed to be burned, as well.

Picking up the phone, he flipped it open, the small screen lighting up and pushing the darkness away, but only slightly. The creatures stopped and stared at him, this man who was lying there on the tunnel floor crying, now seeming to be unafraid of them.

Jonathan waved the cell phone in his left hand, moving it back and forth across the visages of the creatures that were only inches from his face. They swayed back and forth, staring at him and at the phone, fascinated, their eyes wide, their white orbs watching him like he was an ant under a microscope.

With his right hand, he raised the Glock to his lips and placed it inside his mouth. The barrel burned his mouth, the weapon still hot from the recent firings, and he squeezed his eyes shut. The tears had stopped now; he was all out of them.

He held the gun in his mouth for how long, he had no idea, but just when the cell phone began to beep, **Low Battery**, and prepared to die, he did the same, his finger beginning to tighten on the trigger of the gun.

With one final sob, he squeezed the trigger on the Glock.

But instead of a loud noise in his ears as a bullet blasted his brains out the back of his skull, and the sweet oblivion of death took him into its cold embrace, he heard a dry *click*. The gun was empty, he was out of bullets.

He began to laugh, long and hard, and while he cradled his son in his arms, he yelled out his frustration. "Come on then, kill me! That's what you want to do, right? Well then fucking do it!"

None of the creatures moved; but merely stood watching him, swaying back and forth like cornstalks on a windy day. The cell phone was ready to turn off for good, and then the rubble behind him began to shift. Stones were pulled inward as slowly but surely, a hole was beginning to form. The creatures hissed and backed away from him, though only a few feet more. Still, they had retreated.

As the rubble shifted behind him, he slid a foot away from the tumbling debris, his son still cradled in his arms.

If the rubble was moving, then it could only mean one thing.

His jaw dropped and his face went ash white. No, it couldn't be. Not now! Not when his son was gone! Not after he'd killed him!

"No, oh God, no. Not now. Not when it's too late!" Jonathan screamed to the forming hole. He turned to the creatures, his eyes filled with anger and loss.

"Not now, not when it doesn't matter. Why didn't you just kill me when you had the chance! Why did you wait?" he screamed at them. The creatures hissed and swayed, watching the rubble disappear as a small hole began to appear in the side of the cave-in.

Though filled with sadness and loss, the will to survive was strong in him, and though he didn't know how he would go on living after everything that had happened, he moved to the hole, something inside him still happy to be alive and finally rescued.

Ever so gently, he set Billy down on the ground, careful not to jar him, like his son was just sleeping. The cell phone beeped again, warning of its impending death, and he aimed it at the opening in the rubble.

"Oh thank God, I'm here, I'm in here! Help me!" he called out, now wanting to live more than ever, no matter what. He realized it was easy to be brave and face death when there was nothing to live for, but still, he wanted to live! He didn't want to die!

He looked down at the still forms of Trudy and his son, and though it broke his heart to leave them, he wanted to live even more.

The opening was now large enough for him to fit through, the workers still moving rocks and debris from the other side, and he stuck his head and shoulders through the opening, the cell phone now in front of him so he could see. He tried not to think about the creatures behind him and how they could grab his feet at any time if they wanted to.

The phone beeped again, warning him that it was really going to stop working soon, and just before it died, the screen showed him his rescuers at the opposite end of the hole as they moved the last of the rubble blocking his path to freedom.

The dim screen of the cell phone illuminated the opening and his rescuers clearly in its pale ambience, and just as the battery died, turning the phone off forever, Jonathan screamed as the black claws and milk-white eyes came for him, grabbing him by the head and shoulders and pulling him deeper into the darkness he had longed for only seconds before.

CHARLIE

Summer 1979

Blood was everywhere.

It covered the ground underneath the porch, seeping into every crack in the pavement. To a casual glance, it looked like someone had taken a can of red paint and had tried to paint the ground, but on a closer examination, bits of gore and gobbets of skin and hair could be seen.

One rivulet of blood seeped down the small incline, slowly meandering its way out from under the porch and into the bright day.

Above the blood spread out on the pavement on the back porch, a door opened to the house it was attached to. It was a gray, two-family house with asbestos shingles. There was a medium-sized patch of grass on the right side of the house and in the middle of the green lawn was a newly planted pine tree.

In twenty years the pine tree would be as large as the house, but until then it was only four feet tall.

A woman stepped out of the back door. She was pretty, in her early thirties and had her hair tied in a bun on the back of her head. She had a slim face with high cheekbones, and though she wore an old housecoat, the figure within was breathtaking.

Susan Warden looked around the yard, searching for something. She walked to the edge of the porch, one foot hovering over the top stair.

Her eyes scanned the yard and when she didn't see what she was after, she called out, her melodic voice floating on the wind. "Thad! Where are you! Supper's almost ready!" She waited for a reply, but there was no answer. "Darn it, where is that boy?" She asked herself.

She had told her only son to stay in the yard, informing him it would be time to eat soon. She also knew that if he hadn't obeyed her, his father would end up beating him. She hated to see Thad get hit, but she knew better than to get in the way when a father was disciplining his son; though it broke her heart.

With a weary sigh, she stepped onto the top step, the wood creaking under her heel, and it was then that she spotted the thin red line of scarlet seeping out from under the porch.

Curious, though not overly concerned just yet, she stepped down the stairs, her shoes clicking on the painted wood. Once she reached the pavement, she walked around to the side of the porch. There was a small door there, which when opened, would allow access to the underside of the porch. Her husband kept the lawn-mower there, as well as a few gardening tools, such as clippers for the hedges on the left side of the house and a few old knives he used for pruning the shrubs on the front of the house.

Staring at the bottom of the door, she could see the slim ribbon of red was coming out from under it. Not knowing what it could be, she unhitched the small latch and opened it. Whatever she had thought she would find under the porch paled in comparison to what she discovered.

Under the porch, spread out on the ground like a laboratory experiment, was Mrs. Johnson's cat from next door.

The cat was in a hundred pieces, butchered to the point of being unrecognizable. The internal organs were spread out like someone had been taking inventory. The small body had been sliced open, a thin line straight through the abdomen, from its tail straight up to its neck.

All four legs had been severed from the body, each one spread out like chicken wings at a barbecue. But it was the head of the dead animal that was most disturbing—if that were possible.

The head had no eyes, each one having been plucked from its socket. The tongue had been pulled as far out as it would go and then had been sliced off at its base.

Susan Warden stared in horror at the morbid scene before her, her mouth hanging open in disgust, her gorge rising in her gullet from the death smell seeping out into the open air.

A slight movement caused her to look deeper into the darkness under the porch, and as she did this, she saw the sneaker of her son, still on his foot.

For an instant her heart lodged in her throat, but then the sneaker moved and her son leaned forward, showing her his face. He was fine, alive and well.

Sort of.

There was her son, her beautiful seven-year-old boy, sitting on the ground with one of his father's knives in his hand. His hands and face were covered in blood, and as she moved slightly to the side of the door, the sunlight penetrated a little more into the gloom under the porch, chasing the darkness away, banishing it back to the realm from which it came.

Thad looked up at her, an angelic smile on his lips. "Hi, Mom, is it time for supper yet?" he asked, as if he had no idea what he had just done by butchering a helpless animal.

"Oh my God. No, Thad, not again! I thought you were over this," Susan said as she stepped away, falling back on her haunches. "The doctor said you were getting better."

Thad shrugged, the blood covering him giving the boy a devilish appearance. "What's wrong, Mom, why do you look so unhappy? I was just playing with Charlie."

"Unhappy? My God, Thad, look what you did to Mrs. Johnson's cat? You promised you wouldn't do this anymore. You promised me there would be no more Charlie."

Thad only shrugged again. "It wasn't me, Mom, I swear, it was Charlie's idea. I didn't really want to do it and then it was done."

"Charlie? Thaddeus Peter Warden, what has your father and I told you about Charlie?"

Thad's smiling face faltered for a moment as he thought back to what he'd been told. "That Charlie isn't real, that he's just in my imagination."

"That's right, he is, now come out of there right now. We need to clean this mess up before your father gets home. You know what the doctor said. If this happened again, you were going to go into the hospital. You don't want to go there, do you?"

"You mean to go live with the crazy people?"

"Yes, dear, the crazy people," Susan answered back.

Thad climbed out from under the porch, blood dripping from his arms and legs like he had been inside a slaughter house.

"No, Mom, I don't want to go there. I want to stay with you and Dad."

With a weary sigh, Susan walked the few feet to the water hose and began unraveling it as she prepared to wash the blood out from under the porch. Inside her mind, she wanted to scream, but she knew she needed to stay calm, keep level-headed—for her son's sake.

"That's good, honey, I want you stay with us, too," she said, her voice calm. "Now come over here so I can wash you up."

Thad did as he was told, and a second later, he was being blasted with cold water. He tried to turn his face away from the spray, but his mother only yelled at him, making him turn back around so she could wash all the blood off his clothes.

Her head was constantly swiveling like an owl's as she tried to make sure none of the neighbors spotted what was happening in her yard.

Once she was finished with him, she grabbed a rake from the side of the house and began raking up the cat pieces; quickly tossing them into a nearby barrel with a small shovel.

Later that night, when her family was asleep, she planned to sneak back out and bag the remains up properly, but for now this would have to do. Her husband would be home any minute from work, and if he found Thad like this, covered in blood, well, that would be it for her son.

Though she knew there was something wrong with her boy, she knew she still loved him deeply, and as any mother would do for her son, she would lie, cheat and steal to keep him safe.

When he was as clean as he was going to get, she shooed him into the house.

"Now, get, and I don't want to hear about Charlie anymore. I told you before and so did the doctor, when he tells you to do something, you have to tell him *no*."

"Yes, Mom," Thad said solemnly, stomping up the stairs, his clothing soaking wet.

"And take those clothes off before you go into the house. I just did the floor earlier today. And go take a shower, too."

"Yes, Mom," he said again, now stripping his clothes off in the doorway. When he was finished, he dropped the soggy clothes onto the porch and stepped inside to take a shower.

While Thad went into the house, Susan finished cleaning up the dismembered carcass of the cat. The entire time she did this, with the blood and pieces of organs and entrails floating on the river of water she was creating, she kept telling herself that her son was fine. That he was just going through a faze. All boys did. There was a faze when all boys liked to blow up animals with firecrackers and hurt things.

But then they grew up and realized they were wrong and stopped doing such horrible things.

All she had to do was protect her son until he broke out of the faze, that's all.

Then everything would be fine.

Finishing up, she made sure all the blood was gone from under the porch, and once satisfied, she straightened and checked her clothes to make sure there was no blood on them. After wrapping up the hose, she went back into the house to put supper on the table.

Just before entering the house, she paused at the door and made sure to place a large smile on her lips, as if nothing had happened. Though crying inside, she stepped into the house, and hoped she and her son could put the horrible incident behind them.

* * *

"Come on, Thad, it's time to get ready for bed," Susan called out to her son.

Thad was laying down in the living room, watching the black and white television. It was almost seven-thirty at night and he had just finished watching the Electric Company on PBS. After a few commercials, that weren't really supposed to be commercials, the channel saying thank you to all the corporate sponsors, Zoom would be on.

After that he would have to go to bed.

"Okay, Mom, I'm going," he said.

He knew once he changed into his pajamas and brushed his teeth, that he'd be all set to watch his show.

His father was in the kitchen doing paperwork at the table. Being only seven years old, Thad didn't really care much about bills for the water and electricity he used. To him it was all free, like some magical creature sent it into his house everyday.

In minutes he had brushed his teeth, changed, and was ready to watch his show. He could hear his parents talking in the kitchen, and sometimes his father's voice would go up a notch, before his mother would shush him and he would lower it.

Thad barely noticed, engrossed in the start of his program.

At five to eight, the show was over and he entered the kitchen to say good night to his parents. He had no way of knowing his parents had been talking about him. Though Susan hadn't told her husband about the cat incident earlier in the day, she had hinted about Thad's well being.

His father looked at him and Thad could have sworn he saw fear in his father's eyes. But then his father blinked and the fear was gone, if it was ever there to begin with.

His mother bent over and gave him a hug.

"Good night, honey, sleep well," she said and kissed him on the cheek.

"'Night, Mom," he replied, kissing her on the left cheek, as well.

"'Night, Dad," he said to his father.

"Good night, son, be good. I'll see you tomorrow night when I get home from work."

"'Kay," he replied and left the kitchen, the hushed tones of his parents beginning again.

Climbing into bed, he grabbed his favorite stuffed animal from his nightstand—an old ratty bunny he'd had since he was three—and curled up under the blankets.

"Good night, Charlie," he said to the empty bedroom, the room wreathed in shadows.

"Good night, Thad," Charlie answered from out of the darkness of his mind.

Content and happy, Thad closed his eyes and slowly drifted off to sleep.

"Thaaaad. Thaaaad. Wake up, we have work to do," Charlie whispered in Thad's mind.

Thad rolled over in his sleep, grunting slightly.

"Come on, Thad, there are things to do, all kinds of fun stuff. Just get up so we can play."

Slowly, Thad opened his eyes. The room was wreathed in darkness and the small clock on his nightstand told him it was well past four in the morning.

Sitting up in bed, he looked round his room.

"Charlie? Is that you?"

"Sure is, pal, and boy have I got some great stuff for us to do tonight. Mrs. Johnson's cat was nothing compared to what we're gonna do next. You'll see."

Thad slid out of bed, stretching his arms over his head. "Oh, I don't know, Charlie. My mom was awful mad at what you did to Mrs. Johnson's cat. Maybe we shouldn't do anything until she's not mad anymore."

"Aww, don't be a spoilsport. She's not mad, she's just jealous she didn't get to play with us, that's all. Come on, I'd never lie to you. Now let's play before I have to leave again."

"Okay, what do you want to do?" Thad asked.

"Well, first, pally boy, you need to go into the kitchen and get a knife; then we'll go from there."

"Okay, Charlie, but I don't really know if I want to play. I should really be in bed sleeping. The last time Mom caught me up playing with you, she was real mad."

"That's all in the past now, Thad my boy. Plus, she'll never know you were up, I promise."

Thad thought about it for a moment, and decided Charlie was right. He always listened to Charlie. He was much smarter than him and always knew what to say.

"Okay, Charlie, you win," Thad said, impressionable as all seven-year-olds are.

"Good, Thad, now go into the kitchen and get a big knife, then I'll tell you what's next."

"Why can't I know now?"

"Because it's a surprise," Charlie said sweetly in his head.

When Thad entered the kitchen and found a large steak knife in the butcher's block holder on the counter, Charlie nudged him toward his parent's room.

"Why are we going to my mom's room?" Thad asked, curious.

"You'll see, Thad, now you just relax and let me take over and I'll do everything. You just sit back and watch."

"Okay, you can take over. I like it when you do that, that way I don't have to think about anything too much. I can just watch."

"Exactly, Thad, exactly."

Thad walked like a sleepwalker into his parent's bedroom. Sleeping soundly in their bed, his parents were unaware of their son hovering over their motionless bodies.

Charlie smiled as he raised the knife over his father's chest.

This is going to be fun, Charlie thought, and just before he plunged the knife up to the hilt into Thad's father's chest, Thad cried out, understanding what Charlie was doing. But Charlie was in control now and plunged the knife deep into the man's heart. Then he yanked the bloody knife from the twitching body and jumped onto the bed and sat on Thad's mother's chest.

In the darkness, she opened her eyes, and in the wan light of the room, she saw death looking down on her. She managed one fleeting scream before the knife slid into her throat, slicing her vocal cords in two, severing her jugular in half. Charlie was bathed in her blood, and he opened his mouth and let it slide down his throat.

Inside his mind, Thad had passed out from the horror of watching his parent's slaughtered like small animals, Charlie now in full control.

Charlie laughed out loud and began slicing and hacking, dozens of incisions marking the soft flesh as blood soaked into the sheets. Thad's body soon became covered in his parent's blood like he had bathed in it.

With the mattress soaking up the gallons of blood, Charlie continued butchering the two corpses long into the night, Thad now a cowering ball of fear inside his own mind.

* * *

Bright and early the next morning, Mrs. Johnson was out looking for her cat.

Mr. Sprinkles had gone and disappeared on her the day before, and she was ever so worried.

But the moment she walked past the Warden's house, all concern's about her cat vanished when she saw the horrible sight lying on the front porch of the house.

Running toward the small, bloody boy, she almost tripped over the small tree root that crossed the pathway from left to right. Thad's father had been planning on getting to that root any day now, but work had kept him from doing so.

Susan had chastised him constantly, telling him if someone tripped, they could get sued.

Recovering her balance, Mrs. Johnson ran to the small body and rolled it over to find it was Thad, the small boy who lived in the house. He was unconscious, and she could easily see his small chest rising and falling slowly.

She couldn't believe all the blood covering the boy. It was like he had poured a can of red paint over him. She quickly checked for signs of wounds, but in a few seconds was fairly certain the boy was unharmed.

But if that were so, then where did all the blood come from?

Stepping into the open front door, she called out. She almost stopped herself, thinking if there was some insane killer in the house then she would find herself in a real pickle, but concern for her neighbors gave her the courage to continue. Plus, she made sure to be ready to bolt back through the door at the first sign of danger.

Entering the house, she walked through the living room and into the dining room. The bedrooms were off to the right and she slowed at the first doorway.

The door was slightly closed, and with ever so much caution, she pushed it open with her foot. Her heart was beating so fast she hoped she didn't have a heart attack. She was in her seventies and knew not to agitate herself too much.

But when she opened the door and stared inside at the two undistinguishable bodies sprawled on the bed, she found herself throwing up her breakfast across the bedroom floor.

Feeling woozy and knowing she was about to faint, she stumbled away from the bedroom, her eyes looking into every corner of the house, expecting a madman to jump out and kill her, too. But she made it to the kitchen safely and then was out the door, thanking God she was still alive.

For a few seconds she was in a daze, trying to process what she had found inside the house, but she soon came back to the here and now and went back to Thad.

The boy was still there, unconscious, and as she tried to decide what to do next, a police car came into view, casually driving down the street.

The policeman driving the squad car was drinking a cup of coffee, relaxing, enjoying his morning shift when an old woman ran out in front of him, waving her hands and screaming for him to stop.

Slamming on the brakes, hot coffee falling into his lap, he let out a yelp of pain. *Damn that was hot*, he thought. Someone should sue the bastards for making the coffee so damn hot.

Officer Lee Kirkland stopped the police car and climbed out, his pants now soaked.

"Gees, lady, you better have a good reason for running out in the middle of the street or so help me I'm gonna write you a ticket for jaywalking."

Mrs. Johnson ignored him, merely pulling on his arm toward the Warden's house, babbling about murder and mayhem.

With coffee cooling on his pants, Lee was mumbling to himself about what a bad morning he was having as he followed the crazy old lady towards the house as she led him onward.

But after he had investigated inside the house and found the dismembered corpses that were obviously the small boy's butchered parents, and then had to see to the small, covered-in-blood boy that was found unconscious on the house steps, he realized his morning hadn't been going too bad after all.

In fact, next to the small boy's morning, his had been the best one in his entire life.

* * *

The next eleven years went by in a blur for Thaddeus Peter Warden. An orphan of the state, he was bounced from foster home to foster home. He had a tough time of it, even tougher because his friend Charlie had left him the night his parents had been killed and had never returned.

Thad was totally alone in the world, not even Charlie around to keep him company. Some of the foster families he was tossed into were good, while others were worse than going to prison.

Through it all, the only thing Thad had to keep him strong was his bunny from when he was a child. Somehow, after all the years, he managed to keep hold of the stuffed animal.

Of course, when he had entered foster care when he was seven he had other belongings with him, but over the years, they were destroyed, lost or downright stolen from him by other children or his foster parents themselves.

His parent's killers were never found; the murders listed as a break-in gone horribly wrong.

The authorities assumed young Thad had woken up and discovered his parent's bloody bodies and had ended up becoming covered in their blood as he tried to help them.

Since that day, Thad never spoke of that night, blocking it from his memory.

When he had been brought in to the hospital to make sure he was all right, and the police tried to find out what he knew, he had told them that Charlie had done it. The police thought they had a suspect, that is until Thad told them Charlie was his invisible friend. The police had just brushed it off as a coping mechanism for the small boy who couldn't handle the tragic death of both his parents.

After all, no boy would want to think the murderer of his parents was still at large somewhere out there in the real world.

Eventually, the police stopped asking and Thad's case was filed away as unsolved, added to a box with dozens more. Thad was lost in the foster care system, to be absorbed like thousands of other children.

That is, until he was eighteen.

At eighteen, he left the foster family he had spent the last three years with and got a job at a burger joint and began to go to college at night after work.

Six years later—it took longer because of going at night—he graduated with honors, and with his degree, landed a better job.

Three years after that he met a nice woman, dated her for a year, fell in love, and married her.

And four years after becoming happily married, the young couple had their first child, a beautiful little girl they named Susan after Thad's late mother.

Everything was going great. Thad had a good job, a loving wife, and a beautiful daughter.

There was nothing he could have wanted in the world that could make him happier than he already was. There was nothing he wanted that he didn't have. Everything was perfect.

That is, until Charlie came back to visit one dark night.

Summer 2007

Thad was asleep, dreaming of his parents. His mother and father would often come to him in his dreams, telling him how proud they were of him and how they missed him.

He would always hug them and never want to let go, but then the dream would end and his parents would fall back into the void from whence they went every morning when he woke up.

But this night his parents didn't come to him. Instead, he got a blast from the past as the voice of Charlie filled his head.

"Hey, pal, how've you been? Missed me? My you've grown. You're a big boy now, aren't you?"

"Charlie? Oh my God, is that really you?" Thad shook his head, disbelieving the voice. "No, you aren't real; you're just in my head."

"Oh really? Is that you talking or one of those psychiatrists they had you seeing all those years ago. I'm real, buddy boy, just as real as that beautiful wife sleeping next to you."

Thad opened his eyes and looked to his right, his wife sleeping soundly next to him. Jenny was oblivious to the conversation going on next to her and Thad decided to take the conversation into the next room.

Climbing out of bed, he walked out of the room, taking his bathrobe as he left. As he walked by his daughter's room, he paused and glanced inside.

Little Susan was sleeping soundly, his old bunny now her favorite possession. She was almost three and he loved her so much it hurt.

"Oh, isn't she darling, and she looks just like her mom," Charlie said.

Walking to the bathroom, Thad peed and went into the kitchen.

"What do you want, Charlie? If you are real and not just a figment of my imagination then I'm far too old to have an imaginary friend. You need to leave me alone."

Charlie chuckled. "Leave you alone? Oh no, Thad my boy. In fact, I've never left you. I've been in here all along, waiting for the right time to say hello. And this is it. This night, tonight. Don't you know what tonight is?"

Though he didn't want to admit it, he did know what tonight was.

It was two years from the thirtieth anniversary of his parents' deaths.

Charlie picked up his thoughts and purred in contentment like a big ol' alley cat.

"Ah, you do remember. But you don't remember much about that night, do you?"

Thad shook his head, his silent debate filling his head as he sat down at the kitchen table. "No, I don't, Charlie, and I don't want to remember. What will it do? It's in the past now, too late to do anything to change it."

Charlie chuckled again. "Oh, but don't you see, Thad my boy, I can help you remember. I can show you what happened that night and how much fun we had."

Charlie pried open the locked door at the back of Thad's mind, opening it wide and allowing all the memories of that fateful night to come forth.

Like a lightning bolt striking his head, Thad cried out in pain and fell to the kitchen floor as memories of that terrible night slowly crept into his mind. How he had woken in the middle of the night and how Charlie had made him get a large knife and made him go into his parent's bedroom.

But this time Charlie showed him everything, all the bloody details of his parent's slaughter.

Thad screamed out in pain, wanting to shut out the images, but incapable of doing so. Like a movie reel flowing in his mind, he saw his mother's slashed throat and watched her eyes roll up in her head. He saw his father's gaping chest wound and slack jaw as he expelled his last breath, all the while gazing up into his son's eyes as his father's eyes showed the disbelief that his own son could do this to him.

Charlie laughed as he let the images pour forth, relishing in Thad's pain. Image after image flooded into Thad's mind, overwhelming him until he had no choice but to burrow away from the torture. His face was scrunched in torment, tears streaming down his cheeks to pool on the kitchen floor.

At that moment his mind cracked.

"That's okay, Thad, you go and rest; I'll take over for a while," Charlie crowed happily.

Thad barely heard Charlie, his mind fracturing from the brutal realization that it had been his own hands that had killed his parents. It had been him that took their lives, and his own childhood, away in the blink of an eye.

Jenny had come into the kitchen, awoken by his screams. She knelt down next to him.

"Thad, what's wrong, honey, are you okay? Thad? Speak to me."

At first, Thad's head was buried in his arms as he sobbed into the floor. But at the sound of Jenny's voice, he stopped sobbing and then, slowly, looked up at her.

Jenny gazed down at him, her arms around his shoulders, but when Thad's eyes met hers, she saw something different inside him, something she had never seen before.

When Thad spoke, his voice deeper, harsher. "I'm sorry to tell you, dear, but Thad isn't home anymore. But don't worry, he gave me the keys to the house to keep the lights on, so to speak."

Jenny fell back onto her butt, not quite understanding what was happening, and she stared at Thad as he slowly stood up, bent his neck to the left and the right, as if getting used to his body, and moved his arms a little, looking as if he was trying to get comfortable in a new suit. He reached over to the counter and picked up one of the large butcher knives sitting in the dish strainer after being cleaned from dinner that night.

Bringing it to his mouth, he licked the blade with his tongue, actually cutting the tip of his tongue on the long edge of the knife. A small ribbon of blood seeped out of his mouth, and he smiled down at Jenny, still curled up on the floor.

"Mmmm, that's good. There's nothing like the taste of Warden blood. I should know," Thad hissed.

"Thad, what are you doing? Please, put the knife down, you're scaring me," Jenny whispered to him.

Thad chuckled in a way she had never heard before. "Oh, Jenny, don't fight it. If you do it'll only hurt all the more. Tell you what. If you give in to me and let me have some fun with you, I'll do the little girl quick and painless."

Thad was standing over her now, and she realized there was something wrong with her husband. She didn't know what was happening to him, but she knew he had a knife and was threatening to kill her and her daughter. She knew about what had happened to Thad's parents, and though she could never put the pieces together, she wasn't about to let tonight be a repeat of what had happened to Thad's parents all those years ago.

So as Thad walked closer to her, leering menacingly, she found her legs directly under his crotch as he straddled her. With as much force as she could muster, she kicked up into his groin, crushing his testacles and sending them up into his abdomen.

Thad let out a wheeze of expelled air and fell over like a toppling tree. Jenny rolled to the side and jumped to her feet. Snatching her cell phone off the kitchen table, she ran for little Susan's bedroom, slamming the door closed and pushing the small bureau in front of it.

Little Susan stirred in her bed, dreaming fitfully, and Jenny quickly dialed 9-1-1 and prayed help would get to her in time.

* * *

Detective Lee Kirkland was sitting at home when he heard the domestic disturbance call go out on the police band radio.

The second he heard the address, he knew who it was.

Over the years, he had kept tabs on the Warden boy. He didn't know why, but there was something about that kid's story that always bothered him.

It was the way there had been no evidence that anyone else had ever been in the house that night, with the exception of the old lady who had found the bodies. And the way the knife found at the scene only had the small boy's fingerprints on it. It was assumed he had touched the knife when he found the bodies, but Lee never truly believed that assumption.

Though no one would jump to the conclusion that Thad had killed his own parents, the idea had always eaten at Lee's stomach, despite not being able to prove it.

So he kept an eye on the boy through all the foster homes, to the job at the restaurant, and right up until he had was married.

He had actually been in the back of the church and had watched the entire ceremony.

The bride had been beautiful.

He also visited the hospital where Thad's wife had given birth and had seen Thad's daughter in the nursery only a few days after she was born. Often, on many a lonely night when he was too restless to sleep, he drove by Thad's one-family home in the suburbs, checking to make sure things were all right.

Even now, when he was only a few months away from retirement, he continued to keep an eye on the man, though he had to admit it wasn't as often as he would have liked. In the past few years, he had slowed down, trying to focus on his own disintegrating marriage and two ungrateful children.

But he had to admit, in many ways, Thad was more like his son than his own two boys were...the ungrateful bastards.

So when the call went out, Lee was already sliding his revolver into his chest holster and tossing on his jacket, running to his car like he was on fire.

There had never been a problem with Thad in all the years he had watched him, so what could possibly be happening in his house tonight that would warrant a domestic call?

Jumping into his car, he started the engine and pulled out into the street, his gumball light already flashing to warn other drivers he was in a hurry and on police business.

He was only eight minutes away from the Warden home if he didn't stop and wasn't worried about traffic, and if he floored it, he could knock yet another minute off that time. As his foot flattened the gas pedal to the floorboard, he decided he'd see if he could do even better than that.

* * *

Charlie picked himself up off the kitchen floor and winced in pain.

Christ that hurt, maybe being in charge of Thad's body wasn't such a good idea after all, he thought.

Stumbling out of the kitchen, he heard noise coming from little Susan's room, and after a few quick breaths to right himself, he began moving forward with new determination etched on his face.

"Oh, Jenny, you shouldn't have done that. Now I'm going to make you both suffer," Charlie said to the empty hallway.

When he reached the bedroom door, he tried the knob and found it locked. Cursing up a storm, he tried to break it down, but the door was solid wood and wasn't giving easily.

Remembering the knife in his hand, he smiled, and began slamming it, tip first, into the wood. Like a small chisel, the wood began chipping away, small pieces littering the floor by his feet like bits of confetti.

From the opposite side of the door, he could hear little Susan crying and that only made him strike the door harder. Then he remembered Thad kept a few tools under the sink and he ran back to the kitchen, returning a second later with tools in hand.

With a large screwdriver and a hammer, he began working at the hinges, knowing in a few minutes he would have the entire door off. Jenny was crying, screaming for him to leave, that she had called the police, but he ignored her.

After the top hinge was pried loose, he went to work on the bottom one. This one was even easier, and a moment later, he was yanking the door away from its frame to clatter into the hallway.

Jenny was at the window; actually debating the ten foot jump, when he charged inside the room, pushing the bureau to the floor and lunging over it. Grabbing Jenny by the hair, she screamed, now only having one hand free, the other one holding little Susan tightly to her.

"Going somewhere, dear? That wasn't very nice. We have so much to do before I can go away again," Charlie said while waving the reacquired butcher knife in his hand before her eyes like a silver snake.

Charlie twisted Jenny around so she was staring up at him and she saw nothing of her husband in the malevolent face glaring down at her.

"Who are you?" she whimpered in fright, Susan crying into her shoulder.

Thad's face creased into a wide smile. "Why, I'm Charlie, Thad's friend, and I've come for a visit. Do you want to play with me?"

Jenny screamed and Charlie sliced her cheek, causing her to shriek even louder.

Charlie threw her against the wall, laughing in utter ecstasy. "God, have I waited for this!" he yelled to the ceiling before charging over to Jenny. He picked her up again, while in her arms, Susan screamed even louder.

"Shut that brat up or I'll shut it up for you," he snapped as he ripped Jenny's nightdress off, exposing her white skin to the air.

She tried to sooth Susan, completely ignoring her nakedness, and Charlie licked his lips in anticipation of what was to come.

"Oh, this is going to be so good," he said as he moved up and wrapped his left arm around her torso, cupping her right breast in his hand. He squeezed the nipple hard, causing her to cry out in pain, which only aroused him even more.

"I might as well see just what Thaddy boy liked about you for myself."

In the house next door, across from the bedroom window, lights were coming on, the noise Charlie and Jenny were making more than enough to wake the neighborhood.

Deciding it was time to get down to business, Charlie grabbed little Susan by her small arms, yanking the baby free and tossing the small body onto the bed. Susan cried bloody murder as she flew through the air, but was otherwise unharmed. Charlie pulled Jenny to him, his hot breath on her face. The knife was at her throat, and all he had to do was twitch his hand and her jugular was severed.

"Ignore the whelp, it's fine. And don't move if you want to keep living for the next five minutes. Now on your knees, bitch. I have something for you, and if you so much as move a muscle I don't give you permission to move, I'll slit your throat and finish my fun on your daughter."

With tears streaming down her cheeks, Jenny slid to the floor, the knife never wavering from her neck. Charlie undid his pajama bottoms and let free his engorged member.

"Go ahead, bitch, do it," he hissed. "Suck it."

She swallowed hard, the motion causing the blade to cut into her skin. She was fairly certain she was only delaying the inevitable. Sooner or later, he was going to kill her, and then her daughter, and there was nothing she could do about it.

Knowing she had no choice, she prepared to take him into her mouth when a loud crashing sound flooded the house, coming from the front door.

"What the fuck was that?" Charlie hissed.

Kicking Jenny to the floor, he aimed the blade at her eye. "If you move, so help me I'll slice you in half. Do I make myself clear?"

She nodded slowly, utterly cowed by this man that was supposed to be her loving husband and yet was somehow something so totally alien to her it was unimaginable.

Charlie went to the bedroom doorway and stopped when he saw a man charging into the house.

Detective Lee Kirkland looked up from the kicked in front door, and when he saw Thad with the knife in his hand, he aimed his revolver at him.

"Freeze, Thad, or I'll shoot!"

"Shit, the cops!" Charlie screamed while laughing, and ran back into the bedroom. Once inside, he ran over to Jenny, who was just about to risk the drop out the window, her baby in her arms once more. Charlie grabbed her by the hair and pulled her back into the bedroom, using her body as a shield.

Lee had reached the doorway and aimed his revolver at Thad, though with Jenny in the way, he had no shot.

"Don't you even try it, pal, or the woman gets it, and then the baby right after," Charlie said, breathing heavily.

"If you do anything to either of them, I'll shoot you down like a dog," Lee warned, not lowering his gun.

"So, what do I care? If you kill me, then you kill Thad, not me, I'll be fine!"

Lee's eyes creased in thought. "What the hell are you talking about, Warden?"

"Oh please, give me a break. You don't think I haven't seen you all these years hiding in the shadows, do you? Maybe Thad hasn't, but I sure as hell did. I tell ya, pal, you're one guy who seriously needs to get a life."

Lee licked his lips, studying the man across the room, this man who had never done an evil deed in his entire life, not so much as getting a parking ticket. And now he was holding a sharpened blade to his wife's neck, prepared to slice her throat at a moment's notice.

Deciding he had nothing to lose, Lee took a shot in the dark. "Is that you in there, Charlie?"

Thad's face lit up with surprise. "Well, I'll be. The stupid cop isn't that stupid after all. You figured it out, have you? Good for you, not like anyone will believe you, though."

"Maybe not, but I'm not going to let you harm this woman or her baby."

"Uh-huh, and exactly how are you going to stop me?"

While the two men argued, Jenny was trying an idea of her own. She had her left hand free, the other holding Susan, and she reached across the few inches separating her from the small table that still had her cell phone on it.

Though a cell phone wasn't much of a weapon, the antenna on her phone was one of the older models. It extended out six inches from the top of the phone, but a few months ago, little Susan had gotten her hands on it and had broken a few inches off the tip.

Now the antenna was sharp and she had to constantly make sure it was out of Susan's reach for fear her daughter would cut herself with it. She was meaning to get it fixed, but now it looked like her procrastination just might save her life, and her baby's as well.

While the two men debated back and forth, Jenny reached out and picked up the phone, then, with only the one hand, she managed to pull the antenna out the entire three inches still left on it.

Holding it in her hand, she waited for the right moment.

Thad was arguing, and as he did, the knife blade would sometimes move slightly away from her throat. There were the beginnings of a pattern, and as she waited for an opening, counting in her head, she took her chance when it came. With only a guess, she brought the hand with the phone over her shoulder, hopefully going for Thad's eye.

She cringed as the antenna plunged into his left eye, puncturing the orb like a hard-boiled egg. A clear liquid seeped out of the socket to drip onto her naked shoulder, and the arm around her let go, Thad now screaming in pain.

She dropped to the floor and rolled away, Susan screaming in her arms again as she was gently crushed, but not hurt, under Jenny's rolling body.

Then she heard the gunshots.

Lee Kirkland almost didn't take the chance Jenny gave him as her hand came up and stabbed Thad in the eye.

Thad screamed in pain and dropped the knife as his hand went up to his punctured eye. Jenny rolled away on the floor and there was Thad, standing like the police manual's perfect target, exposed and unwilling to surrender.

Just before Lee fired, Thad was already refocusing his anger. Bending over, he picked up the knife and charged at Lee.

For a heartbeat, Lee didn't fire, too amazed at the ferocity of Thad's anger. But then he broke free of his shock and fired three bullets into the man's chest. Thad was thrown back against the bedroom wall, missing the window by a few inches.

He fell to the floor and landed on his knees. He looked up at Lee and smiled, as if he knew something Lee didn't, then he slumped over, his head falling forward to touch the floor.

It looked like he was just praying instead of dying.

Lee ran over to Jenny and knelt down next to her, helping her to sit up. There was a baby blanket on the floor and he picked it up, draping it over Jenny's nude body. She was crying. If they were tears of joy at being saved, relief, or sadness, he didn't know.

Since he had burst into the house, only a few minutes had passed, the time seeming like forever. Little Susan cried in Jenny's arms, but Jenny soothed the child and eventually Susan responded to the soft words of kindness from her mother.

"Is he...?" she asked in a whisper, tears on her cheeks. She had a small cut on her neck, superficial, but still bleeding slightly.

Lee nodded. "Yeah, he is, I pumped three rounds into him. I'm sorry."

She only nodded as he helped her up. As they were shuffling toward the doorway, and were just about to leave the bedroom, Lee paused at the soft rustle of movement behind him.

Not knowing what it could be, assuming it was Thad's body settling on the floor, he told Jenny to go into the kitchen and wait for the arriving police. He stopped and turned back around, planning on taking care of Thad's cooling corpse. Leaning on the doorframe, he lowered his head to stare at the body of Thad Warden.

Lee's eyes went wide as Thad slowly sat up. The bullet wounds in his chest were still apparent, still weeping blood and Lee's mouth fell open when Thad smiled at him. It was the same smile that said, *I know something you don't.*

Lee froze, forgetting about the gun in his hand as he watched the impossible happening. Thad was dead, there was no question about it, the bullet holes were proof. Hell, one was exactly over the man's heart!

Thad reached over to his right, picked up the butcher knife, and turned it on himself. Starting at the top of his head, he cut down, over his face, past his neck and down his chest.

He stopped at his waist.

He now had a red line splitting his body in half, like he was trying to separate the left and right sides.

With that knowing smile never leaving his lips, he reached up and dug his fingernails into the red seam splitting his face in two. He began pulling like he was taking off the skin of a chicken, actually peeling the skin away.

Red gristle seeped out of the exposed skin as he slowly peeled off his face and hair and then began tearing open his chest. It was like he was a giant orange and he wanted the skin off himself at all costs.

Lee stared in awe as the man across the bedroom pushed the old skin off his body and stood up. Like his skin was a pair of pants, he pushed downward. One leg and then the other were slid out of the skin suit.

The skin of Thaddeus Peter Warden now lay on the floor like a balled-up piece of laundry, but what was now standing in front of Lee was not a skinless man.

Instead, there was another face, and hair and chest, all perfectly formed.

The face underneath the old one was a hard face, with frown lines around the mouth. Where Thad's eyes had been blue, this new person's eyes were light green, and what was most amazing was the punctured eye was whole again.

The man shook his body like a wet dog after a bath, blood droplets spraying everywhere. Seeing his nakedness, he reached over to the small bed and pulled off the sheet hanging over the side of it.

Draping it over his body, he now looked fully at Lee.

"Thank you so much for your help, Detective. I've wanted a change of clothing for almost thirty years. I just haven't been able to figure out how to do it."

Lee's mouth hung open, and he swallowed hard, his throat jumping with the motion.

"Is that you now, Charlie?"

Charlie smiled. "In the flesh." He laughed, long and loud. "I like that, seems to fit."

Suddenly, more voices filled the house as the on-call policemen arrived to investigate the disturbance.

"Police!" the first officer called out to the house, his partner right behind him.

"Over here! I'm in here!" Lee called out, taking his eyes away from Charlie for a split second.

But when he turned back, the man was gone, only a pool of blood on the floor and a handprint on the windowsill to ever prove he was there. On the floor, the skin suit that had been Thad Warden was gone, taken when Charlie had escaped.

Lee ran to the window and looked outside, his revolver leading the way, but when he looked onto the grass, there was nothing but a few red footprints that faded away as the blood on Charlie's feet were wiped clean in the wet grass of the morning dew.

A shuffle at the bedroom doorway caused him to turn around and he saw one of the police officers staring at him.

"Detective, I didn't think I'd find you here," the officer said in a surprised voice.

"Yeah well, I was in the area, so I took the call," Lee said.

"At four in the morning?" the officer asked.

"Yeah, at four in the morning. Look, quit your yapping and get an APB out on a naked man in a sheet. Oh, and he's covered in blood. That shouldn't be too hard to find, huh?"

The officer hesitated, as if the description was ludicrous, until Lee barked at him to move. The officer did as instructed, moving back to the front door to start looking outside, the hand radio in his left hand already talking to dispatch while his partner saw to Jenny.

As Lee went to console Jenny, he had a feeling that Charlie would never be found, no matter how thorough a search.

And he prayed that no one else would ever find him.

ZOMBIES VS. MUMMIES

"Hurry, they're right behind us!" Carly yelled to the others. The small group of refugees struggled to keep up, but each time they rounded a corner, Carly was always a few more feet ahead of them.

The reason for this was obvious to anyone who was watching the rag-tag group of survivors.

Carly was in her early twenties, with long brown hair and a trim figure. Even though she was malnourished, she was still healthy enough to run.

Meanwhile, behind her, the group of ten survivors was either old, wounded, or infirm to the point they could barely walk.

The reason for this was simple as well. They were all that was left of the residents of the Greenwood Nursing Home, and Carly was the last of the nurse's aides still alive. She lived over an hour away from the nursing home and when the dead began to walk, and accidents and society imploded in less than a day, she knew she could never get home safely. So she stayed at the nursing home and took care of the people who depended on her. In many ways they were her second family. After all, she spent almost as much time with them as she did her own parents and little brother.

They had all stayed barricaded on the second floor of the nursing home, safe but hungry. The kitchen had been on the bottom floor of the two-story building, and with the dead swarming the ground floor, there was no way to get access to the food.

And then the dead had managed to break into the second floor and Carly had desperately gathered the remaining residents and had helped them escape. Many were left behind, and Carly could still remember their screams as the undead tore into them. Many were ripped apart like ravenous dogs were attacking them, and Carly knew the images of internal organs being ripped and pulled from geriatric bodies would haunt her to the day she died. Not that she knew if that would be a long time, of course.

Even now, as they made their way down the street into downtown, she knew they were all about to meet their maker. A large crowd of undead was following them and it was only luck that had kept them from catching up to the aging group of survivors.

And Carly.

Carly had been like a slave driver, yelling, pushing, and pulling to get the residents to move.

She knew if they didn't find shelter in the next few minutes, all her work would be for naught, for they would all be run down and killed, some then returning while others would end up as food for an undead palate.

A shriek floated from the end of the group and Carly turned to see the dead had finally caught up to them. An old man, in his early eighties, complete with walker and sleeping gown, was pulled away from the others as the quickest of the undead grabbed him. He yelled for help in a voice hoarse from smoking, and though he had cancer and only had a few more months to live, that was now taken from him as the dead tore into his mottled flesh and pulled out his failing organs.

"Come on, leave him, it's too late!" Carly yelled to the others who cried, shrieked and begged for their god to save then from the Hell they now found themselves in.

With the old man's dying gasps following them, the rest of the group moved on. Some of the dead stayed with the old man, wanting to feast on the corpse, but most of the zombies continued onward, wanting the fresh kill of the infirm group of residents.

Carly rounded a large building that had a bank on the first floor to see another building that could either be their salvation or their doom.

The Natural History Museum was before her, the large red and white banner hanging over the doors stating that, ***The Egyptian Mummy exhibit was now open.*** Her eyes took in the stone walls and the heavy glass doors and she knew if they could get inside safely, they would be safe from the dead. At least for now.

"Across the street, run for the museum!" Carly yelled to the others as she dashed between two stalled cars and made her way to the stone steps that bordered the front of the museum.

As she ran, her eyes glanced to the right, under the car closest to her. A bloody hand protruded, the limb marinating in a congealed pool of blood. She turned her head away, already feeling herself grow sick from the sight, then continued onward.

So much death, so much carnage, and the answers to why the dead walked still unknown. Before the cable went out, the news had scientists on who tried to decipher how the dead could be walking. It was scientifically impossible, one man said and he remained adamant of his opinion, even after the newsroom was overrun and he was torn apart on live television. Carly was thankful when the screen went dark and a technical difficulty sign had appeared, a low beep replacing the screaming as the newsroom was slaughtered.

Carly stopped at the bottom of the stone steps leading to the museum, turning to see if the group was still following her.

She let out a low howl of sorrow at the sight before her.

Half of the group was now taken down, while the rest ran as fast as their withered legs would allow.

"Hurry! Hurry up!" Carly yelled, her mind willing them to speed up.

Behind the small group, more of the residents of the nursing home were torn apart. Chests were ripped asunder and hearts and kidneys pulled forth, the undead feeding like ravenous dogs. A low growling could be heard, as if the dead were angry at the living.

But for all Carly knew, the growling was in her mind, something created to put a reason to this madness. For if the dead truly hated the living, at last then there would be a reason for the bloodshed, and the death. But if the dead wanted to kill the living for no justifiable reason, then her entire world would be pulled out from under her and she knew she would likely go mad.

"Hurry!" she yelled again, for there was nothing else to say.

As the much smaller group reached her, she turned and began running up the stairs. Her breath came in gasps and she felt faint from lack of food. It had been days since she'd eaten anything substantial. Once they had left the nursing home, she and her charges had been on the run, always one step in front of the undead horde. As she reached the glass doors, she sent a silent prayer to the heavens that they were unlocked.

When her trembling hands pushed on the thick glass, she expected it to remain firm, but she let out a soft squeak of relief when the door slid inward on greased hinges and the cool air of the museum greeted her.

Turning, she opened the door wide, and called out to the group as they ascended the stairs.

Though old and slow, they were still more adept at stairs than the zombies, and as each second passed, they made better time as they climbed them.

Carly ran out and helped the first resident inside, then went for more.

As the last old codger was led inside and into the atrium, Carly practically threw the old man before her so she could close the door. As it slowly hissed shut, the hydraulics slowing it purposely, Carly pushed on it with her shoulder to speed it up.

As it seated in its frame, she shot the bolts on the top and bottom, then went to the other doors to make sure, they too, were secured.

As the first ghoul slammed into the glass, she jumped back and let out a bark of victory. "Hah, you can't get in! I beat you!" she yelled at the pale and bloody face that slid its visage across the glass, leaving a snail trail of pus and gore. More dead countenances collected beside it until more than a dozen were there.

Laughing as if she'd won the lottery, she turned and smiled at the residents as they lay sprawled on the floor. "We did it, we're safe. Now we just have to make sure that none of them are in here and then we can wait for help to come."

The residents nodded, most too tired to speak. They were on the verge of exhaustion and most felt as if they were already dead.

"Come on, let me help you to a chair, then we'll see about finding some water," she said to the first of the group. Falling back into her duty as caretaker, she began helping the first resident up to a standing position. Off to the right, there was a small area with chairs and tables. There was a coffee shack with its gate down, a perfect place for a cup of coffee and a bagel when the museum was open.

She decided that would be a good place to get comfortable. With luck, she could break the lock on the coffee shack and get at the food within.

As she began to help each resident, she had no idea that on the opposite end of the museum, something stirred, something once dead but now reanimated by the same force suffusing the zombies, but something far more ancient.

* * *

"Okay, everyone try and relax," Carly told the residents as they sat huddled in their chairs. "We're safe now. Those things can't get at us in here."

"How do you know that?" a small, tired voice said.

Carly looked to see it was Mrs. Haroldson, a seventy-three year old woman with varicose veins and bleached white hair.

"Because I said so, Mrs. Haroldson. I've taken care of you this far haven't I?"

The old woman nodded before going into a coughing fit.

At the edge of the tables, Walter Randall sat slumped in his chair. He had barely made it through the city, and near the end, when Carly had led the group into the museum, his chest had begun to hurt as well as his left arm. As he sat in his chair, his vision began to grow dim, and before he was able to call for help, a massive heart attack seized him. It was over before it began and Walter's chin touched his chest as his head slumped forward.

As the rest of the group gathered themselves and took stock, no one noticed Walter had died. To the casual eye, it just looked like he had dozed off after all his exertion.

If the world had been how it was a few weeks ago, that would have been the end of it, but whatever mysterious force was bringing the dead to life, quickly entered Walter's body and filled him with renewed life, albeit an undead one.

Walter's eyes snapped open and he looked around the atrium. He saw dozens of bodies, all warm and looking tasty. His mouth watered and he felt a hunger grow within him, one he had never felt before.

There was a hollowness inside him, one he felt could only be filled with human flesh.

Carly was working on getting into the coffee shack, and the first sign she heard that there was a problem was when Mrs. Haroldson screamed. Spinning, she dropped the makeshift tool she was using and stared in horror at the sight before her.

Walter was sitting on Mrs. Haroldson's lap, his teeth an inch deep into her right cheek. Mrs. Haroldson waved her hands in terror as Walter reared back his head, tearing off a thick piece of flesh and swallowing it whole.

"Walter, what the hell are you doing?" Carly screamed at the old man from across the atrium. Walter turned his head and glared at her, a few bits of cheek still protruding from his mouth. As Carly watched, he slurped the meat into his mouth, like a lazy Italian eating spaghetti.

The rest of the group erupted into chaos as each one tried to escape Walter. No one went to help poor Mrs. Haroldson, each resident only worried for their own welfare.

Walter ignored the running prey and went back to feasting on Mrs. Haroldson. As she waved her hands in the air in futility, Walter lowered his face into her withered neck and tore at the wattle below her chin. Like taffy being stretched, the liver spotted skin began to pull, until it snapped, sending a burst of blood in all directions. Walter slurped down the flesh like it was the skin of a roast chicken, then dove in for the glistening muscle and tendons now exposed. Mrs. Haroldson had time for one last screech before Walter's teeth crushed her jugular and tore it free. As warm blood splashed his face, he lapped it up like an old dog, relishing in its essence.

Mrs. Haroldson spasmed as her blood shot from her body, then mercifully, she went still.

The group of residents was now huddled in a corner of the area designated for the coffee shack, each shaking and crying in fear.

As Mrs. Haroldson went limp, Walter fed for a few more seconds, then lost interest. Climbing off the old woman, he turned to face the cowering group. His face and chest, as well as his crotch area, were now slathered with blood and he licked his lips as dead eyes took in the group.

He took a step forward, his dead brain trying to decide who was next, when there was the sound of footsteps coming up from behind him. He began to turn at the sound, but before he had halfway turned, a large brass pedestal—one of many in the museum used to hold velvet ropes and keep customers from touching the exhibits—came crashing down onto his head like a lead weight.

His head didn't so much as crack as implode, the base of the pedestal weighted to support the ropes and more than sufficient to break a skull. Walter was forced to the floor where his head met polished cement, and his brains splattered in all directions, reminding many to witness it of a watermelon struck with a baseball bat.

Carly stood over the very dead old man, breathing heavily as she stared down at the carnage she had wrought. She tried to tell herself it wasn't murder, that Walter had somehow become one of the undead, but deep inside her heart she felt guilt.

"Is everyone okay?" she called to the rest of the group. At first no one replied, but soon voices were sent into the air, each saying they were scared but fine. Carly stepped over Walter, careful not to slip on his brains and blood now coating the polished cement. It was like walking on ice where her feet touched blood.

She held the pedestal in her arms, despite its weight, and she went to investigate Mrs. Haroldson. When she was within a few feet of the old woman, it was very obvious the woman was dead. Her eyes were still open in death, but they were vacant, absent of life. Carly left her, not wanting to move too close.

Carly turned and faced the others and said, "Okay, it's over now. We need to get moving. See what's in this place that can help us survive. Besides, we need to make sure there's no one else in here that can hurt us."

As Carly talked, her back facing Mrs. Haroldson, she didn't know the old woman's eyes had begun moving once more. The pupils had a haze over them now, as if advanced cataract had formed in death. Slowly, the pupils darted back and forth and her left hand began to twitch.

As the group listened to Carly, they saw none of this as Carly was blocking the old woman from their view.

"So we all need to gather whatever we have and in a calm and orderly fashion walk into the main part of the museum. Once there, we'll see which way to go. Any questions?"

Carly was looking at one face to the next when she heard the scrape of the chair behind her. She went rigid, and her face went slack as she realized someone, or something, was behind her.

As she faced the group, she saw the terror in their faces as they looked past her at something that was even now coming for her.

Carly was frozen in fear.

She may have stayed that way, and died right there, but at the last second, as a low moan caressed her ear and she felt a wisp of wind on her neck, she broke from her stupor. Yelling like a Viking going into battle, she spun around, letting the pedestal lead the way.

The heavy base, now coated in blood from Walter, struck Mrs. Haroldson dead center on the left cheek. Bone cracked and the old woman went down like a ton of bricks dropped from a pulley. As the old woman fell to the floor, Carly raised the pedestal and once more brought it down. Metal met bone and bone lost, the head popping like a rotten egg.

As brains and blood squirted out in a circle, Carly let go of the pedestal and stumbled backward, the pedestal falling to the floor with a loud clang. Meanwhile, Mrs. Haroldson's limbs jerked and spasmed as dead receptors and nerve endings went dark for the final time.

"Oh, Christ, she was dead, I saw it plain as day," Carly said.

As she stared at the remains of the old woman, it became too much and she turned and vomited, the warm liquid mixing with the gore. She heaved until she thought her organs were next. When she was finished and rose up, she looked at the residents, all still where they had been, too afraid to move.

It was at that moment that Carly realized they were like sheep, and she was the sheepdog. The wolves outside wanted them and she was all that protected them.

Wiping her mouth with the back of her hand, she sucked in a breath, stood a little taller, and waved to the group.

"Come on, let's get out of here; move out, folks."

As she went to them and began gently shoving them in the right direction, she tried not to glance over her shoulder at the two dead geriatrics.

As the last of the group moved deeper in the museum, she glanced one more time at the two dead souls, the two dead people she was supposed to protect, and at the zombies outside as they banged on the glass, desperate to get inside the museum.

Then she followed the others.

Within minutes of Carly leaving the atrium, the zombies seemed to grow agitated; as if they were angry their prey was leaving their line of sight.

They banged continually, more than once a hand becoming so mashed that bone was exposed. The glass was soon covered in blood and gore as the ghouls relentlessly pounded on the glass. Then, one of the zombies bent over and picked up a brick. The brick was once used to prop the doors open on spring days and the ghoul stared at it, not quite understanding what it held.

As if something from its memory of being alive surfaced, the zombie pushed its way through the throng of undead and began using the brick as a bludgeon on the glass.

At first nothing happened, other than a corner of the brick was broken off, bits of it falling to the ground, but as each blow grew more aggressive, the glass began to relent, and with one last blow, the glass splintered and cracked, to then cascade down, small crystals falling to the floor of the atrium.

It was as if the gates at a rock concert had given way as the undead mass of rotting humanity began to pour into the atrium. Their moans filled the air, rising to the high ceiling, then bouncing back to reverberate in all directions.

Stumbling over one another, a few paused to feed on the two dead geriatrics sprawled on the floor, but most continued onward. They wanted living prey, not old meat, and they knew in the back of their dead brains that the group of codgers had gone deeper into the museum.

With the dead crowd growing by the second, they swarmed inside the museum.

The museum appeared empty and for that Carly was thankful.

As the group made their way from exhibit hall to exhibit hall, each room was devoid of life.

Fifteen minutes later, she found herself and her charges in the back of the museum, in the section set aside for the Egyptian Mummy exhibit.

As she walked into the large room with its massive ceiling, she couldn't help but be amazed at the grand designs and textures on each sarcophagus, totaling ten in all.

Off to the left were seven glass cases the size of a standard coffin, six feet in length, and in each one lay a preserved mummy. Behind these cases were paintings and murals depicting who the mummies had been in life and how they had come to be mummified.

As the group of geriatrics found places to sit, Carly began moving around the room, as if all the death and suffering she'd been exposed to was lifted. In this large room, time stood still, and the past was laid out before her, the future still not written.

She walked over to the closest glass case and placed her hands against the surface. Leaning so close her breath fogged the glass, she felt drawn to the face of the mummy. Wrapped in ceremonial bandages, she could still tell the body was that of a woman and she found herself fascinated.

She was so enraptured by the mummy that she barely heard the moan of the zombies echoing through the museum.

"What was that?" an old man asked as he looked around the room.

"It's them, they're in here," an old, small woman said. She was barely above five feet tall, her body having shrunk from age.

Carly turned to look at the remaining survivors, and as she did so, she missed the movement when the mummy's head turned to look at her. The idea that the mummy could actually *see* her was silly, but nevertheless, the face turned in her direction.

"It's probably nothing," Carly said. "They can't get in here. We're safe."

Glass breaking caused Carly to spin around and her eyes went wide in shock and terror to see that the mummy had sat up, its rising head shattering the glass of its clear coffin.

Carly had her mouth hanging open, her head moving back and forth in denial as she stared at the mummy as it began to climb out of its case.

"But how? It can't be, it's dead...has been for thousands of years..."

Carly was correct, but whatever force was animating the dead cared nothing of the passage of time, only that dead tissue could be reanimated. More glass breaking caused Carly to look at the other cases, where here too, the mummies burst from their crystal coffins to walk once more.

Behind her, each sarcophagus began to open and more bandaged dead stepped forth, their silence all the more horrifying. Where the zombies were vocal, growling and moaning, the mummies were silent, their mouths bandaged, their lungs missing.

"This can't be happening, it's impossible!" Carly screamed as she took a step backward to join the aged group.

And old man stepped up to Carly as he stared at the mummies. "More impossible than the zombies outside the museum? My child, dead is dead, it makes perfect sense these creatures would rise as well."

"But...but..." Carly began but nothing else would come out. She had managed to grasp that zombies were real, that the dead walked. In her upside down world she had managed to regain herself, had dealt with the dead walking, but this...thousand year old corpses also rising? It was too much to take.

"We need to go, we have to get out of here," Carly told the others as they gathered into a tight group. "Everyone, turn and follow me. We can try to get out the rear exit."

She turned to lead the group out of the exhibit hall, but as she spun around, she saw the first of the zombies that had entered through the atrium doors.

At a fast walk they filled the hallway, swarming directly towards her and her charges.

"Oh, no, they got in somehow!" Carly yelled. "Run, you all need to run!"

But there was nowhere to run to.

As Carly turned around and tried to escape, the mummies were on her and the aged survivors. Seconds later, the zombies had joined the fray.

Carly found herself in a battle for her life as a mummy wrapped its bandaged hands around her throat, squeezing, wanting nothing more than to kill her. She found it ironic that the mummy wanted to murder her, while the zombies wanted to eat her.

As she fought, her right hand punched into the chest cavity of the mummy, but there was no resistance. Pulling her hand out, it was covered in dust and rotting bandages and once more she wondered how this could be.

The mummy continued to squeeze her neck, choking the life from her. Over the mummy's shoulder, Carly could see the rest of the group she had so desperately tried to save was also being attacked. Zombies flowed in and began tearing the senior citizens limb from limb, feeding on their moist organs, tearing at their withered, liver spotted flesh.

Carly was losing consciousness and she took solace in knowing she would be dead long before the first zombie found her and feasted on her corpse. The mummies continued the assault and so did the zombies, feeding on the corpses, blood splashing the stone tiles.

When all the survivors were dead, and Carly lay at the feet of a mummy, her bulging eyes open in death, her tongue poking out of her mouth, the mummies turned on the zombies and began to attack them.

Though the mummies grappled with the ghouls, the undead defenders felt no pain, and they too began to fight, tearing at limbs and trying to eat the ancient dead. But no sooner would they sink their teeth into the dried bandages then they would spit it out as foul tasting.

Carly revived then, sitting up slowly amidst the carnage as all around her the other dead residents slowly reanimated.

Standing on unsteady legs, Carly reached out and grabbed a mummy, trying to strangle it as it had done to her only minutes ago. The mummy wrapped its own hands around Carly's throat, trying to kill her once more but with no life, no need for oxygen, the gesture was meaningless.

They danced back and forth as the other zombies and mummies battled, a battle neither side could win for each side was already dead.

The halls of the museum loomed over all, watching silently as the undead, both ancient and new, fought for all eternity.

For the battle would be raged forever, and not until the last defender was too badly damaged to attack would there ever be a victor. And no matter what the result, the only true victor was death, who hovered over all, laughing as his pawns fought on.

ONE MORE HAND

Far beyond the reaches of time and space, in the ethereal void where planets are formed and destroyed, live the supreme beings of our universe and countless others.

They go by many names, though for the sake of discussion let's just call them, God, Buddha, and Allah.

Though they are three separate entities, each powerful being practices many of the same ideals, such as love, caring and compassion for your fellow man, or alien being, as the case may be.

This tale takes place long before the Earth was formed, in fact, the Earth does not exist yet. But to beings that are immortal, this means nothing.

Though omnipotent, one and all, they are still beings with minds, which need something to keep them occupied.

So once a week, they get together, where the rifts of time and space clash for dominance, and they have a friendly game of cards.

This is one such night.

* * *

God leaned back in his chair as he stared at his hand. He knew he had nothing, but the trick was to keep his fellow players from knowing that.

Across the table from him, Buddha lit yet another cigar, blowing the smoke away from the table. The smoke floated out into the vast void where it would end up forming the basis for a new galaxy, not that Buddha particularly cared.

Allah wasn't watching; his nose buried in his own cards.

God knew Allah was the one to beat, as the deity had a nasty habit of bluffing that he had nothing, when he, in fact, had a fantastic hand. God had been trying to figure out if Allah had a *tell* for more than a thousand millennia and it would probably be another thousand before he actually found it.

The problem was that God wasn't really a skilled poker player. Sure, if you needed a universe put together quickly, he was your deity, but poker? Well, he just didn't have the knack for it, though he did a pretty good job of fooling his two companions.

"Come on, God, ante up or fold," Buddha said as he waved his cigar around. The embers flew off the tip, where they floated away into the void. Eventually they would settle in a far away galaxy and a new sun would be born.

"Forget it, I fold," Allah said, tossing his cards onto the table. "I've got nothing."

God decided to go for it and he called Buddha on his hand. Buddha smiled and God knew what that look meant.

Slapping his cards down hard on the table, Buddha grinned at God. "Ha, four of a kind, all kings. What do you have?"

God frowned and placed his cards on the table. Buddha glanced at them and looked back at God, bemusement on his face. "A pair of eights, God? You thought you could beat me with a pair of eights?" He started laughing, the anger in God seething until the Big Bang began to form somewhere a million, trillion miles away from where he sat, his wrath compressing matter and then releasing it.

"So I lost, let it go, Buddha. Sheesh, you are such a sore winner," God told him as he picked up the cards and shuffled them again. Allah had decided to fold, so his cards didn't matter.

God shuffled the cards and dealt another hand. Once he was finished, he set the deck down, picking up his own hand. He wanted to sigh, but knew better as he stared at his cards, not wanting to give anything away. What a bunch of crap his cards were. He glanced over the tops of his cards to watch Buddha, and the deity appeared quite pleased with his hand, or though that could just be him acting, a big show for him for the other players.

God reached out and picked up his glass of alcohol. As he brought it to his lips, he realized the glass was empty. With a weary sigh, he placed it back on the table, but he misplaced the glass and it tipped over, spilling ice.

"Jesus Christ, now that's just great," God said loudly in frustration as he stared at the spilled drink.

Sandaled footsteps could be heard coming from down the long hallway outside the door, and a second later, Jesus Christ appeared in the doorway to the cosmic room.

"Yes, Father, you called for me?" Jesus asked in a monotone voice.

God turned and looked at his son. "Um, yeah, I guess I did. I spilled my drink, son, would you get me another one?" he asked while picking the ice off the table and placing it back in his glass.

"Of course, Father, you know I live to serve you," Jesus said flatly, the sarcasm apparent to all within earshot.

Both Buddha and Allah chuckled lightly at Jesus' subtle art of rebellion. Like most children, Jesus was trying to find his independence, which was infinitely more difficult when your father was the creator of the universe.

God turned so he could see his son better. "Oh, come now, son, don't be like that. Here, could you please get me another bottle of wine? And make sure it's from a good millennium, too, not any of that new stuff. Blah, that stuff's horrible," God said while shaking his glass, the ice clinking inside it.

With a weary sigh, Jesus left the doorway and a moment later returned with another bottle in his hand. Inside the bottle, stars twinkled and moons clashed for dominance, all swirling around in a maelstrom of fiery brilliance.

Jesus placed the bottle on the table and stared at his Father. "There, you happy now? May I leave?"

"What's wrong, boy, why are you so down?" Buddha asked as he sent another puff of smoke out into the cosmos.

"What's wrong? What's wrong? I'll tell you what's wrong, Uncle Buddha. There's nothing for me to do around here. I don't have any friends and there's no excitement. That's what."

God patted his son on the shoulder. "Okay, I get it. You're young and you want to have some fun. I remember those days. Tell you what, as soon as I'm done with cards today, I'll see if I can get something together for you. How about a nice planet where people think you're great. Hey, you'll be like a rock star."

Jesus just shrugged.

"Maybe your father could finish that planet he was working on, what was it called?" Allah asked God.

"Earth? You mean the Earth?" God asked. "Yeah, I could do that, but it's more of a hobby, a pet project I was doing when I'm not so busy." He turned back to Jesus. "There you go, son, I'll just finish making the Earth and you can go there for a while, how's that sound?"

"Whatever, look I have to go. I've got something on the stove," Jesus said solemnly. He left the room, leaving the three deities to stare at the doorway he exited.

A second later, after a door had slammed further down the hall, harsh rock music floated into the room, coming from Jesus' bedroom.

Allah shook his head. "You've got a real problem with that one," he said.

God poured himself a drink and looked up at Allah. "Yes, don't I know it, now come on; let's play some cards."

As the three deities studied their cards, Buddha grunted with an idea. "Hey, God, you know, I've got some light and perpetual darkness lying around in my closet somewhere. You could use that for your Earth planet," he suggested.

Allah's eyes perked up as he got the gist of what Buddha was saying and he added, "Hey, that's right, and I've got some water and sky I've been meaning to use, but I just can't find the time. If you want, you can use that, too."

God's brow furrowed as he gazed back at his two companions. Scratching his white beard, he considered their proposals.

"And what, you're just going to give them to me out of the kindness of your hearts?"

Buddha chuckled, waving his cigar around. "No, of course not. We can use them as currency in the game. That is, if you're up to it."

God considered it. He had a few planets at the tip of the galaxy he wasn't using, not to mention there was always that supernova lying around in mothballs. And he knew he had at least a few items the other deities could use for their own endeavors.

His mouth curved up into a slight smile and he nodded. "All right, fellows, fine, I'm in."

Buddha slapped the table with his hands, a rumbling reaction flowing off into the cosmos. Somewhere far, far away, another galaxy began to form as matter collapsed in on itself to explode outward into a hundred thousand stars.

"Wonderful, finally we're going to play for something that matters," Buddha exclaimed as he glanced back down at his cards. "Now the game is gonna get interesting."

Both God and Allah looked at one another, nodded politely across the tops of their cards, before both deities concentrated on their hands.

The game was most definitely about to get interesting, and the creation of a world was being held in the balance.

* * *

God studied his cards, more than pleased with his hand. This was the first hand with the new stakes and he really wanted to win. If he could play well today, really, really well, he could end up with all the supplies he needed to finish his pet project, the Earth.

And once done, maybe his son would have somewhere to hang out instead of moping around the cosmos all day.

Sending his will across the cosmos, he formed the basis for the planet Earth, bringing debris and rocks from a million miles away to condense and form the basis for the planet. Though for God this was a blink of an eye, at the center of the galaxy that contained the Earth, this took a full day.

At the end of the day, the Earth was formed, though still nothing but barren rock.

God stared at his cards, not very pleased with the results. Both Buddha and Allah were concentrating on their hands and so it was God who made the first move.

"All right then, boys, I'm in," God said, tossing a substantial amount into the pot.

Buddha did the same, adding light and darkness to the growing pot, grinning as he stared at the potential. Allah did the same, as well, adding sky and water.

"Okay then, so who wants what?" Buddha asked as he stared at God and Allah. God examined his cards, not sure what he should do. Deciding to take a chance, he asked for two cards, discarding the ones he didn't want.

Buddha tossed God the two cards he asked for and then turned to Allah. "How 'bout you, sunshine, what'll it be?" Buddha asked Allah playfully.

"I'll take three," Allah said unhappily.

Chuckling, Buddha gave the deity three cards and then did the same for himself.

"And I'll take three," he said out loud.

Both Allah and Buddha looked at their hands, at one another, then back at God.

God had the perfect poker face on, though he had nothing in his hand. He only hoped he was doing a good job of bluffing. He was the first to add to the pot, his face full of confidence in his hand. Deciding it wasn't worth the risk, both Buddha and Allah folded.

"Not bad, God, I didn't want to risk anything else on that hand," Buddha said as he collected the cards.

God merely shrugged. It had worked, his bluff had worked. Collecting light, water and sky, he sent them across the vastness of space to the distant floating dead rock of the planet Earth.

In an instant, the light appeared, off set by darkness, the planet split in half so that there was always light on one half of the planet and darkness on the other. Soon blue sky appeared, filling the space over the Earth, and in a horrendous crash of cascading power, water appeared across the globe, filling the holes and craters of the pockmarked planet.

In the Earth's cycle of life, these actions took two days and at the end of the second day there was light, water and sky on the planet Earth.

God leaned back in his chair, satisfied with himself. If he was able to keep playing this well he would end up with all the supplies to build the Earth, all thanks to the two suckers across from him.

It was Allah's turn to deal and the deity took the deck of cards, shuffling them happily.

"All right, boys, next hand is for the land for the Earth. You know, grass, seeds and trees, stuff like that." He began dealing the cards.

Buddha nodded as he accepted his cards. "I'm adding the stars to the pot, too, if it's all right," he said to God.

God shrugged. "Sure, it's okay, I need those anyway. Otherwise, it'll be pretty boring when you look up at the sky on my new planet."

Allah dealt the cards and all three measured their hand, each asking for new cards, with the exception of God who only asked for one card. When he picked up his new card, he almost wanted to jump for joy. He had a full house, three sevens and a pair of threes. Not bad for his second hand.

The pot was filled and he actually raised two times before Allah called him.

Slapping down his cards, he grinned from ear to ear. "Read 'em and weep, boys," God said proudly.

Buddha slapped the table angrily, and a trillion miles away a black hole collapsed in on itself. Allah smiled at the hand for he had been bluffing and had lost dismally, but as wont with his nature, he took it in stride. "Congratulations, God; well played," Allah complemented him.

God smiled again and took the pot, sending the land, trees, and seeds across the void of time and space. This was followed by the stars, thanks to Buddha, which filled the sky surrounding the Earth.

Back on Earth, the land appeared, separating the water into separate oceans. On the land, trees sprouted up, filling the land with vast forests. Grass spread across the landmass, coloring the world green, while seeds were planted in the soil, soon to sprout a thousand different kinds of flora, fruit and vegetables.

By the time the grass had finished filling the world and the trees and landmass had settled down, it was the end of the third day and all was well with the Earth.

Across the cosmos, God took his next hand, picking up his cards to study them.

He had already taken two cards, his companions doing the same.

On the table, between them, was the large pot. Allah had placed *life*—such as the birds and bees—in the pot, and Buddha had added the rest, such as rodents, bacteria and other organisms that make up a planet's ecosphere.

God studied his hand.

With the five cards he had received in his first deal, he already had a pair of sevens—one in spades and one in clubs. The other cards were a four of clubs, an ace of hearts, and a two of diamonds.

He had a tough choice to make. Should he keep the pair and try for something else? Or should he toss them away and hope he could maybe end up with a straight or even three pair?

Decisions, decisions.

Buddha was tapping his fingers impatiently as God tried to decide. Next to him, Allah asked for only one card. That couldn't be good. Buddha had taken only one, as well, which means the deity had to have a good hand.

Far away, across the universe, suns lived their life spans and died in the time it took God to decide what to do, as time was irrelevant to him, but finally he decided to keep the pair of sevens and let luck take him by the hand.

"Give me three," God told Buddha.

"Ho, ho, he wants three cards, Allah, guess he doesn't have anything good this time," Buddha said to Allah as he handed God his three cards.

As for Buddha, he inspected his cards and then added to the pot. This time he added the Sun so the Earth would be warmed and continue to flourish after God had departed.

"All right, then, fellas, what has everyone got?" Buddha asked as he leaned on the table. He let out a fart that caused solar storms to ravage a far away galaxy, snuffing out two planets in their fury.

Allah went first, laying his cards gently on the table. "Two pairs, fives and eights," he said as he showed his cards to the other two deities.

Buddha nodded at the hand. "Not bad, Allah old boy, but not good enough."

Buddha slapped his cards down on the table and leaned back with his arms behind his bald head, a wide smile creasing his face.

"Ha, beat that boys," he said as God and Allah studied the cards. On the table in front of Buddha was a three of a kind, all threes.

God said nothing, only glancing at his own cards again. Buddha saw him waiting, and was about to lean over and take the pot, when God held up a hand.

"Ah, wait a second, Buddha, I haven't shown you my cards yet," God told him.

"Okay, then show them already if you got something," Buddha snapped back, aggravated that he might not have the best hand.

God lay his cards down, and low and behold, he had a straight. He had taken a risk and it paid off handsomely. He had thrown down the seven of spades, the two of diamonds and the ace of hearts and had gotten back three more cards he could use; a five of hearts, an eight of spades and a six of diamonds.

He had a straight, plain and simple.

"Son-of-a..." Buddha spit angrily but stopped himself.

Allah clapped his hands happily. "Outstanding, God, well played. My, you're getting better at this game with every passing millennium."

God smiled a thank you and took the pot for himself. With a wave of his hand, he sent the pot to Earth where the next items were added to the planet.

Back on Earth, birds appeared chirping in the trees and in the ocean fish began to swim and small mammals crawled across the land. In the sky overhead, a Sun appeared, casting its warm and glowing brilliance on a grateful world.

When everything was finished and in its place, the fourth day was complete and God was pleased.

So far so good, he thought, as he took his next hand of cards.

Jesus entered the room, wearing a mask of unhappiness.

God turned to stare at his son, admiring the family resemblance. "What's the matter, son?"

"Is the Earth done yet? I'm so bored!" He stretched the word *bored* to emphasize its meaning.

God smiled at him. "Yes, my son, just give me another thousand years and I'll be finished, then you can go play with your new friends."

Jesus let out a sigh, throwing his hands in the air laconically. "Good, I'm sure once I get to Earth, then I'll be happy." He turned to leave the room, waving as he left. "I'll be over at Wilma's place, just let me know when you're finished."

When he left, Buddha leaned forward and in a conspiratorial tone asked, "Who is Wilma? Some pretty thing he's got on the side?"

God nodded, slightly. "As far as I know. He's at that age when he doesn't tell me anything. Frankly, it'll be good if he goes to the Earth. Let him study abroad for a while, so to speak."

"Hey, are we going to play cards or what?" Allah asked as he tapped his fingers on the table.

"Keep your robe on, Allah, we're playing, we're playing," Buddha said and picked up the cards. "So who's deal?"

God gestured magnanimously to him. "You can deal, its fine with me," he told Buddha. He looked to Allah and asked, "How about you, is it okay with you?"

"Fine, sure, let's just go here, I'm losing my shirt today," Allah said impatiently.

"You don't wear a shirt. You wear a dress," Buddha quipped at the deity.

"It's a robe, Buddha, you just said it a second ago, now quit teasing me about it or we can start talking about why you have no hair and are so overweight."

Buddha seemed slightly hurt. "Hey, it's a glandular problem, leave me alone. And as for my hair, it's a fashion choice, you should try it sometime."

God raised both hands in front of the other two deities, trying to calm the argument. "Fellows, please, we're supposed to be above all this. Remember who you are."

Buddha and Allah frowned at one another, but both stopped bickering.

God nodded, pleased that he managed to stifle the altercation. These two were like brothers, always bickering and teasing one another. He was just glad Mohammed wasn't here, as well. With the three of them together, God could barely manage to keep them from killing each other; such was the sibling rivalry.

Buddha lit a new cigar, and after squeezing it between his lips, he picked up the deck of cards and began dealing.

When he was finished, each deity picked up their cards to see what they were given.

God frowned slightly, not wanting to show how unhappy he was. He had nothing, a mish-mash of different suits in a scattered out-of-sync numerical order.

Deciding he had nothing to lose on this hand, he asked for three new cards.

He idly noticed both Buddha and Allah did the same, each deity taking three cards each. That bode well for him.

Perhaps they had been as unlucky as he?

Buddha quickly passed out the new cards and God inspected his new hand.

He had nothing, though he did have a king of hearts, though without any accompanying cards, it was useless.

"I'm in," Allah said as he added *cattle and beasts* to the pot. God needed these for the Earth if he wanted to complete his project. He needed to win this pot despite the lack of a good hand so he decided to bluff.

The bickering went back and forth until Buddha finally called him on his hand. He hadn't expected that, and God knew he was caught in his bluff.

Sighing, he laid his cards down on the table only to find his were still the winning hand. Neither Allah nor Buddha had anything, and God's king was the high card.

He had actually won the hand, despite having absolutely nothing.

Accepting the pot, he sent the *cattle and beasts* across the void to join the planet Earth.

And so on the fifth day on Earth, all was well and God smiled.

Only one more hand to win and the Earth was finished. Buddha passed the deck of cards to God. It was his turn to deal.

God accepted the cards and dealt them across the table, trying not to look too closely into either of the other deity's eyes. He didn't want them to know how bad he needed to win this last hand.

Setting the cards down, he picked up his cards and studied them as Buddha and Allah did the same with their own hands.

After a few moments, Buddha asked for one card, and then Allah asked for two.

God decided to go with two new cards. He kept a queen, ace and ten of hearts, discarding a five and seven of spades. He knew his chances of getting what he needed were slim, but it was all or nothing at this point in the game.

After the last hand, he really doubted he could bluff his way through this hand. He either needed to get something extra special or just fold and give it up, scrapping the creation of the Earth for the foreseeable future. Jesus would be upset, but he would get over it.

Buddha grinned as he looked at God over his cards. He grunted and reached out into the void and brought something back with him. Setting the prize on the table, he grinned and said, "All right, God, this is it, the big one, so to speak. Here's my ante. *Man* in all his glory. If you win this hand, you can have mankind for the Earth.

God gazed down at the glimmering form of man as it hovered above the table. "Fair enough. What do you say I just call and end this right now?" he asked both Buddha and Allah.

"I'm game, if you are Buddha," Allah shrugged as he spoke to the bald deity.

Buddha nodded again and smiled widely. "Okay, it's your funeral, God." He slapped his cards onto the table, the tremor vibrating out into space where a sun went supernova in a distant galaxy. "Straight flush, five high," Buddha preened as he stared at the other two deities, making eye contact with each one.

Sure enough, he had a straight flush, all diamonds. He had an ace, and then two through five; an excellent hand and sure to be the winning one.

Allah was next. He laid his cards down gently, leaning back when he was finished. He managed a straight, a five through nine, but it was hopelessly inadequate next to Buddha's straight flush. It was the second best hand to have and so Buddha was more than confident he had won the game.

"Sorry, God, looks like I win. Better luck next time on that whole Earth thing," Buddha smiled while reaching over the table to take the pot. But just as Buddha was reaching over the table, God held up his hands to stop the grinning deity.

"Wait, Buddha, don't you want to see my cards before you jump to conclusions?" God asked.

Buddha shrugged. "Sure, why not, go ahead and show them off. Not that it matters."

God smiled widely, indulging in a rare modicum of self-pride and superiority over the other deities. Upon laying his cards down casually, Buddha's cigar fell from his mouth as he stared at God's cards.

God had pulled off a royal flush. After discarding his two cards, he had actually had a miracle happen—one that he didn't perform himself, mind you—and he had picked up a jack of hearts and a king of hearts, thereby completing his hand.

He had won.

And with Buddha staring at the hand, God took the pot and whisked *man* to the Earth, telling him to multiply and be happy.

On the sixth hand of poker, and the sixth day of the creation of the Earth, God leaned back and smiled.

The Earth was finished, his pet project complete.

On the seventh day, God decided to stop tinkering with the Earth, not wanting to push his luck.

God looked up across the poker table at Buddha and Allah. "Well, fellows, that was an excellent time. Thank you for all your wonderful items for the Earth. Now, what do you say we get something to eat? I'm starving."

Buddha reluctantly agreed and the three deities left the cosmic room to eat and laugh and be merry.

Next week there would be another card game and at that time anything could happen.

*　*　*

The next week went by quickly—thousands of years in Earth time—and before any of the deities realized it, the week was over. As they were omnipotent beings, the actual time was nothing in the grand scheme of the cosmos.

Gathered around the table in the cosmic room, Buddha leaned back in his chair, his cigar hanging from his mouth, as always. "So, God, how's that Earth thing working out for you?" Buddha asked with the cigar moving slightly up and down as he talked.

God poured himself a drink, shrugging slightly. "All right, I guess. My son has recently returned from there and he's been acting funny. I have a sneaking suspicion something happened to him while he was on the Earth. It's hard to tell what exactly because he won't talk about it."

Allah's eyebrows went up in curiosity. "Oh, how so?"

God stood up from the table, and waved the other two deities to follow him.

"I think it will be easier if I just show you."

The three deities walked down a long hallway to a door. God knocked on the door, but there was no answer. Turning to gaze at Buddha and Allah, he opened the door, exposing Jesus' room.

Jesus was in the corner, curled up in a ball, writing diligently in a book. When the door opened, he looked up, but went back to writing in his book immediately, ignoring God and the others.

His face was filled with manic passion as he scribbled page after page of drawings. On the walls were the pictures of crosses, different shapes and sizes, all with multicolored colors and odd shapes.

"Since he returned from Earth, all he does is stay in his room and draw crosses. It's like he's fascinated with them."

"And all this started when he came back from Earth?" Allah asked.

"Uh-huh, I don't know what those people did to him down there, but it sure messed him up."

Stepping back, God closed the door of Jesus' room and they all went back to the cosmic room.

Buddha sat down in a heavy slouch, sucking on his cigar. "Look, God, he was probably just teased or maybe he had trouble with a girl. I'm sure it's just a faze and it'll blow over soon. Just give it time."

God only sighed. "I hope what you say is true, Buddha. I tell you, it's times like this when I wish I had someone else to talk to about being a parent." He looked at both Allah and Buddha.

"Hey, don't look at me," Buddha said nervously, "I like being a bachelor. No wife and no kids, makes things easier."

Allah only shrugged and smiled sympathetically. He was also a bachelor.

Buddha picked up the deck of cards lying on the table, shuffling them like a card shark. "So, are we going to play our weekly game or what?"

God and Allah consented, and Buddha was about to begin dealing the cards when a smoke cloud appeared in the middle of the room, filled with fire and brimstone.

The theatrics disappeared as soon as they appeared, leaving behind a suave looking deity in a pin-striped suit and a walking cane.

"Oh, great, it's Lucifer," God said under his breath, then turned to smile at the new arrival. "Lucifer, what brings you by here today?"

Lucifer smiled with fanged teeth and moved closer to the table.

"I heard through the rumor mill you fellows were getting together for your weekly card game. I thought if it was all right, that I might join you for a few hands."

"Why's that? Is Earth getting too boring for you?" God asked snidely.

"On the contrary, my dear friend. It's going swimmingly. In fact, I have a plan in motion that will surely rock the galaxy." He casually leaned on the table with his left hand. "So, may I join your little group?"

God considered Lucifer's request. Lucifer had an ongoing disagreement with God going on a few thousand years now and had since departed Heaven to go to Earth.

Now Lucifer was the tenant that didn't pay rent and refused to leave. Not to mention he was always playing his music too loud and breaking things.

It was true that God was mostly finished with the Earth. Now that his son had left, he stayed out of the way of the populace of the planet, though for some reason the population of Earth just wouldn't let him go altogether. They were like a crazy girlfriend who wouldn't take no for an answer.

He would have thought after a few thousand years of not doing anything to show the people he truly existed that they would get the hint, but instead, some were more fanatical than ever, assuming because he did nothing to help them that it was *His will*. Like he had some divine plan to let them die in floods, hurricanes, plagues, famines, and mud slides, not to mention all the wild fires that burned up thousands of acres of land and the thousands of killings that man committed on each other on a daily basis, and sometimes even in *His* name.

Atrocity after atrocity, year after year, it never stopped. Man's ability to heap pain and suffering on one another knew no bounds and had no comparison to any other being in the universe.

Sometimes it made him regret ever making the planet.

And the population's divine belief that all that misery was somehow in his grand design was maddening.

Oh yes, he had planned for all that...not.

Fools. Every last one of them.

Crazy they were, which was why when he usually created a planet, he usually left the *making in his own image* thing out. It just became too complicated.

God closed his eyes as he thought all this and then he opened them and acquiesced to Lucifer's request. "It's okay with me, but you still have to ask them," God said, pointing to Allah and Buddha.

Both deities assented, and soon Lucifer was sitting at the table, studying his cards.

The game went well, each deity winning a hand and losing a hand; with the exception of God. While the week before, when he had won everything he had needed for the creation of the Earth, this week he was back to his old tricks, that is, not playing very well. He was almost out of chips, or what the deities considered chips, and he was not feeling too positive for the next hand, at least until he picked the cards up and saw them.

As he received his five cards for the last hand of the night, he studied them carefully, seeing a possibility of four of a kind, or perhaps even a straight. He already had three of a kind, all jacks, though that wasn't much to use as he went into the last hand of the night.

Also, he hadn't been very lucky this night and so was hesitant to try anything risky. Almost as if Lucifer could sense his trepidation, he turned to God, smiled that smarmy smile he always used and said, "So, God, what do you say we make this last hand something special, hmm? A little more interesting than the other ones," Lucifer suggested.

God leaned forward in his chair, his eyes going back to his cards. He sure did have a good hand, full of promise. If he decided to risk it and take a chance, that is.

"Maybe, what did you have in mind?" God asked.

"What do you say we wager the Earth?" Lucifer said.

"The Earth, why?" God asked, confused.

Lucifer shrugged. "Let's just say I'm getting bored with it and I think it's time to wipe the slate clean and start from scratch. I truly believe I've done everything I can with that pitiful little mud ball. It's time to start fresh."

God considered it. Though he was finished with Earth, he was rather fond of it, what with the people worshiping him and all.

"Tell you what; just to make things interesting, I'll throw that planet in the Quasar Nebula into the pot. I know you've had your eye on that one for quite some time," Lucifer said with a lecherous grin.

It was true, he had. It was a small planet, perfect for molding into another Earth, only this time he would make sure to do it right. That way maybe the populace wouldn't feel the need to constantly kill one another all the time in wars and conquests.

Deciding it was worth the risk, God nodded and said, "You've got yourself a deal, Lucifer, let's go."

Lucifer glanced at Buddha and Allah. "What about you two. Are you in?"

Buddha tossed his cards to the table, shaking his head. "No, not me, too rich for my blood."

Allah did the same, dropping his cards onto the table with a shrug.

"Well, then, God, it looks like it's just you and me," Lucifer grinned malevolently.

God ignored him, used to his machinations.

Deciding he had a good chance of winning, God tossed two cards to the table, and asked Buddha for two more. God kept the three jacks he had, deciding to discard the seven of spades and the ten of hearts, deciding to try for four of a kind. He had to admit that he was a little nervous now. If he lost this hand, then so too, would the Earth be destroyed in the blink of an eye. And all thanks to Lucifer's short attention span.

Lucifer only asked for one card, which made God even more nervous. That must mean he had a good hand already and was trying for something even better.

Lucifer smiled slightly as he picked up his new card, though it could have all been for show. After all, he wasn't called the Master of Lies for nothing.

As for God, he was pleased with his two new cards. He had himself four of a kind, picking up the jack he sorely needed. Lucifer grinned widely as he leaned on the table. Sulfur floated to God's nose from Lucifer and he tried not to sneeze.

"So, God, here it is, the hand that decides the fate of that simple little planet. Show me what you have," Lucifer prodded.

God swallowed and laid his cards down on the table. Buddha whistled softly and Allah nodded, impressed.

"Not bad, God, not bad," Buddha said as he admired the four jacks.

God smiled, feeling good about himself. Buddha was right, he did have a good hand.

The Earth was hanging by a tenuous string; the cards Lucifer held deciding the fate of a world. Across the galaxy, far away on Earth, the people living there went about their daily lives, not knowing their fate was hanging by a thread, nothing but game pawns in a high-stakes game of chance by immortal beings of light and power.

God turned to stare into Lucifer's eyes and his forehead began to perspire with the tension. God wiped his brow as he licked his lips, never breaking Lucifer's gaze. Allah and Buddha's attentions were focused on Lucifer, as well.

Buddha's cigar ash began to grow long as it was ignored, and Allah held his breath, too worried to breathe. Both deities were riveted to the high-stakes poker game where millions of lives hung in the balance of a simple game of cards.

This was it, the moment of truth. Did Lucifer have a better hand than God or was it all just false bravado?

His face impassive, giving nothing away, Lucifer carefully laid out his cards in a fanning motion.

All eyes were on the cards in Lucifer's hands as he gently spread them out on the table, face up.

A collective murmur floated across the table as each deity gazed down at Lucifer's cards, the hand there for all to see...

To be continued...hopefully forever.

THE LAST TARGET

James Travis lay sprawled on the rooftop overlooking 22nd Street in New York City. It was late, and though there was still traffic, the volume was much less than earlier in the day. Every hour that passed saw a diminishing amount of vehicles and pedestrians.

It was cold on the rooftop, just a little above freezing, a two inch layer of snow covering the rooftop.

James was sprawled out under a white blanket, almost entirely hidden from chance view if someone happened to glance his way from one of the nearby buildings, but he wasn't worried about that. From where he lay, the higher windows were at an odd angle, and unless a watcher knew exactly where to direct their gaze, he would remain hidden from view, and even if they did look at him, the odds of him being discovered were slim.

He had been in this position on the rooftop for almost three hours, patiently waiting for his next target. It had been hard staying warm, not to mention keeping his extremities from freezing. But he had learned isometrics years ago and as he lay immobile on the rooftop, he continually exercised muscles, keeping blood circulating and flowing freely.

Glancing through the night-scope, he grunted when he saw no movement, his target still not arriving. Checking his watch, he realized the target was running late.

He grinned slightly. He had been paid handsomely for this contract and was looking forward to completing the job and going home for the night. Conveniently, New York was his home, as well, and so this particular target had required the least amount of effort of all his others, which there were many.

A car door being slammed sounded across the street below him and he placed his right eye against the rifle's eyepiece once again, the magnification on the scope more than ample enough to see the street below.

"There you are," James whispered under his breath, the air fogging out in front of his mouth.

The man who he referred to had just exited a Rolls Royce and was the head of a large, multinational company. His name was William Astin and he was a father of three, as well as a loving husband. He was a good man, always giving major sums of money to charities and to homeless shelters in his place of residence, that being New York. He was an activist on the environment and was so good to his mother that any other man would be ashamed of himself.

But none of that mattered to James. Good or bad, right or wrong, he had no conscience.

All he saw was a target; one that would be extinguished in a brief moment.

There was no fanfare, like in the movies. No threatening music played over the background, no camera angles zoomed in to witness the assassination of a good man. Instead, there was just James. He carefully lined up the man's head in his gun-sight, and when he acquired his target, he squeezed the trigger.

The target in the street never felt a thing. One second he was stepping out of his car, the next he was sprawled on the cold sidewalk with half his head missing.

The police would do a thorough investigation of the incident, but James' employers would bribe the right men and women and the entire investigation would be whitewashed.

Did James care that the men who had hired him were now going to make a hostile takeover of the dead man's company, thereby diffusing it and dismantling it until all the good the man had done would be lost in time?

No, of course not. He did what he was paid to do and that was it.

Rationalizing could be left to the bleeding hearts and liberals.

With the target bleeding out on the sidewalk, James backed away from the edge of the roof, and once inside the roof access door, he quickly gathered up his few belongings. He quickly moved down the stairs. His job was complete and he was cold and tired.

When he reached street level, he quickly walked two blocks over from the crime scene and then headed for his car which was parked in a side alley. No one noticed him, the few pedestrians who were out this night were far too cold to care who they shared the street with.

He climbed into his car, a nondescript Oldsmobile, used for just this reason, and pulled into the street and drove away. He drove silently through the streets, weaving his way through one intersection after another until he was almost home. When he was only a few blocks away and relaxing, pleased at a job well done, he slowed at a red light, waiting patiently for the light to change to green.

He glanced out his window to study the pedestrians as they moved back and forth on the sidewalk and his jaw dropped when he spotted a face he knew. And to top off the sighting, the face was staring directly at him, the eyes piercing through his car window directly into his soul.

Then the face was running away down the street.

Before he knew what he was doing, James pulled his car into a parking spot, not caring that he was in a loading zone, and jumped out of the car, running after the face he had seen only seconds before. He felt the reassuring weight of his revolver in the folds of his pocket, and with his breathe pluming in front of him, he dashed down the dimly lit street after the man who shouldn't exist.

But that was all right. James was never a man to ruminate too hard on any given subject. If the man was still alive, then he would just have to remedy the situation...permanently.

Running on the snow covered sidewalks, careful not to fall and break his neck, he chased his prey for five blocks. Just when he thought he had lost the alluring form, a brief glimpse of a black coat would catch his eye and he would dart after it.

Each time James thought he would catch up with the man he was pursuing, the figure would turn a corner again. When James would reach the corner and round it, the man would once again be out of reach, always at the next corner, turning it to be gone, only to be found once more.

If James was concerned, he thought nothing of it, only wanting to confront the man who should be dead and finish what he had been paid to do. For the face he had seen staring back at him, was none other than the face of William Astin, the man he knew was lying across town with half his head blown off and his brains painting the sidewalk.

Running down the next street, James realized he was entering the business district. Once again the figure was tantalizingly distant, but this time when James turned the corner, he saw that the man was standing at the main entrance to a non-descript building, and almost as if he was making sure James was still following, he darted inside the doorway to be lost from sight once more.

James took the bait, needing to unravel this obscure mystery. Running to the doorway, he tried the door and found it unlocked. Opening it, he stepped inside, stopping in the foyer to let his eyes adjust to the dim interior.

Now that he was inside, away from prying eyes, he pulled out his revolver. The finish was black so as not to catch the light and it had a soft rubber grip to protect sweating hands from losing purchase. Not that James' hands were ever sweaty. On the contrary, they were dry, very dry.

He was like a rock, confident and sure. He would unravel this strange occurrence and finish the night off with a nightcap at his apartment.

With his eyes adjusted, he stepped into the foyer, his footsteps silent on the floor. Heel to toe, heel to toe, he walked, careful not to make a sound.

There! Up ahead, the face, poking out from a doorway.

When the man saw James, he quickly disappeared back into the doorway, and James, never one to hesitate, darted after him, charging around the corner and into a room of dim light and soft shadows.

James paused for a moment, assessing the situation.

As he waited, he spotted the man in front of him, his face hovering six feet off the floor, and before James could think about it, his instincts and reflexes kicked in, and he brought up his revolver and fired three quick shots, two in the chest and one aimed at the head.

But what should have happened didn't. Instead of his target falling to the floor in a pool of blood, James felt the impacts of the bullets strike his own body. One at a time the rounds entered his flesh, and he let out a gasp and fell to the floor, gazing up at the ceiling.

Suddenly, the room was bathed in bright light, and though he was rapidly losing consciousness, his blood pooling under his body and spreading across the floor, he managed to see the room he was in a little better, now seen much easier with the lights on.

The room was empty with the exception of polished metal covering the walls. They were polished to a mirror finish and were angled in such a way that as long as a gun was fired from the doorway, the rounds would be reflected back to the shooter. A geometric trap that was foolproof.

A perfect trap, actually. One James had fallen for hook, line and sinker.

His chest felt like knives had been implanted under his flesh and were slowly being turned on a spit of fire. He breathed out and blood splattered across his chin and neck, acid flooding his veins in waves of agony.

The man he had pursued stepped into the light and gazed down at James with a sad smile.

"Thank you for killing my husband for me, James, I can't thank you enough," a woman's voice said from under a rubber mask. James tried to get up, to raise his revolver, but he was too weak.

As he watched, she reached up and peeled away the mask she was wearing over her face, the true visage now looking down on him a familiar one. After only a moment had passed, he recognized the wife of William Astin from the photographs he had studied in preparation for his mission.

"What? Why?" he croaked with the last of his strength.

The woman continued to gaze down on him, smiling slightly.

"I should think that should be obvious. You see, I'm the one who hired you. My husband might seem like an angel from God to the public, but try living with him. He's an abusive tyrant who delights in debasing me. So I decided to kill him, with your help, of course. But I can't have you walking around and knowing my secret, now can I. So I devised this clever trap to have you kill yourself."

Her cell phone rang and she answered it, as the growing pool of blood spread across the floor around James like a halo. She stepped back a bit, not wanting to get any of the viscous fluid on her designer shoes.

She listened to the caller on the opposite end of the phone and said, "Thank you," before hanging up.

"Well, that was the police. It seems my husband has been shot. I have to be going now. I need to play the grieving widow. Thank you again, James, especially for being so gullible."

She turned and was gone, her footsteps echoing down the hall-way until they faded to nothing. He lay on the floor, gazing up at the ceiling and suddenly began to chuckle, though it caused him great pain.

She was a clever woman, he had to give her that, and maybe it was for the best, anyway. After all, thanks to her machinations he had been forced to hunt himself, and he always got his man.

As his eyes closed and he fell into oblivion, he continued laugh-ing. He never would have thought his last target would end up being himself.

REGRETS

Eyes closed tightly, the wind whistling around my head. My hair feels like it's in a tornado. My body feels weightless, as if gravity doesn't apply to me any longer.

My heart is heavy with loss, dragging me down. My wife has left me. It's not my fault. I lost my job and then the unemployment ran out. Though I should have tried to find work, I found myself lost in a sea of depression.

Finally the mortgage became past due, and in time, the house was taken from me...and her.

She couldn't take it anymore and she packed up her bags and left me.

Now I have nothing. No house, no wife, no job.

How to explain the deep sadness and loss that fills my heart and soul at this very minute?

The wind still buffets me, sending me twisting and turning. I don't care, I relish it.

At least it's a sensation, something to remind me I'm alive.

So I took a room at the Y, at least until they found out my check bounced higher than a child's kickball at recess.

Tears slip out of my eyelids, crawling up my cheeks. I ignore them, thinking of her, letting her image fill my mind.

God how I hate her for leaving me. God how I still love her despite her betrayal.

How to put into words how one feels when everything that defines you, everything that tells others who you are, is pulled out from under you like a slippery rug on a hardwood floor.

My heart is beating so fast it feels like it will simply burst, shattering organs with the shrapnel it leaves behind.

I've lost everything. So what's the point of going on?

Why even try. Sure, there can be sunnier days to come, but when the love of your life walks out on you, spitting on your shoes as she slams the door in your face, well, how do you go on after that?

Is there ever a time when you say, No more, I've had enough. I'm tired of being tortured and thrown and pulled into five different directions at once!

When do things come back down to reality and save me from myself?

The wind howls in my ears, a massive maelstrom, filling my head with sirens of long dead friends and family. What would they say about my predicament?

Would they reach a hand out to help me, or would they slap me in the face with the same hand, telling me I'm pathetic and that everything I do is of my own device.

Sounds of traffic pierce my consciousness, filling my head with a symphony of civilization. A staccato of horns, honks and beeps play like an orchestra of thousands, all there to merely entertain my attentions.

"Sally, wait, please don't leave me, I love you, we'll find a way!" I begged her as we stood on the front porch of our soon to be lost home.

"Oh, really, John, and what have you been doing for the past six months? Where have you been when the bills kept piling up and our savings dwindled to nothing?" She picked up her luggage and began walking down the stairs.

"No, John, I'm leaving and I won't be coming back." She hesitated then, almost as if she was anguishing over the next words. "I met someone, John. Someone who is responsible and knows how to treat me right." Another hesitation. "I'm sorry, really. I still care about you, but I need to look after myself now." She looked down at her feet, studying her shoes. "I'm sorry." She walked to the checkered cab which had just arrived, and upon climbing inside, it drove away.

She did not look back at me.

She had found someone else to take my place.

How to explain the betrayal I felt then and now. How to even try to place into words the series of emotions that fills my mind when you find out the woman you have been faithful to for ten years has not only decided to leave you, but has found someone else? Someone who will hold her, tell her sweet nothings and that she is the most beautiful woman in the world?

The wind dries my tears as fast as they leave my eyes. My limbs flail about me as I scream to the world that I...have...had...enough!

So what do I do? Do I get a gun and kill people indiscriminately as seems to be the fashion nowadays. Then taking my own life when I'm through, thereby leaving more misery in my absence, as if that could somehow seal the wound in my soul?

No, of course not. Though I'm miserable, I'm not psychotic.

Wait, what about if I take my own life. How would Sally deal with that? How would she accept the fact it was her dagger that pushed me over the edge, that caused me to throw myself into the tempest of oblivion?

How she would cry at my funeral, realizing I was the man she had first and truly loved. That would be when she came to her senses, realizing she had thrown it all away for nothing.

But it would all be too late. Too late for anything.

I open my eyes then, and they go wide with fright. The pavement rushes at me, far too fast to comprehend.

And in that moment, that instant before I strike the sidewalk a thousand feet below, I realize that all my problems could be fixed.

Everything I anguished over was but one drop of water in the ocean of life. None of it mattered and the slate could be wiped clean, to start fresh, like a spring day after a rainstorm.

But it's too late.

Far too late to do anything but plummet to the hard cement below.

If only I could have the last minute back, I would have never stepped off that roof. I would have found a new job and met another woman and lived a good life.

If only...

ONE NIGHT STAND

The nightclub was in full swing, the band playing hard rock, the rhythm of the tune so strong it threatened to tumble the entire building down onto the heads of the revelers.

On the dance floor, Peggy danced like there was no tomorrow. No past or present. She had her eyes closed and she let her body move with the song, letting it take her away to somewhere not of this earth. Her body gyrated to the music, her ample breasts bouncing under her tight blouse, antagonizing the eyes of every man in the room.

But Peggy didn't see them. She was focused inward, on the beat, beat, beat of the bass and of the smell of a hundred other bodies all sweating and dancing around her.

It was intoxicating.

The song stopped and a lull floated over the heads of the crowd.

Suddenly, just as quick as the music had stopped, it began again, the bass bouncing off the walls like hail, the crowd gyrating once again.

Deciding she needed a break and a drink, Peggy moved through the warm bodies and slumped against the bar, waving to get the bartender's attention but with no luck.

"Hey, can I have a beer, please?" she called out to the bartender. The man nodded her way but continued mixing the drink in his hand. In due process, he finished what he was doing and handed her the beer she craved like a fish on dry land needs water.

Gulping half the bottle in a heartbeat, her throat moving slightly as the liquid slid down her slim throat, she opened her eyes and smacked her lips.

And immediately fell in love.

The man standing next to her was absolutely gorgeous. He had broad shoulders and piercing blue eyes that made her want to jump into them and swim around naked for the next hundred years.

His jaw was firm, his cheeks just slightly red, and when he smiled, her legs felt weak and a warm sensation began to grow between them.

There were not many things in the world that Peggy was sure of, but she knew she wanted this man to make love to her. Well, maybe that wasn't the right description.

She wanted him to screw her until her head blew off.

"Hi, I'm Paul," the man said, his voice slicing through the din of the crowd like a knife.

It was like they were the only two people in the club; which was aptly called: Hell on Earth.

"Peggy, Peggy Walton," she said, her throat moving as she swallowed her nervousness. Her smile grew wider and he leaned closer to her, almost as if he could sense her attraction to him.

"Nice to meet you, Peggy Walton," he said slyly. He looked around the club, all the bodies twisting and rubbing one another as the band rocked on well into the night. "Look, you want to get out of here and go somewhere and talk?" he asked her with a twinkle in his eye.

She nodded, her head bobbing like a toy dog on the rear dashboard of the family car.

He smiled so his teeth were showing, and Peggy saw they were a clean white, with two of his incisors slightly larger than the others, almost like fangs, but not so predominant.

Must be Sicilian, she thought, as she let him escort her out of the club.

In moments they were stepping outside into the cool night air, the perspiration covering her body tingling as it evaporated into the night.

Now that they were outside, and she was standing close to him, she could smell his scent and it drove her wild. God, she had to have him.

They walked out of the parking lot and down the street. Above the closer buildings, the cityscape blinked like a thousand stars that had fallen to earth to light her path.

She was slightly chilly now that her body had cooled, but walking next to her, Paul seemed fine, despite the fact that all he wore was a light cotton shirt.

"What are you thinking?" he asked as they walked arm in arm down the street. She had no idea where she was going, but as long as she was with him, she was content.

"Do you really want to know?" she asked, her heart beating in her chest so fast she thought it would simply rip itself out and run away down the street to find a new home.

"Yes, I do," he said, his voice husky and cool.

She swallowed again, her throat rippling with the movement, and she decided to go for it. "I was thinking that I want to make love to you, tonight. Is that wrong? I mean, I know we just met, and I don't want you to think I'm promiscuous. I can't describe it but..." she stumbled for the correct words. "I feel we have a connection that I just can't explain. I..."

He placed his finger on her lips, stopping her from saying another word. "No, it's all right. I feel the same about you. I can't explain it, but it's like I was drawn to you. When I saw you on the dance floor, I knew I had to possess you."

Peggy blushed and began to perspire, despite the cool night. Next to her, Paul was cool and calm, the icon for the perfect Casanova.

She didn't care, all she knew was that she wanted to kiss him. She turned to him then, raising her head slightly, pursing her lips seductively, and just as she hoped, he leaned in and kissed her.

His lips were cool, like the rest of him. As cool as the night air surrounding them. She pressed her body against him and grinded her hips like a common whore.

Deep inside, her rational side screamed at her. *What are you doing? You just met this man. Think, lady, think, before you do something you'll regret!*

She pushed the voice down where it could do no harm and concentrated on the passion writhing within her. She was growing warmer, and as his tongue probed into her mouth, touching her tongue, she felt like she was going to faint.

"My apartment is just around the corner if you'd like to come up for a drink," he breathed, his lips pulling back just enough so he could speak, then he nuzzled her neck, his five o' clock shadow rubbing her soft skin, causing her to tingle all over.

"Uh-huh, that would be nice," she gasped, ready to orgasm right there on the street.

He stopped and she wanted to scream for him to keep going. They could rut like dogs right there on the sidewalk for the entire world to see; she didn't care anymore!

Taking her arm in his hand, he escorted her across the street and down a side alley. She barely saw where she was being led; only wanting to feel his lips on hers once more. It was like she had been mesmerized by this man, this gorgeous hunk of meat.

Before she realized where she was, they were standing in front of a doorway, with the number 6 on it. Without preamble, Paul unlocked the door and led her inside the apartment.

"Do you want something to drink?" he asked, the perfect gentleman, even though he was about to have sex with a strange woman.

She shook her head and moved closer to him. "No, all I want is you inside me," she whispered.

He smiled, his teeth flashing in the light of the room. His slightly pointed front teeth gave him an air of cruelty, despite the warmth of his eyes.

"Come here," Peggy breathed, and walked to the couch, holding out her arms so he could embrace her.

Paul nodded, as cool and calm as if he was deciding what he might watch on television later that night. He moved across the room and sat down next to her, his eyes glinting in the warm lighting of the room.

Just as he was about to lean in and kiss her, he stopped and seemed to draw away from her.

"What's wrong, are you okay?" she asked, scared that she had somehow offended him.

"Yes, I'm fine, it's just, that cross on your neck, could you take it off for me? I can't really go into specifics, but I can't stand the sight of them."

She glanced down at the small gold cross on her neck and nodded. "Oh, all right, if it means that much to you." She slid the slim chain over her head and placed it on a small side table next to the couch.

"Better?" she breathed, leaning back and opening her legs to him, her dress riding up to her thighs.

He smiled cruelly, and licked his lips. "Much better." He bent over and pressed his body against hers, nuzzling her neck once more. He could feel her pulse beating under the thin layer of skin on her swan-like neck and it drove him wild.

He opened his mouth, prepared to dive in and taste her. It had been so long.

Wait, what's this? he thought.

Suddenly there was a pain in his neck, as iron-like hands held him fast.

Something warm was dripping down onto his chest and shoulder.

He tried to cry out, but he found his voice taken from him, washed away like a plastic cup in a flood. He could feel his heart beating in his chest and he swallowed hard, his Adam's apple bobbing with the motion.

Still he couldn't move. Soon he felt himself growing weak and he closed his eyes, falling into oblivion to never awaken again on God's green Earth.

Peggy stood up, wiping her mouth with her blouse sleeve. Her teeth were stained a deep red, scarlet still tinting her lips like lipstick.

She gazed down at the dead form of the man she had only met an hour ago, sighing deeply with regret.

A shame really, she thought. She had really just wanted to screw him, but she had become lost in the moment and had lost control of her primal urges.

Ah well, at least now she wouldn't have to feed for a few days, her belly more than full. He had tasted wonderful, and she hadn't had Italian for quite a while.

She leaned down and picked up the cross, chuckling to herself.

Crosses, just one of many myths that were false. Such as sharp front teeth. A normal set of teeth were more than ample for biting into the flesh of a victim.

She placed the chain over her head and moved to the door, pausing at a cork bulletin board nailed to the wall.

Her eyes roamed over the papers tacked on the board until she came to what looked like a lawsuit form. Paul's name was written in as the plaintiff and the Catholic Church was the defendant.

She grunted at that. Evidently, Paul had some trouble when he was a child, as an altar boy, perhaps? That would explain his distaste of the cross.

Shrugging, and deciding it was irrelevant; she opened the door and stepped out into the hall. As she moved gracefully down the long hallway, she wondered if she should go back to the club or just go home.

Deciding on the latter, because she had work in the morning, she stepped out into the street and hailed a cab.

Climbing inside the cab, the driver turned around in his seat and his eyes gazed at her slim form. "Why, hello there, pretty lady, how can I be of service to you?"

She looked down at the cab floor, checking her shoes before looking up to glare at the driver. "Forget it, pal, I've already eaten tonight, now get going before I report you to your supervisor for harassment."

Rejected, the driver turned back around, and after receiving her instructions on where to go, he drove off into the night.

A DAY AT THE PARK

"So, how do you like Somerset Falls?" Karen Talmadge asked politely as she gazed at the handsome man standing next to her with a sexual hunger. She was almost forty, but still had an air of beauty about her, though a subtle whiff of desperation could be detected if the right man was perceptive enough to notice. She hoped this man might.

Tom Scottsdale nodded politely as he glanced at her, not meeting her gaze.

His son, Bobby, should have been over by the concession table at the edge of the baseball field, hanging out with the other children. He was there a few minutes ago, he was sure of it.

The baseball game was in full swing, at the top of the fifth inning, and the crowd was quite large for a small town, all cheering their small time heroes.

"Oh, it's fine, fine," Tom said. "It seems like a nice place to live."

Karen nodded. "Uh-huh, that it is. And where did you say you lived before?" Her eyes drifted to his strong chest and muscled arms.

Tom glanced over at the concession table again. He was looking for Bobby's blue and red jacket, but for the life of him, he couldn't find it.

"Uhm, New York. We came from New York." He stepped away from Karen, moving closer to the concession table like a smaller planet trapped in the orbit of a larger one.

"Oh, really, and why did you leave there? Was it because of the rash of murders I heard about on the news?" she asked.

"No, of course not. I needed to change jobs, that's all. Don't be silly."

"They say there's something evil prowling the streets of New York right now," she continued. "Over twenty found dead so far, is that right? They say the bodies were ripped to pieces. Like some kind of animal did it." As she talked, she kept moving closer to him so that he could smell the fragrance of her hair.

Tom took a step back, slightly rattled by her aggressiveness, before regaining his composure. Once more he looked around the park for his son, still not seeing him.

"Listen, I gotta go, I need to check on my son. I don't see him anywhere."

Karen frowned a little, but let him go, though she did follow by his side.

"So, is there a wife waiting for you at home, Tom?" Karen asked as she continued trolling for a new boyfriend...or perhaps, if she played her cards right, maybe even a husband?

"Huh, what? Oh, no, there's no one like that. It's just me and my son, Bobby."

"Oh, well, that's great, actually. Listen, if you're not doing anything tonight, I was thinking..."

Tom stopped her with a hand in front of her face and she went silent. She looked up into his eyes, waiting for what he would say next. She found herself almost hypnotized by the intensity of their penetrating gaze. They were a deep blue, with flecks of green. She could get lost in those eyes, she thought.

"Listen, uhm, Karen is it?"

She nodded.

"Well, Karen, I really don't have time for you right now. I can't find my son and I need to go look for him."

"Oh, of course, Tom, what was I thinking? Do you want me to help?"

He gave that a thought and nodded. "Yeah, sure, that would be great. Keep an eye out for a blue and red jacket. That's what he's wearing."

"Okay," she said as Tom left her behind, searching frantically for any sign of Bobby.

Tom walked through the crowd until he was at the table he had last seen Bobby at. The table was filled with hotdogs and pizza, pretzels and chips, soda cans piled high. Two old ladies with sun hats on their heads served the food and helped the customers. As for payment of the food, there was a small cardboard box at the edge of the table, all very small-town in its set-up, where everyone trusted everyone else to put in what they owed.

His son was nowhere to be seen. He remembered seeing other children near the table, also, and now those children were gone, as well. Not wanting to yell out and make a scene, he craned his neck over the other spectators as he tried to find Bobby.

Finally, he spotted a group of six boys across the field, near a copse of trees. From a previous walk earlier in the week, he knew there was nothing down there but the old defunct concession stand and a rather steep hill that led to the highway.

Deciding it was worth a look, he began running across the park, taking the long way around the field, though everything in his bones wanted him to just cut across the field while they were playing the game, and to hell with them.

Upon reaching the edge of the trees and shrubs, he looked down into the gulley. He could see the boys' jackets and hear their voices, but if his son was with them, he couldn't tell.

His son was nine years old, and no matter where they would move to, his son always seemed to become the target of bullies. Countless schools and countless towns had passed through their lives, and in every one of them, Bobby had been terrorized by bullies and children who took pleasure in making him, and others like him, suffer.

Running down the small path lined with trees, Tom reached the group of boys. His heart was beating faster now as he stared at the faces of the children. Though he didn't know these boys, their faces told of cruelty and pettiness. Eyes were hard and mouths were curved up in sneers of contempt.

Though an adult had fallen into their ranks, they weren't the slightest bit intimidated.

"Have you guys seen my son?" Tom asked politely. "He was wearing a red and blue jacket. He's new here in town and maybe you guys took him with you? Look, I don't care about anything like that, no one's in trouble. I just want my son back."

As he finished his questions, Tom's eyes were pulled to the old concession stand on his right. It was a cinderblock and stone building with faded paint and water stains and mildew on its sides. It was still a good, strong building, and if the town had needed to, they could have easily made the building into something else, a club house or a gardening shack for the groundskeeper. But as it was, the building was abandoned and probably quite the hangout for the older kids to drink and smoke in at night.

"So, guys, do you know where my son is?" Tom prodded.

The boys, all around twelve and thirteen years old, stared at Tom, and then at each other, each snickering like Tom was the biggest in-joke of the month. One boy, near the back of the gang, had a bright shock of unkempt red hair and freckles on his cheeks. Despite this, he had a look of a troublemaker. Nothing you could put your finger on, but just a gut sense adults would have sometimes when they measure up children. The other boys seemed to defer to Red Head and that told Tom he was the leader of this little gang of delinquents.

"You, do you know where my son is?" Tom asked, moving through the boys until he was looming over Red Head.

Red Head shrugged inconclusively, but his eyes involuntarily glanced at the abandoned building. Tom caught the look and turned to stare at the building, as well.

"He's in there?" Tom turned and crossed the twenty feet to the building and called out.

"Bobby! Bobby! Are you in there? It's okay now, it's Dad. Just yell out so I can get you! Bobby?"

Nothing. If his son was inside, he was either too scared to call out or God forbid, somehow incapacitated. Tom stepped closer to the building and tried to listen for his son. Behind him, all the boys stood silent, though continually tossed smiles at one another. Oh yes, they knew something, but weren't talking.

Tom stepped against the faded wall of the refreshment stand and strained his hearing.

Then, suddenly, he thought he heard something. Was it sobbing? Softly, barely perceived over the traffic of the nearby highway, just eighty feet from where he stood, but yes, he was pretty sure.

The door to the old building was open and Tom ran inside, looking up at the chipped ceiling and old ductwork. The ductwork ran around the ceiling and disappeared into the walls and ceiling at the edges of the main room, from there it would lattice through the entire building until it reached the ventilation and air conditioning units at the rear of the structure. From the size of the inside room and the shape of the outer building, there was probably no more than two more rooms besides the one he was standing in.

Tom looked around the room, having no idea where his son could be, or even if he had truly heard him.

No, he had. He had to go with his instinct and follow it. If his son was trapped somewhere in the building, he needed to get to him quickly. There was no time to call for help on his cell phone. By the time help arrived, it could be too late. Not to mention Tom would prefer to leave the law out of it if he had a choice, too many questions to answer.

"Bobby, are you in here? It's your Dad, son, call out to me if you can hear me!"

Nothing. The other boys were standing by the doorway, watching him. They seemed to be enjoying the afternoon's revelations. Perhaps because they had caused the problem in the first place?

Tom spun on his heels and stared at the young, insolent faces glaring back at him.

"If you kids know where my boy is, so help me if you don't tell me."

None answered, but Red Head smirked widely from the back of the group. That was enough for Tom. Obviously this kid knew something.

Crossing the few feet separating him from the boys, they all scattered, resembling pigeons when a car drives through a flock as they mill about on the ground. Stretching his right arm quickly, Tom's left hand reached out and grabbed Red Head by the scruff of his jacket and held him fast.

They were outside again, and for a brief second, Tom thought he heard muffled crying again coming from inside the building. Then it was gone like it was never there in the first place.

Tom was growing more and more frantic as he worried about his son. Not to mention the valuable time he was wasting here if it ended up that Bobby hadn't gone with the boys. What if someone else had taken him; kidnapped him? No, it was too much to consider and so he needed to deal with what was in front of him. If these boys didn't know where Bobby was they sure were up to no good.

But when he stared at the face of Red Head, he knew that wasn't the case. If Bobby was here, then why were the boys so damn cocky? And why hadn't they run away when they had the chance? Nothing was stopping them, unless they were enjoying the torture he was experiencing with the anguish over his missing son.

Tom was about to ask a question when a splash of color struck his right eye, just out of the corner of it. He followed it and spotted what might be Bobby's jacket lying under a pile of leaves. With Red Head still in his grip, he moved across the overgrown walkway until he was looking down at the red and blue jacket; it was definitely Bobby's. There on the sleeve was the rip he had gotten only a few days ago. He had fallen off his skateboard in the driveway and had ripped the jacket on a sharp rock lining the edge of the pavement and the lawn.

With his free hand, Tom picked up the jacket and shook it off. Upon inspecting it, he could see the jacket was covered in mud and bits of grass and bits of decayed leaves. Someone had tried to hide it, but as most children are wont to do, had done a terrible job.

"If my son isn't here then how do you explain this?" Tom asked Red Head as he shoved the jacket into the boy's freckled face.

Red Head turned his face and spit out a wad of phlegm onto Tom's shoes, curses flowing out like water to insult Tom's mother and heritage. Tom quickly learned Red Head may be a child, but the boy's vocabulary had graduated him to adulthood.

In disgust, Tom dragged the boy with him as he moved back to the abandoned building, his heart pumping in his chest so fast he wondered if it would explode.

"Where's my son, you little bastard? Where did you put him?" he screamed while shaking the boy.

His eyes drifted over the other boy's faces again, but none of their countenances showed anything he could use as a weakness to try and exploit. These kids were hard, used to dealing hurt and pain on others and then laughing about it later.

A muffled sob carried on the wind and Tom's head swiveled to the building again.

"That was Bobby's voice, I know it." He began to shake Red Head like he was a rag doll. "Damn, you, where the hell is my son?"

Red Head only smiled back, enjoying the entire situation, knowing Tom couldn't hurt him. If Tom hit him, any of them, the boys knew they could get him in serious trouble.

Tom moved back to the door of the building and glanced inside again. Moving into the kitchen, now nothing but a frame of what it once was, he tried to see where his son could possibly be. Red Head struggled for a brief moment in Tom's arms, but when Tom squeezed harder and shook the boy again, Red Head stopped moving, becoming docile. The snide smile never left the boy's face.

Tom knew if he let the boy go now, after he had shone Red Head and his gang his anger and what he might do to them, it was highly possible Red Head and his friends would run away, leaving Tom to fend for himself.

"Dammit, kid, where the hell is my boy? He's only nine, for God's sake!"

Red Head's eyes reflected only amusement, not seeming to care in the slightest.

"Screw you, old man, I don't know nothin'. None of us do," Red Head spit.

Tom knew then that he needed to take drastic measures if he wanted to find his son.

Taking Red Head's right arm in a firmer grip, he twisted it behind the boy's back, pulling up so hard the boy actually stood on his tip-toes to try to lessen the pain.

"Alright, you little bastard. I'm through playing with you. Tell me where my son is or so help me I'll break your arm like a chicken wing and feed it to you fingers first."

Red Head let out a yelp and his friends ran inside, all gathering by the opening to the kitchen. If Red Head was going to talk, he quickly shut up as the eyes of his friends fell upon him.

Tom shuffled to the door with his charge and slammed it closed, blocking out the lingering gazes of the others.

"There, now we're all alone. Just you and me. Now tell me where my son is or I'll break your arm." To emphasize how serious he was, Tom added more pressure, causing Red Head to yelp in pain.

Sweat began to bead on Red Head's forehead and Tom could feel his breathing begin to grow heavier in anticipation of finding where his son was.

Red Head cried out again and this time he called out to his friends at the door. A second later and the door was kicked in and there were the boys again. Only this time each held a knife, while one held a small wooden bat with bent rusty nails on its tip.

"You just made a big mistake, old man," Red Head sneered happily, though he ended up wincing in pain from his bent arm.

As the boys moved closer, Tom realized it had all been a trap. Perhaps the boys had done it before, probably countless times. First they take a lonely child away from the park, and when the fretful parent goes looking for him or her, they lead the parent to the abandoned concession stand where they must rob and probably beat them. Then they threaten the parent not to say anything or risk further problems.

A perfectly controlled mugging. But if it had happened before, then why was the building still standing? Why hadn't the police boarded it up or even just torn it down?

Questions that had no answers at the moment. All that mattered was that his son was still missing and now five boys with weapons were advancing on him, while a sixth was still in his grasp. Another sob filled the building and Tom looked up to the water-stained ceiling. Ductwork was overhead as well and that was when he put it all together.

"He's in the ductwork, isn't he? You put my son in the damn ductwork," Tom growled.

Red Head seemed to deflate a little as the mystery was solved, but then he barked out an order to his gang of young thugs and they surrounded Tom, closing him in a ring that was growing ever tighter.

"Hang on, Bobby, I'm coming to get you!" Tom screamed as he slowly backed up, his butt coming up against the old stoves for the kitchen. This time there was an answering sob and Tom heard a tapping coming from the ductwork.

As the first boy moved closer to Tom, waving his knife in the air menacingly, Tom grinned widely. A feral snarl crossed Tom's face and he eyes creased so only the slightest hint of his dark orbs could be seen. He leaned down until his mouth was so close to Red Head's right ear that he could have bitten it off if he wanted to.

"I tried to do this right, you should know that. I tried to change my ways, start over, get a new job and live the good life; just me and my son. But you had to screw it all up for me, you little bastard."

Tom spun Red Head around until the boy was gazing up into Tom's face. But it wasn't the face of a frightened parent looking down on him anymore. Instead, there was the face of a predator. A hunter.

"You just picked the wrong father and son to fuck with," Tom growled and then his face shot down and tore Red Head's nose off his face like a wild animal, the nose coming off like it was a piece of taffy, the boy screaming in pain as he reached up to stop the staunch of blood with his hands.

With the taste of blood in his mouth, Tom's eyes played over the other boys who had stopped in their tracks, all in shock at what had happened to their leader.

Tom dropped Red Head to the dirty floor, where the boy rolled around, screaming in pain as blood shot between his fingers in thick gouts.

"I told you boys when I got here that we could do this the easy way or the hard way." He took a step closer to the first boy with a knife. "Which way do you think I'm going to do it now?"

Tom blanked out then, not remembering anything that happened. That was what always happened. It was like his mind shut off, not wanting him to witness the animal ferocity of its carnal nature.

Screams of absolute terror and torture filtered out through the walls of the building, to be lost with the noise from the highway before quickly growing silent.

Minutes later, without remembering how he had gotten there, Tom realized he was standing outside the old building again, his son in his arms.

Tom was covered in blood, like he had bathed in it, but his son was fine.

Bobby looked up at Tom and wiped some of the blood off his father's weary face.

"Oh, Daddy, not again. I'm sorry I was so scared and didn't call out to you when I was inside the vent, but did you have to go and do that to all those kids?"

Tom chuckled at his son, hugging him tightly. "Yeah, son, I guess I did. Come on, let's go pack again. I hear Boston's nice this time of year."

Father and son walked up the pathway and away from the charnel house smell of the old concession stand, as a pool of fresh blood trickled out from under the main door of the building.

Though another place of refuge had been destroyed and it was time to move on, that was okay. They were still together and would remain so for a long, long time to come.

SECRET TALENTS

The carnival was in town today; the rides and games of chance filled with screaming children and frazzled parents. Just past the ticket booth were the games of chance, and the rides were in back, near the edge of the lot the carnival had rented for the month of June.

"Win one every time!" screamed one of the men behind a counter. He was tucked in his booth like a soldier defending his territory. Behind him were floating plastic frogs on light green and yellow plastic Lilly pads, all sitting in a large swimming pool filled with dirty water that would probably send a human being on an acid trip if consumed internally.

At the moment, there were three people playing the game. The first was a young woman of twenty, with her boyfriend watching silently behind her. The second was an older man with too much time on his hands, so he spent the hours at the carnival whenever it came to town, and the third was a young boy of around seven. He had just spent his last quarter and had already used two of his three trys.

"Come on, son, it's easy. A winner every time, guaranteed," the large fat man said from behind the counter. He wore a bright red shirt and white pants that hadn't been washed since Nixon was in office.

The boy scrunched up his face and tried one more time, tossing the small rings of plastic across the few feet separating him from the pool of plastic frogs.

The ring rose into the air and the old man and the young couple stopped breathing as they watched, all believing the ring was going to land on the middle frog's head. But just as it landed, it bounced off and fell into the water with a *splunk*!

"Aww, great try, kid, really, better luck next time," the vendor said with no regret in his voice.

He moved closer to the boy and touched the boy's hand. The gesture seemed casual, but it was far from it.

"Maybe you could come back later and I could teach you how to do it right," the vendor said under his breath, no one else in the crowd hearing him.

"Well, I don't know, mister, my mom might not let me."

The vendor leaned slightly closer, only pausing for a moment to take a quarter from another customer and pass the man three plastic rings. "Then don't tell her, it'll be our little secret. Look, do you wanna learn how to win or what? Just come by later after we close and I'll show you how to do it. I'll even get you some ice cream, how 'bout it?"

The boy looked into the man's perspiring face and then back to the plastic frogs, waiting tantalizingly in the pool for him to try again. He was about to say yes, that he would come back, when a woman's shrill voice cut through the din of the crowd.

"Timmy, what are you doing here alone? I told you to stay by my side," the boy's mother snapped at him as she came up to his side and grabbed his left shoulder in an iron grip. "I was worried sick."

"Aww, Mom, I'm just trying to win the game. I want that stuffed bear."

Timmy's mother would have none of it. "I don't care, I told you not to wander away. Little boys and girls disappear all the time from these places. There are very unsavory people who work here. Drifters and criminals who need a quick dollar. Now you come with me, young man, we're going home right now!"

Timmy looked at the vendor's sweating face and the boy's face was sad.

"Sorry, mister, I gotta go," Timmy said.

The vendor only grunted as the boy was pulled away into the crowd to be lost from sight. "Ah, well, there's plenty more where he came from," the vendor said lecherously under his breath. "It's too bad, though," he sighed heavily, "he was so young and sweet. What I would have done to him."

And he had, too. Many times before.

Many other boys in past cities had felt his malevolent touch after succumbing to his enticements, only to become another face on a milk carton days or weeks later. He had never been caught, always moving on with the carnival before an investigation into the missing children's fates could find him.

The vendor looked up as two new customers slapped a few quarters down on the counter, eager for their try at winning a bauble or a stuffed item.

With an evil smile of what might had been, he went back to work.

* * *

A tall, dark man walked into the carnival. He was well over six feet. He was dressed entirely in black with the exception of a small pin on his lapel. The pin was gold and it flashed in the sun. On closer inspection, the pin looked just like a small pitch fork.

The man had a strong jaw and a wide brim hat on his head, also black. In his left hand was a cane, a dark wood of unknown origin, and on its tip was a carving of the fabled Cerberus, the three-headed dog from Hell.

Though it was a hot day, the temperature well in the nineties, the man didn't perspire. In fact, he seemed comfortable as if he was sitting by the pool with a cold drink in his hand, lounging in a set of swim trunks.

As he moved through the crowd, men and women unconsciously moved out of his path. It was nothing that could be perceived openly, it was something entirely unnoticeable, like the wind blowing a paper bag gently across an empty parking lot.

The man glided through the carnival until he came to the fat vendor with the plastic frogs. The vendor didn't notice the man at first, as he was engaged in a private conversation with a small boy of no more than nine. The vendor had one of his meaty paws on the boy's shoulder and he was whispering something into the child's ear.

The man in black stepped up to the counter and slapped a quarter down on the faded and peeling wood. "I would like a try please," the man said in a low voice, almost inaudible.

"In a second, pal," the vendor said, trying to seal the deal with the young boy.

The man in black slapped the counter with his cane, making the other customers jump. The vendor looked up, and deciding he had no choice, he reached under the counter, took three plastic rings from a basket, placed them on the counter, and retrieved the quarter from the counter.

"Here ya go, pal, good luck, a winner every time," the fat man said, but his attention was still focused mainly on the small boy.

The man in black only grunted in reply before tossing the first ring. It arced out over the frogs to drop effortlessly onto one of the plastic heads. It never bounced, but just seemed to settle on it like a feather landing on the surface of a lake.

As the other customers clapped at the success of one of their own, the vendor looked up from the boy, seeing the ring lying precariously on the plastic frog.

"A winner!" the vendor said, reaching up and grabbing a small stuffed animal that was worth a dime to fifteen cents when it had been new more than five years earlier.

The man in black ignored the faded relic and tossed the next plastic ring. Once again, the second ring flew threw the air, almost as if on its own volition, and seemed to stop in mid-air before dropping onto the next plastic frog in line, the ring settling so that one end dipped into the dirty water.

The vendor stopped talking to the boy and looked up, his face annoyed and shocked that the man had succeeded twice in one session.

He ignored the boy now, his honor and pride at stake. Who was this man to win on his fixed game? The head's of the plastic frogs were just slightly too large so that the rings could never land on top of them unless they were dropped from directly over the frogs, and then from only an inch or so in height. What the man in black was doing was utterly impossible.

The vendor took the cheap stuffed animal away and replaced it with another equally worthless prize. "Well done, pal, well done, so take care now," the vendor said, trying to get the man to leave.

"I'm not done yet, I still have one more try," the man in black said.

The vendor frowned, but he stepped back and waved the man on. "Go ahead then, do it already."

The man in black did, tossing the ring into the air. The boy stood next to the tall man, his eyes wide as he watched the plastic ring glide across the distance to the frog like it was on a cushion of air, then it seemed to suddenly stop and drop easily onto the frog's head.

"You did, it, mister, you did it," the small boy clapped, slapping his hands together in happiness.

The vendor frowned, but took away the stuffed animal and handed the man an ashtray worth fifty cents, if anything at all.

"Congratulations, pal, now take off will ya? I got a business to run."

The man in black said nothing, but instead, slapped another quarter down on the counter next to his growing pile of winnings. "Give me three more trys" he said quietly.

The vendor stared at the man, clearly not wanting to, but in the end he sighed and reached under the counter, taking three more rings and placing them in front of the man.

"Here ya go, buddy, good luck. A winner every time!" he yelled the last part out to other carnival goers. A few people decided to take a chance and he handed out more plastic rings, sliding the cash into the money belt on his waist.

The man in black picked up the new plastic rings and this time tossed, one, two and then three, back to back. Each one flew threw the air to then drop onto a separate frog's head. The other customers clapped at this, glad to see someone winning for a change.

The vendor frowned deeply. This wasn't funny anymore. This was his livelihood. If people started winning, he'd never make any money, or make as much money as he wanted to.

With the crowd cheering, the vendor reached up and pulled down a fancy mirror, its surface etched with a butterfly.

"Here ya go, pal, use it in good health," he barked, then ignored the man and began seeing to other customers.

Like the crack of a breaking branch, the man in black slapped another quarter down on the counter. The vendor's eyes flashed anger and he stared at the quarter as if it were poison.

"That's it, pal, only two trys per person."

"What? Yesterday you let me go four times," another man from the crowd called out.

"That's because you weren't winning yesterday. Hell, he probably would have let you go ten times if you'd wanted to," another man called off from the side. He had cotton candy in his hand and some in his mouth.

By now a small crowd was slowly growing around the vendor's stall as curious passersby wanted to see what all the commotion was about.

"Give the guy his rings," a woman said.

"Yeah, give him his try," a seventeen year old boy called.

The vendor frowned deeply, but decided to give in to the crowd's protests. He reached under the counter to grab three more rings. But this time he reached into another basket, this one filled with rings that were slightly smaller than the regular ones, his failsafe. He had never had to use them before but decided it was time. It was absolutely impossible for the dark man to win now.

The rings were dropped on the counter and the vendor took the man in black's quarter. "Good luck, pal, you'll need it," the vendor said flatly.

The man in black said nothing in reply, but instead tossed the first ring into the air. The ring glided through the air and landed on the first frog in line, but due to its smaller size, it merely rested precariously on the green and chipped head, looking as if it would slide off, but didn't.

The crowd went wild, clapping and cheering.

The vendor pursed his lips and grit his teeth angrily. He was being fleeced and there was nothing he could do about it. Reaching up, the vendor pulled down a large stuffed animal, actually worth something to him.

But the man in black shook his head. "Not yet, I still have two more trys."

The vendor frowned deeply, but stepped away from the pool. The man in black stood taller and the vendor held up his hands. "Wait a second there, pal, no leaning, stay behind the counter."

"I wasn't leaning; I was just going to toss it."

"Leave him alone, ya jerk, he's doin' it fair and square," a heckler called out.

"Yeah, leave him alone, let him play," another angry voice snapped out from the crowd.

The vendor knew he was outnumbered and stepped back. "Okay, okay, maybe I was wrong, just watch it," he said.

The man in black only grinned slightly, a mysterious grin that said many things and yet nothing at the same time.

With his second ring in his hand, the man in black tossed it over the pool of plastic frogs. The ring crossed the distance easily and then seemed to gently settle on the head of a frog near the back of the pool.

The crowd went wild, clapping and laughing. It was about time someone won. Though no one could prove it, almost every game was fixed in some way or another, so it was almost impossible to win, each game more deceiving in its own right.

The vendor's jaw went taut and his throat moved as he swallowed. He reached up and pulled down his most expensive present, a cassette radio that was outdated years ago, but was still actually valuable.

"Here, ya go, buddy, now what do ya say you leave now, huh?"

The man in black pushed the radio away. "Sorry, but I've still got one more try left."

"But you've got everything I have to offer. I don't have anything else you would want."

The man in black tilted his head slightly and leaned forward so that only the vendor could hear him.

"Oh, I wouldn't say that. Tell you what. How about this? One more try, and if I win, I get whatever I want."

The vendor's eyes became slits. "Oh, yeah? And what if you lose?"

The man in black shrugged.

"Then you get everything back and I leave. Tell you what. I'll even step back two feet from the counter, just to make it interesting."

The vendor chewed his lip and rung his hands, thinking about it. He needed all the junk the man had won and it would vindicate him to the crowd if the man in black lost. Not that they would cheer for him, all of the crowd were on the man in black's side.

Screw the crowd, he had his pride to gain back and this man was making him look the fool. "All right, deal," the vendor said.

"Shake on it," the man in black said.

The vendor reached one chubby hand out and shook the dark man's hand. The hand felt cold, despite the heat and the clothes the man was wearing, and then the vendor felt a pinch in his hand.

"Oww what the..." he said as he pulled his hand away. In his palm was a tiny pinprick, a small bead of blood showing.

"Something pricked me," the vendor said curiously.

"Yes, that happens sometimes," the man in black said cryptically.

"Why the hell did you do that?"

The man in black ignored the vendor's protest, but proceeded to raise his arm and take two steps backward. The crowd around him clapped and cheered him on the entire time.

Behind the counter, the vendor was sweating worse than ever, his hands squeezed into fists as he crossed his fingers and prayed the man would miss.

The man in black took one deep breath and gently tossed the ring into the air. This ring was a dirty yellow, slightly bent and not a full circle but more of an oval.

The ring flew into the air, and for just a moment it seemed like it was going to miss the pool entirely, and end up landing on the dirt floor of the booth, but at the last moment, like a gust of air had struck it, it turned to the left and angled downward toward the head of a plastic frog on the edge of the pool.

The ring landed on the head, not bouncing, but just resting softly, and the crowd went wild, laughing and cheering as they applauded the man in black's good fortune.

The vendor was about to yell at the dark man, knowing the man had to have cheated somehow, when he felt a sharp pain in his chest. His mouth began opening and closing like a landed fish as he crumpled to his knees behind the counter, his hands going to his chest. It felt like there was a giant hand on his heart, squeezing and pulling at it like it was taffy.

Around him, no one noticed what was transpiring, all celebrating the man in black's victory.

The vendor sprawled on the dirt floor, his chest heaving up and down in cadence to his breathing until he just stopped breathing. There was no succession, one instant he was gasping for air, and then he wasn't, like his heart had simply disappeared from his body.

Suddenly, one of the cheering women in the crowd noticed the vendor on the ground and let out a cry of shock that soon had everyone else in the vicinity doing the same. Men hopped over the counter to try and help the vendor, but it was far too late for the rotund man.

In all the confusion, no one noticed the man in black had simply disappeared, along with the radio, leaving the other prizes to lay abandoned on the counter.

But one small boy happened to look behind him as the crowd began to panic at the vendor's collapse, and he spotted, for just an instant, the man in black moving away from the stall and into the crowd.

The boy never told anyone about what he saw that day, but as he watched the man move away, he could have sworn he was holding a heart in a jar, and in his other hand was the cassette radio. Perhaps it was just a trick of the boy's eyes as the sun glanced off the glass jar, but he could have sworn he saw the heart beat, a steady pulsing despite the fact it was inside the jar.

Then the man in black moved behind a crowd of three revelers, and when the crowd had passed, the man was gone like he was never there to begin with.

Paramedics were called for the vendor, but it was too late, and the vendor was pronounced dead on site. What was even stranger was that at the autopsy, the coroner reported that the man was missing his heart, like it had been surgically removed from his body, despite the fact that the vendor had no scars or wounds on his chest or back.

In the dead man's belongings, a small gold pin shaped like a pitchfork was found, the pin discovered attached to the man's chest, just over where his heart should have been. It was filed in a box and forgotten, with the rest of the miscellaneous items the man had on his person. The vendor had been a loner, no family to notify.

In the end, the entire incident was pushed into a file and buried, never to be spoken of again with the exception of rumors and innuendoes around the water cooler at the morgue.

After everything that had happened, the carnival decided to pack up and leave the town early. But they would return in another year...minus one vendor, of course.

ONE OF THOSE DAYS

Byron Greenwald lay under the folds of his bed, half in and half out of sleep. As he lay there, he idly wondered what time it was.

Assessing his body as to how tired he felt, he tried to guess what the bedside alarm clock would read when he stuck his head out from under the blankets and checked.

He knew he had to get up at seven a.m., his alarm set to that time exactly, as it was every morning, and he tried to gauge the depth of the sunlight filtering in through the blanket.

Feels like it's six-thirty, he thought.

At times he would wake up before the alarm clock, beating its annoying buzzer to the punch. Before he had chosen the buzzer to wake him, a modern day rooster in a plastic box, he had set the radio to a music station. But after three days of listening to the disc jockeys droning on about this and that, he couldn't stand it any longer and had reverted back to the buzzer.

His bladder alerted him to its fullness and he decided he would just get up, but when he pushed the blanket off his head and gazed over at the alarm clock, he saw it was seven-thirty.

"Oh, no, I'm late!" he screamed to the empty bedroom, a single man for all of his forty-five years, and happy to be a bachelor. Reaching over and checking the alarm, he suddenly realized he had set it to six p.m., instead of six a.m.

Remembering the day before he had wanted to go in early and beat the traffic, he had messed with the clock and had ended up setting it to the wrong time.

"Great, what a way to start the day," he mumbled to himself as he climbed out of bed and walked to the bathroom.

Sitting down on the toilet, too lazy to stand at this juncture in the morning, he peed and then realized he had to poop. Squeezing his cheeks tightly, he let out a slight moan, as what felt like a watermelon passed through him. His face scrunched up like he had eaten a lemon, and when he thought it couldn't get any worse, he sighed as the massive object broke free of him and plopped into the toilet water, a few drops splashing on his exposed butt cheeks.

With relief he sighed. Then, opening his legs and peering into the bowl, he expected to see a large turd floating in the water, something he could take pride in inside the confines of his bathroom. A creation only he could make, one that only he could appreciate in all its magnitude. After all, it came from him, from inside him and anything that came from the internal world of Byron was a wonderful thing.

Something so big he could say: "I did that. It's beautiful isn't it? Put it on display in the Smithsonian for all to see and admire."

He could imagine thousands of people passing through the west wing, where his work of art was on display, and perhaps for a price, to a lucky few, viewers could take a piece home for themselves to enjoy in the privacy of their living rooms.

But when he opened his legs and gazed into the bowl, the dream was shattered when all he saw staring back at him was a small round ball, only slightly larger than a marble.

What the hell was up with that? It felt like he was passing a baby, for Christ's sake! Or so he assumed, listening to women whine about how hard it was to give birth. Personally, he thought they made a big deal about nothing and he was happy to stay buried in his male ignorance. And perhaps this standard of being so unsympathetic was why he was still single.

When he knew he was done, only a few seconds passing, as he had no time to enjoy this morning's bowel movement and not wanting to be late for work, he reached out to grab the toilet paper mounted to the wall.

It was empty, nothing but a cardboard tube staring back at him.

"Dammit," he cursed and reached into the nearby vanity for another roll. But when he opened the vanity, he was only mildly surprised to see it was devoid of a replacement roll.

Sighing, saying to himself that it was going to be one of those mornings, he stood up, but had to stay bent over or risk making a mess in the crack of his ass.

He knew he had more rolls of toilet paper in the linen closet, just outside the bathroom door, and so, wobbling like a duck with hemorrhoids, he moved into the hallway, hoping nothing would fall off him to land on the carpet and soil the material.

Opening the linen closet, he looked up on the shelf where the toilet paper should be. But instead of a neat row of clean white tissue, there was a note.

Byron, get more toilet paper, it stated in his handwriting.

"Oh, you've got to be kidding me," he said to the empty hallway.

With an aggravated grunt, he waddled back to the bathroom, and after a moment of soul searching, he pulled down the washcloth from its hook and proceeded to wipe himself.

After he was finished, he filled the sink with water and dropped the soiled linen into the liquid. He would deal with it later when he returned home from work that night.

With one problem solved, he brushed his teeth, but when he was about to spit, he realized the washcloth was in the sink, its brown stains taunting him. Adapting quickly, he spit into the shower, proud of himself for solving this new little problem and not getting aggravated.

After finishing in the bathroom, he went back to the bedroom, planning on getting dressed. His shirt went on without a hitch, as it should, a common chore he did every day of his life, but when he slid on his pants, he didn't pay attention very well and the skin of his right testicle caught in his zipper as he zipped his fly.

Screaming in pain, he cursed himself for going commando today of all days, and with ever so much care, he tried to unzip the bear-trap on his nuts.

But just as he knew it would happen, his balls protested, pain shooting into his stomach to make him gasp out loud. He knew what he had to do. Like a band-aid coming off, he had to do it quick.

Closing his eyes, he counted to three, and with a loud yell that threatened to shake the walls of the bedroom, he unzipped his pants. There was a brief pain and then nothing but bliss, minus a dull throbbing in his crotch.

Checking his package, he was pleased to see no lasting damage, just a very small spot of blood. After sitting on the bed for a moment and thanking God his jewels were safe, he finished dressing and went downstairs to the kitchen to make a slice of toast before heading off to work. He checked his wristwatch and was pleased to see he was only slightly behind schedule.

Hopefully he could make it up on the road.

Entering the kitchen, he opened the bread box to find the empty plastic bag where the bread should be.

Gritting his teeth in anger, he pushed his frustration back down. There was no one to blame but himself, and it was a small thing in the scheme of life. Hell, he could get a donut or something when he was on the road.

Deciding it was time to go, needing to make up precious time, he slid into his overcoat and prepared to leave, opening the door and passing through it.

Just before he locked the door behind him, he reached into his pocket for his keys, but at the same time, he continued closing the door out of habit.

As his right hand dug into his pocket, finding his cell phone, some chewing gum, and...no keys?

The door clicked shut.

"No, wait, my keys are on the counter! Dammit to Hell!" he screamed. Now he remembered, he had tossed his keys on the counter when he had returned home late from work last night. Usually he left them in his pocket; after all, if he left the house, he wore a coat and what better way not to forget them?

Realizing this was one more nail in his coffin for the day, he walked around to the back of the house. He needed his keys. He had to get back into the house.

Checking all the windows, hoping he had been negligent and forgot to lock one of them, he soon found out he was out of luck.

Stepping back into the driveway and staring at the house, he looked up at the second story window and saw it was cracked an inch or so.

"Ha, there you go, my luck's changing," he said, clapping his hands in joy.

There was a small ladder on the side of the house and he retrieved it, climbing up to the window. He had to break the screen, but under the circumstances it would have to do.

Climbing into the house, he fell onto the carpet in a heap of limbs and then ran back downstairs and grabbed his keys off the counter. With keys firmly in hand, he went to the door and started all over again.

Checking his watch, not happy with the time, he ran to his car, jumped in, and drove off, finally on the road to work, though it had been a rough morning.

The clock on the dash read 7:52. He was late, but not that late, he could make up the time if he was lucky.

A small *ding, ding* sounded on the dash and he looked down to see the gas gauge was on empty and the little picture of a gas pump began to flash, telling him he was an idiot for letting it get so low. He needed to get some gas before he ran out.

He was about to start yelling, knowing there wasn't enough time to get gas, but instead held it in check, like a cauldron of hot water not able to boil over thanks to the tight seal on its cover.

Weaving into traffic, he got every red light. And I mean every single one. It was like there was someone deliberately messing with him. Finally though, he reached an open area, but then the *ding, ding* sounded again, and though he knew he would lose precious time, he pulled into the next gas station, envious of the traffic as it continued to drive past him.

As he pulled into the first slot of pumps, he turned off the motor and climbed out, only to see plastic bags over all the nozzles. **THIS PUMP CLOSED, PLEASE PULL UP**, was printed in messy script.

"Oh, you have got to be kidding me," he cursed under his breath, but what was he gonna do? He needed gas, so climbing back into the car, he drove to the middle pump. Looking in his rearview mirror, he saw another car pull up behind him. There was a car in front of him too and now he was stuck between the two vehicles.

Mentally crossing his fingers that the driver in front of him would be fast, he waited patiently, tapping his fingers on the dash, watching the seconds turn into minutes.

The nozzle of the gas pump was already in the Lincoln Navigator's fuel spout, and when Byron leaned forward and looked out his front windshield, he could see the meter on the pump rolling away, racking up the vehicle's price.

"Good God, was this guy driving on fumes before he pulled into the station?" he mumbled to himself as he watched the meter hit twenty gallons and keep on going.

Meanwhile, to his right, people were pulling in and filling up their tanks and then leaving. He had definitely picked the wrong side of the gas station to get fuel on.

Finally, the pump clicked off, but the driver didn't get out of the SUV. From Byron's vantage point he could see the Navigator's side mirror, and when he squinted to get a better look, he saw a middle-aged soccer mom talking on a cell phone. She was oblivious to the fact her gas tank was full, gabbing away happily.

His hands squeezing into fists, Byron honked his horn. He saw the woman look back at him, but she didn't seem to care.

Suddenly, an image flashed through Byron's mind. How he would start his car and rear-end the Navigator, pushing it out of the way like so much trash. He could imagine the look on the woman's face and it made him smile. But he couldn't do it. Not only would he get in trouble for hitting the woman, but it would make him even later for work.

Byron leaned on his horn, his face red with anger at the inconsiderate bitch. Finally, she climbed out of the SUV and took the nozzle out of the spout. She flipped him off and climbed back inside the tank she called transportation and pulled out of the lot.

"About time," he said to the empty car and drove up to the next pump. Climbing out, he read the sign on the front of the pump. **PLEASE PAY FIRST**.

Sighing, he started walking to the small store/gas station/lottery ticket vendor, not to mention you could get the newspaper, milk, beer and the most important thing to half the country...cigarettes, at the lowest bargain prices the law would allow.

Stepping inside the small store, he moved up next to an old man in his late seventies.

The man was talking to the cashier, a young girl of eighteen or so with a ring in her nose, spiked hair tinted purple, and black fingernails. The moment he saw her, Byron knew she was an underachiever.

The old man was talking to the cashier. "Yes, dear, give me two quick picks, three Jackpots and a Megabucks."

Byron gritted his teeth. He needed gas and now he had to wait while this guy pissed away his social security check on lottery tickets?

Tapping his leg with impatience, Byron waited for the cashier to meet the old man's needs, but then the old man began scratching the tickets right there at the counter. Byron couldn't get to the cashier because the old fart thought he was about to become a millionaire!

"Hey, buddy, could you do that somewhere else? Some of us still have to work for a living," Byron said in a disgusted tone.

"Huh? Oh, my, I'm so sorry, didn't think, there ya go," the old man said as he gathered his tickets and moved away from the counter. With a smile, the old man waddled away, much the same as Byron had earlier in the morning when he had shit on his butt.

The cashier gave him a dirty look after how rude he was to the old man. Her eyes bore into him and her lips turned up into a sneer. Byron saw that look and it made him so mad he slipped into another vision where he reached across the counter and grabbed her by her nose ring, ripping it out of her nostril with one mighty yank. Then he grabbed her by the back of the head and slammed her face into the counter so many times her face looked like a mangled piece of meat from the butcher's shop.

He snapped out of it just as she was asking him how she could help him, though her tone signified the exact opposite.

"Ah, yeah, hi, can I get twenty on pump..." he turned to look where he was parked and saw a five in black spray paint sprawled on the side of the pump. "...On pump five, please."

Reaching into his pocket for his wallet, his eyes opened wide when it wasn't there. He immediately remembered he had left it on his desk in his home office after having to search through it for a client's business card.

He was actually thinking about how he could fill his car with fuel and take off without getting caught when he found a twenty in his pocket, left over from the previous night.

Finally, something was going right, he thought and slapped it on the countertop, his face elated, not that the cashier knew or cared why he was suddenly so happy.

The cashier looked at him with mournful eyes, rolled her tongue, then took the twenty; all without saying a word after the initial greeting.

Byron never hesitated, as soon as he knew the price was inputted, he turned and left, almost sprinting to his car to make up the time he was losing with every passing second. He ran by the old man like the man was standing still, the geriatric only having eyes for his scratch tickets.

Reaching the pump, Byron undid the gas cap and jammed the nozzle home, counting the seconds as the meter scrolled to twenty dollars.

Finally finished, he put everything in its place and jumped back into his car. He pulled back onto the main road with a miniscule amount of honking from his fellow commuters.

And so began the true commute to work. It moved fairly average, until his front tire began giving him trouble. Realizing something was wrong, he pulled over and climbed out, while commuters drove past him on their own morning odyssey.

"Oh, you've got to be kidding me?" he said to the air, holding his hands out in front of him.

His front tire was flat, and on closer inspection, he saw a nail protruding from the middle of the tread.

He wanted to scream. He wanted to jump around like a child having a tantrum for a toy he had seen at the store yet couldn't have, but he stopped himself.

Deciding he better get to work changing the flat, he went to the trunk, got the spare and did what he had to do, all the while cursing and grumbling to himself about how much life sucked.

Twenty minutes later he was finished, and so aggravated that if someone had stopped and tried to talk to him, he would have probably attacked them with the tire iron.

Tossing the flat tire into the trunk of the car, he climbed back in behind the wheel and started the engine, heading off to work once more. Checking the clock on the dash, he saw it was almost eight thirty and he decided he should just suck it up and call work to tell them he was going to be late.

Reaching into his pocket, he pulled out his cell phone. Upon opening it, he saw it was already on, he had forgotten to turn it off the night before. He was preparing to dial when he saw the screen flicker for a brief moment and then turn off.

Thinking he did something wrong, he turned it on again, and was greeted by the low battery sign in the middle of the screen before it flicked off again.

The anger began to rise within him like a newly awakened volcano, but he pushed it back down. No, he was a civilized man. These things happened in life, welcome to the twentieth century. So instead of going ballistic, he tossed the phone onto the back seat with yet another weary sigh.

He didn't want to look at it anymore. Besides, men and women had survived decades without cell phones; surely he could make it through one morning commute. He had a charger at work and could charge the phone's battery there.

And he could still pull it off and make it to work almost on time. If it was 8:30, and he had a forty-five minute drive, he would only be fifteen minutes late. Not that bad considering the morning he was having.

He continued moving in the bumper to bumper traffic and in less than five minutes realized his lane was the only one that wasn't moving. After changing lanes, he sighed with relief for a few seconds as it moved, but then his lane stopped moving. Then he saw cars passing him on his right in the lane he had just vacated.

Grunting in frustration at the waste of precious time, he worked his way back in line in the previous lane and fought the traffic like a seasoned warrior.

Just as he reached his exit, he saw why the traffic was particularly bad this morning. There were two cars on the side of the road, blocking one lane of traffic. From the looks of it, one had tapped the other on the bumper and now they had to change insurance papers. It didn't seem to cross either driver's minds to pull out of traffic so everyone else could make decent progress.

Furious as he passed the drivers standing by their cars, he imagined what he would do if he was free to let his ego loose.

When he was close enough to the two cars, he would step on the gas, his car shooting forward with a surge of force. His front grille would strike both drivers head on, knocking them away to land on the pavement; then he would drive over their prone bodies, crushing them and flattening their corpses into the asphalt like road kill on the road for far too long.

When he was done, he would beep twice and keep going, all to the applause of his fellow commuters who had to suffer in traffic because of those two idiots.

He snapped out of his fugue and took the exit off the main highway that would bring him to his destination. Checking the time, he was still hopeful. The road he was on was the last leg of his commute, a one lane road on both sides and it was five miles long. There was a double line in the middle so there was no passing allowed.

Just as Byron pulled onto this road, he had to literally hit the brakes. There was a car in front of him that was going twenty miles an hour in a forty-five mph zone. At first he didn't understand why the vehicle was moving so slow, but as he followed along behind it, he was able to see inside the car through its rear windshield.

He saw only a small tuft of gray hair, just barely visible over the driver's seat, and with him so close to the other car, he was able to easily see the rearview mirror of the vehicle he was following.

Two beady eyes stared back at him, surrounded by wrinkles.

What every motorist in a rush dreaded the most had just happened to him. There was a driver well over eighty behind the wheel of a car and they were in front of him.

Banging his right hand on the steering wheel, he cursed his luck. He was so close.

As they meandered down the road, he looked over the car he was following to see the light change to green at the coming intersection. He knew this was a long light, allowing three other roads to intersect, and the light took almost a full five minutes to rotate. If he hadn't had this old goat in front of him, he would have easily made it through with time to spare, but instead the light remained green as they slowly coaxed their way up the road. Looking in his rearview mirror, he saw the inevitable parade that was starting behind him, resembling a funeral because of the speed, instead of harried commuters on their way to work.

Upon reaching the traffic light, he stared at the forehead of the old woman in the vehicle's rearview mirror, wishing he could send a heart attack her way.

The minutes ticked by until the light finally changed and the old woman began to moved forward with infinite slowness. Byron was now actually leaning forward in his seat, as if that act alone would make the car in front of him move faster.

But alas, it didn't, and the minutes crawled by and the old woman cruised down the road without a care in the world.

He didn't understand any of this. If you were old and death was at your door every second and every minute of the day, then wouldn't you be in a hurry to get things done because you might not be alive the next day to finish them?

With miles still to go, Byron screamed in his car in anger. That was when he decided it was time to do something about his predicament.

Checking all his mirrors for the telltale signs of a police car, he made sure the area around him was clear. When the oncoming lane was as clear as it was going to get, he floored the gas pedal and shot over the double yellow line, driving past the old woman. The old crone never wavered, never looked to the left to see a car passing her on the wrong side of the road. She was in her own world, myopic to the day they ripped her license from her arthritic hands.

Byron let out a yell of happiness and pulled back onto the correct side of the road, the old woman quickly disappearing in his back trail.

He did it, he was home free now!

Only a few miles to go and he'd be at work, though still a little late, he could make it up at lunch with none the wiser.

Leaning over in his seat, he turned on the radio, finally in a good enough mood to enjoy some music. But when he looked back up and checked his rearview mirror out of habit, his jaw dropped when he saw the recognizable blue and red lights of a State Trooper's squad car.

His heart sank into his feet and he felt butterflies in his stomach. The squad car whooped a few times, telling him to pull over to the side of the road, and he glanced one more time at the hard-faced trooper driving the squad car.

His imagination took off yet again, and he imagined himself saying "screw it," flooring the gas pedal, and shooting forward like a rocket. The squad car would take off after him, the eight cylinder, turbo-charged engine sounding like a caged monster, and Byron would try to lose the trooper on the side streets.

Other police cars would join the chase and he would drive on sidewalks and over people's manicured lawns as he tried to escape the long arm of the law.

Eventually, the police would block him in and he would stop, his car idling in the cool morning. The men in uniforms, guns in their hands, would yell at him, telling him to get out with his hands up! He would decide to go out in a blaze of glory and would floor the gas pedal, surging forward to break through the barricade of police cars. The police would open up on him, firing their Glocks and 38's into his car like he was a training exercise dummy.

Bullets would tear into his flesh, breaking ribs and piercing organs until there was nothing left of him but a mass of deformed meat. As he died, his foot would come off the gas pedal and he would crash into a squad car, the chase over, the perp taken down. The End.

The squad car whooped again and Byron came back to reality. Realizing there was only one true option, he pulled over to the side of the road and waited as the trooper climbed out of his vehicle with his hand on his gun. While Byron waited for the trooper to walk over to him, the old woman drove by, the geriatric head never even looking his way.

"License and registration, please," the trooper said as he gazed into Byron's car. With the dark black sunglasses covering his eyes, all Byron could see was his own reflection staring back at him from the polished lenses.

He did as asked, already cursing his foolishness. Now his insurance rates would go up, rates that were already through the roof as it is. He handed the trooper his registration from the glove box, but then realized he didn't have his wallet on him. He quickly explained this to the trooper who frowned down at him.

"So you don't have your license, but you say this is your car?"

"Yes, sir," Byron nodded, his voice squeaking slightly. To say this man was intimidating would have been an understatement. This trooper had the look down pat.

"Stay here, I'll be right back," the trooper said and walked back to his car.

Byron sat there, angry, mad, and scared at the same time. He never got into trouble and even getting pulled over was a traumatic event for him. As other commuters drove by, he felt their accusing eyes studying him.

"There's the bad man who couldn't wait like the rest of us," some eyes said. "There's the man who thinks he's better than us, driving over the line," other eyes said. "He deserves what he gets."

He hated them all, and in his humiliation, he silently waited for the trooper to return. Ten agonizing minutes later, the trooper walked back to his car and handed him his registration.

"Okay, I was able to check your picture and you're who you say you are," the trooper told him.

No shit, Byron thought, but kept his mouth shut. He was in enough trouble as it was. The trooper had his ticket pad in his hand and he ripped one ticket and then another one from the pad, handing them to Byron.

"I'm citing you for crossing the double line and for driving without a license. If you choose to protest these charges just follow the instructions on the back of the tickets. Have a nice day."

"Uh, thank you, officer, you too," he replied and immediately cursed himself for saying that. Have a nice day? Was he serious? Byron gazed down at the tickets and read the fines. Two hundred dollars for both tickets, plus whatever fees his insurance would surcharge him with. No more safe driver credits, no more discounts, all ruined because some old fossil decided to go for a drive this morning.

The trooper pulled out and drove off, leaving Byron staring at the tickets.

He sat there for another five minutes, his mind blank.

Finally, he snapped out of it enough to drive and get to work. Checking the clock on the dashboard, he saw he was hopelessly late. Pulling into traffic, he drove the rest of the way to work in a modicum of silent surrender.

When he arrived and pulled into his parking spot, he was only mildly surprised to see there was a car in his space. Still numb from the tickets, he parked in the visitor's section, and walked to the main door of his office building.

He was feeling so low he thought he would die.

What a morning.

Well, at least it was over. He was at work now and could get on with his day and in a few days would probably just laugh about everything that had happened.

If his insurance rose too much in price, he could always work some overtime or even try to get a part-time job to make up the difference.

Life would go on and he would be okay.

Stepping into the lobby, he saw the receptionist behind her desk. She waved him over and he turned away from the elevators and went to her. It was a wide, oval affair with marble inlay, placed there to give visitors who entered the building a taste of the luxury to come.

"Hi, Byron, I had a great time the other night," she said with a hint of a smile. "You all right, you don't look so good."

Byron nodded. Her name was Tina and she was referring to the rendezvous on his desk the other night. She had stayed late, and one thing had led to another, and they had ended up having sex on his desk.

"Hi, Tina, yeah, me too. Hope we can do it again sometime. And thanks for asking, but I'm fine. I'll be okay. I just had a rough morning, that's all."

She nodded and handed him a slip of paper. "Mr. Feldman wants to see you in his office right now. He's been calling for you since nine."

That wasn't good news. Feldman was the CEO, and if you had to see him it was almost always bad news.

"Thanks, Tina, I'll go up there right now."

The phone on her desk rang, and she waved bye to him, having to answer it. Byron headed for the elevators and rode one to the top floor. Stepping out, he saw the security guard standing near Feldman's door. Byron's gaze couldn't help but fall to the handgun on the man's hip.

Walking across the lobby, the receptionist held up her hand and picked up her phone. A moment later she hung it up and gestured for Byron to enter Feldman's office.

"Mr. Feldman has been waiting for you, he'll see you right now," she said sweetly.

His throat moving as he swallowed, he opened the door and entered the office of the ultimate boss of his company.

"Ah, Byron, sit down, we need to talk," Feldman said in a stern voice. He was an average sized man with a small belly and a receding hairline in his late fifties.

Byron did as he was told and sat across from Feldman, a large oak desk now separating them.

"I have some bad news to share with you, Greenwald, but before I do, I want you to watch something with me." He turned in his chair and picked up a remote control. A plasma television turned on behind Feldman and he dimmed the lights slightly so Byron could view the screen better. On the screen, was black and white security footage of him and Tina having sex on his desk. The entire incident was there, including when he had flipped her over and taken her from behind.

Feldman turned off the screen and the lights went up. Byron heard a scuffling and looked over his shoulder to see the security guard now hovering near the doorway.

"Greenwald, did you know that Tina was my daughter?"

Byron's mouth fell open and he found he couldn't breathe.

His head moved from side to side. "No sir, I didn't," he whispered.

"Well, she is, and as I'm a protective father, what do you think I thought about this when I saw this footage?"

Byron didn't want to know and only shrugged.

Feldman sat up higher in his chair, his back rigid. "I'll tell you what I thought. I wanted to kill you, that's what, Greenwald. But seems I can't do that without going to jail for life, I'm going to do the next best thing in my power. I'm firing you and making sure your 401K is history. When I'm done with you, you'll be living in a cardboard box under the freeway. Every company in this city and beyond will know what a lowlife you are. I'll personally see that you never work in this city again."

"But I've worked here for twelve years. You can't fire me," Byron babbled. "For God's sake, I didn't know who she was, she never told me!"

Feldman nodded. "She wouldn't have. She likes the anonymity, not wanting to be daddy's little girl and such. She wants to make her own way in the world."

He looked over Byron's shoulder at the security guard. "Chester, take him away, will you please? I don't want to see this cockroach again."

"But I didn't do anything wrong," Byron pleased. "I'm sorry I had sex with her. I didn't know, wait! Get you hands off of me, goddammit!" he yelled at the security guard.

Feldman had already turned away from him, picking up the phone and talking on it like firing Byron and ruining his life was the smallest thing in the world.

The security guard ignored Byron's protests, grabbing him by the shoulders and pushing him roughly through the doorway. Byron was so shocked at what was happening to him that his mind went inward and his imagination took over once more.

In his mind, this was the last straw of a truly horrible day. He imagined himself reaching down and pulling the security guard's handgun from its holster. Turning, he would shoot the man in the face, the head morphing into a hideous mass of meat and brains that painted the wall red. Then he would turn to the receptionist, his mind completely snapped now, and shoot her in the chest, the force of the blow making her tumble out of her chair to lay silent on the floor, the red carpeting becoming darker with her blood as her legs twitched in her death throes.

Then he would step back inside Feldman's office. The man would stand up, surprised at first, but then real fear would appear, and Byron would walk across the office until he was standing in front of the man's desk.

"Who's in charge now?" he would scream and shoot three rounds into the man's chest. Feldman's body would jerk and jump from the impacts and blood would splash across the room, droplets splattering across the plasma television screen, rivulets coating the screen.

As Feldman collapsed on his desk in a heap, Byron would walk across the office and out to the elevators. Riding one down to the lobby, he would walk over to Tina, and as she looked up at his blood-drenched face, he would snarl, "You bitch, you should have told me!"

Before she could reply, he would shoot her in the face, the bullet penetrating her nose to disappear inside her skull. The lobby would quickly become a mass of screaming, frightened people and he would turn and start firing at whatever moved. A woman fell screaming with a gunshot to the leg, an older man in a brown suit would flop to the floor with a shoulder wound and then try to crawl to safety as he trailed blood. Another woman would be shot in the stomach, blood seeping into her pinstriped power suit, staining it a rich vermilion.

Three more security guards, weapons drawn, would come charging into the lobby, and just as Byron fired his last bullet at a lawyer with a brown satchel under his arm, the guards would open fire, riddling Byron's body with bullets until he dropped his now empty gun and fell to the already blood-soaked floor.

He would blink twice, his eyes trying to focus, but it was no use. His heart had been nicked by a bullet, and as it beats its last, he would leave his stupor and came back to reality just before he imagined taking the security guard's gun and going on his imaginary rampage.

But that didn't happen this time, and as his heart beat one last time in his shattered ribcage, he realized this time it was for real and he had acted on his impulses.

He tried to speak, to say it was all a mistake, but all that came out was a red froth mixed with bubbles.

He closed his eyes and slipped into death.

*　*　*

White light, intense heat, and a searing pain in Byron's chest snapped him awake.

Opening his eyes, he found himself surrounded by fire. He was chained to a wall, and a red man was stabbing him in the chest with a pitchfork.

If that wasn't enough to tell him where he was, then the red tail and the two horns on the man's head sealed the deal.

"Oh my God, I'm in Hell?" he said to no one. "How'd I get here?" he asked through the awful pain flowing through his body like acid.

The Devil smiled as he jabbed the pitchfork deeper into his chest, yanking out Byron's still beating heart, only to have it reappear inside his chest yet again an instant later, so the Devil could do it repeatedly for all eternity.

"Sorry, buddy, guess you're just having one of those days," the Devil said with an evil grin. As Byron screamed in utter agony, he jabbed the pitchfork in again and again until the end of time.

A TALE OF A WRITER

Once upon a time there was a writer named Joe.

Joe had never written anything his entire life, in fact, Joe could barely write a letter.

Then one day, Joe was watching a zombie movie, his favorite form of horror was zombies, and as he watched, he got an idea for a book.

A book? he thought. *Me? That's crazy, I can't write.*

But despite this he went to the computer and began to write the first chapter. He used word pad as he didn't have Microsoft word and actually never used the computer before this. He didn't have email and only used the internet casually by going to the library and using their computers.

But despite this, Joe sat down and wrote a chapter of a book. It wasn't big, only a thousand words and it took him over two hours. With word pad there were so many mistakes it was ridiculous, for on top of everything else, Joe couldn't type!

Two fingers, one for each hand was how he typed the chapter.

The next morning, he woke and couldn't wait to tell his wife what he'd done the previous night. She stared blankly at him, happy for him but at the same time wondering if what he said was true.

She wasn't interested in reading it but still supported her husband.

Joe got the same reception from friends, too. Whenever he told someone he was writing a book, they would nod, not very interested. After all, Joe had never shown the slightest inclination he could write.

But write he did. The night after writing the first chapter, he sat down and wrote another chapter, then another.

He was so excited that he was really doing something he had only dreamed about. See, Joe loved to read and was always amazed at how a person could write a book, to fabricate a world in their mind.

When he finished the book, he did what every new writer does, he began sending it out to publishers.

That grew old real fast. After only a few rejections, Joe began to look into self publishing.

See, Joe was independent. Some might say too independent, but he was proud of what he'd created and even if it wasn't perfect, it was his.

He found a small press that specialized in zombie horror but they said that you had to send it in and if they liked it, give them some cash, and they would make the book. Joe thought this was stupid. Why wait for someone to tell him if his book was worth it and then he had to give them money as well?

No, better to self publish completely and to hell with everyone else.

So he did publish the book and it was soon on the internet and no one knew it was there.

Joe didn't care. He had found he actually had an artistic talent and he was overjoyed. He was happy to write for family and friends. His father, an immigrant, was so proud he wanted to explode.

The first book was small and under two hundred pages. He knew though a fun book, that it could have used some more character development. See, Joe had been so excited to finish the first book he had rushed it just a little. But that was so he could actually show people the finished book. The editing wasn't perfect as Joe was all alone in the work so he did it all himself. He trudged on, determined to do his best.

On the second book, he took his time, trying to create better characters. The book was almost double in size, and when it was done, Joe went right ahead and self published it.

Why not? He didn't care about all the bullshit that writers played to get a book made. He was simply proud to write and make the book and let his children, family and friends get to see it.

He loved what he did so much that he began to write full time. Non stop, sometimes for hours on end. Many books were written, and then when more than fifteen were done, he got an email from a small horror publisher.

It was the same one that used to charge money to make their books. Joe mentioned this to Jake, the owner, but he was told he was incorrect. Still, Joe remembered what he read on the website but figured back then, the small press had been just starting out.

The owner offered Joe a ten book deal, wanting to acquire all his zombie books. He didn't offer much in money but to Joe who had been all alone with no one reading his books, he was very pleased by the offer to get his book out into the world under a professional press, though small.

But to give away ten books? That was a lot of books that were already out in the world as self published books. And worst of all, the horror publisher wanted to put one book out every six months, which with ten books would be forever. Joe was offered a five year contract and in that five years if he ever wrote another zombie book he would have to offer it exclusively to that small press first. But, if they took it, then one of the other books would get bumped.

But Joe wrote a book every three months and the deal would curtail that to the point it could be years before the books would all be out again. And with a five year contract on each, he would never get them all back.

But to be published to what Joe considered a *real* publishing company was a tempting thought. But to sign away what was basically his life's work was a tough decision. In one way he wanted the recognition any writer wanted, but on the other hand, he didn't want to give up his books already in print, nor his freedom to produce what he wanted, when he wanted.

And on top of all this, Joe still wasn't on the internet and didn't know that his books were catching on, that people were now reading them, and though they had some grammar mistakes, most everyone liked them, which was why the small press wanted them so badly.

Very clever actually. The small press would let an author write a book, spend the cash to make it. And if it became popular, they would swoop in and scoop it up. No risk on their end. And Joe was naïve to all of this, the perfect pigeon to pounce on.

But Joe was on the fence the entire time. Like it was stated before, Joe was very independent and so stubborn of people messing with his writing to be obsessed.

So he and the owner, Jake, began to talk on the phone about how things would happen and about the editing of his books. Joe made it very clear that he was very, very protective of his writing. He knew it wasn't perfect, but it was his. To him, who had began writing later in life, writing was an art and not to be messed with by others—other than copyediting.

Joe was stubborn, but he was proud of it. For good or bad, it was his writing and he didn't want it messed with.

So the writer and publisher talked and Jake was always available by phone whenever the writer had a question. See, the writer didn't use email, nor have internet in the house.

They talked about editing and how things would go and the writer was told emphatically that he would be allowed total input on editing. That any problems could be worked out and that the small press just wanted to put out a good book.

Finally Joe decided to go for it. Why not? Jake was a nice man and had always been available to talk and answer any questions.

So Joe signed the contracts and trusted Jake to be a man of his word about the editing. Jake told Joe that he was an honest man and to him a handshake would be good enough but in today's world of course there had to be contracts, which Joe agreed also.

Joe went with his gut and trusted Jake that everything they had spoken about would be adhered to. The contract had none of this in it about editing, a mistake on Joe's part. A rookie mistake but a mistake nonetheless.

And then the first book began to go into editing. The editor began doing things Joe didn't like and when he protested, he was told simply, "You signed the contract. Do what you're told or we're going to have a problem."

Joe was upset but he did as he was told and tried to work with the editor. But time and again, words were changed, twisted, until Joe wasn't happy at all. By this time, Joe had given up with a dialogue with the small press. He felt screwed. Jake had been available when he had questions, but once the contracts were signed, he never had time to talk to Joe by phone. It was all email, which Joe didn't like to use.

Joe was miserable, but he tried to put it put of his mind and work on other projects.

He decided he had made a mistake in selling his books and decided to throw up his hands. At the time, Jake didn't know this but Joe had written off his books with Jake as a big mistake. See, Joe had signed the contract and he was man of his word. He would have to wait for the five years to be over for each book. He decided to write non zombie books then as Jake had no claim to them.

He wracked all of it up as inexperience and knew many writers had had it far worse than him.

And then Joe found out the small press wanted to chop out the first ten chapters of his third book. Now this pissed off Joe to no end. The book in question was a character based book, with the action after the tenth chapter. It was slow for a reason. As it was the tenth book written by Joe, he wanted it to have a different feel. And to have all that taken away was too much.

He argued once more with Jake and had to write an email describing why he felt the ten chapters should stay in the book. Despite this, it was ignored, and the book would be made as planned.

Joe was furious. This wasn't what was agreed to on the phone. Verbal or not, a man is as good as his word. He felt manipulated, fooled, but because a contract is a contract he was trapped.

He yelled at Jake, telling him how upset he was, who decided to give Joe back seven of his books, leaving Jake with three. Joe could deal with that. At least now he didn't have his life's world trapped with one press, and best of all, he could now write whatever he wanted and didn't have to offer it to Jake as the man had released him of his exclusivity.

The second book was made and released and Joe was fine with the edits when he first saw them, though he had only glossed over them as by now he just didn't care, as he was so disgusted with Jake and the antics of this small press.

A different editor edited the second book and that one only changed words like *run* to *dash* or *happy* to *glad*. It seemed silly to Joe but he decided it wasn't the end of the world. Joe wasn't pleased to find out the editor had never published a book himself, not even self published, and felt the editor was very inexperienced, but he was beyond caring, accepting the mistake he'd made in going with the small press. This was when he finally realized the small press he had gone with was really nothing special, just a bunch of guys getting together and making some books, no experience required, or very little.

When the second book was done and in print, Joe read some of the book one day when he was bored. And what he found almost immediately made him explode.

See, for some insane reason, the editor had inserted the word *motherfucker* into one of the most touching scenes in the book. This touching death scene *actually* now had *motherfucker* in it, and Joe was furious to no end.

What editor in their right mind would ever do this to another writer's book? And not so much as an email sent out to let Joe know this was happening? Impossible, no one could be that unprofessional and inexperienced.

Knowing Jake wasn't interested in speaking with him about these items, Joe was so upset he wrote a letter and posted it on his website so any readers would know this. This letter detailed all the editing issues he had and that he'd had enough with the small press.

He had now disowned his books from Jake and would move on to new things. Love or hate the books with Jake, he didn't care, he was done with them. They weren't his as he had no input on the editing.

Jake found out about the letter on Joe's website and emailed him, very upset. Joe said he stood by what he said and Jake and he should talk about it on the phone. Work it out.

Jake said no, he wanted to do it all by email. Joe hated email and said use the phone or nothing. When Jake decline, Joe stopped emailing him, deciding they were at an impasse and that would be the end of it.

But Jake was a sore loser and he was so mad he posted a private email between him and Joe (between publisher and writer) on an open message board for all to see. Any respect Joe had for Jake disintegrated in a flash when he did this. It was unprofessional, unethical, and cowardly.

Jake wouldn't deal with Joe himself for some unknown reason, so he let his fan club on the message board fight his battle. See, Jake was passive aggressive to the point it was maddening for Joe who believed in saying what he felt and never hid behind semantics and lies.

And so a war began, with Jake's fanboys insulting Joe on the message board and writing and attacking as a group, with Jake sitting back and watching it happily. Joe didn't have a chance. No matter what he said, it was twisted and warped to the point Joe gave up and decided to stop saying anything. Meanwhile, the high school antics continued as the mob mentality went into full gear.

Months later, more highjinks ensued when one of Joe's books went under fire for reasons irrelevant to anyone but Joe. Once more he was attacked by people who had no business getting involved, but as we all know, the internet is full of people who feel it is their god-given right to know your business.

Now, a week earlier, before all the business about the book under fire, Joe was offered to buy the third book back from Jake if Joe wanted to give Jake three thousand dollars. Joe refused, he wasn't going to be suckered like that.

But then Jake didn't like all the publicity with the book under fire. People were talking and he got scared, as Joe had two books with him, so he decided to just give Joe his third book back which wasn't made yet, and freed him of his contract.

Joe was thrilled. That was what he wanted all along. Now Jake only had two books and Joe owned the rest of his books lock, stock and barrel.

And better still, with the help of a new friend, Joe started his own horror press, that in time would become a direct rival of Jake's press.

Joe forgot about Jake and worked on creating his new horror press, though deep down inside he was driven by something more than he knew. After what he'd been through he wanted justice and the only way to fully get that was to make his press as great and big as he could.

So he focused on that and worked hard, opening doors for many writers who may not have had a chance on their own. Many writers that Jake's small press wouldn't have given the time of day to.

And then Joe wrote a sequel to one of the two books Jake had the print rights to but not to the sequel. When Joe posted on a publicity release on an open forum that the new book was out and that he didn't consider the book Jake had as part two, Jake replied back with a snotty remark like always.

Well, Joe should have kept his peace, but he was so pissed off this time he decided not to take the high road. He took the lowest road he could. He wrote a long letter on the open forum telling Jake off and that he could take the two books he still had and put them where the sun doesn't shine. Coarse? Yes, but Joe was never one for beating around the bush, especially if he was upset. A hot-blooded man, he would bite first and regret it later.

Well, Jake read the letter and because Jake had other deals going with larger book companies, lucrative deals, he decided it wasn't worth fighting with a writer on an open forum and having the big companies find out (or at least that was what Joe thought) so after leaving a catty remark on the open forum, Jake sent an email to Joe, and in this email, he released Joe from his contract on the two books and would pull them from distribution immediately as well as apologizing.

Joe was elated at this news. He had fought for what he believed in and had not bent over and took his spanking like a good little boy. He finally had his books back, and best off all, he'd won when many writers have stayed silent and gotten screwed. Unlike many writers out there that had been sucked into publishing with a book company only to find out their books were mangled in editing, Joe fought back and took back what was his.

Unlike many writers who only cared about seeing their name on a book, regardless of the content, Joe felt if it wasn't his work in that book, then it was a lie to put his name on it.

No one messes with a painter's work, why should writing be any different?

And best of all, because Jake hadn't treated him better and worked with him more, and treated him with the respect Joe deserved, Joe had now started his own horror press which was doing great. Something that never would have happened if he had stayed with the small press.

To Joe it was all over.

Jake had apologized by email, telling Joe he should have known that Joe was stubborn and shouldn't have taken his books at the beginning, at the first time Joe argued about editing. Joe had accepted the apology, although deep down that was so far from the truth. Jake had done things that couldn't be taken back by a simple apology, some things can't be washed away. But trying to be professional, Joe accepted.

After the apology, Joe told Jake if he ever wanted the bad blood to go away, he would have to pull that terrible blog where he had posted the private email and his fanboys attacked. Jake complied immediately.

Jake even went on the message board and said how sorry he was so all his fanboys would love him still, not that it mattered, they kissed the ground he walked on which was why he let them do his dirty work in the first place.

So Joe and Jake went their separate ways and that should be the end of the story. But there was one more thing, see, Jake was a sore loser. A *real* sore loser.

He had battled with Joe on his books and had lost miserably. Joe had never broken a contract, Jake had given all the books back of his own free will, but Jake wasn't about to let losing stop him from getting even.

As the internet was Jake's battleground, he created an anonymous hate blog, and then searched for anything he could find on Joe that would show him in a negative light, even the stuff that Jake personally had created in his unprofessionalism and posted on his message board.

When Joe found out he was obviously quite upset, he saw this blog and wondered what had he done to someone out in the world to make them want to create this? In a weird way it was flattering, too. For someone to be so obsessed over another human being was strange to say the least, and especially since Joe was really just a no-name horror writer with a few books out. In the scheme of the world and vast internet he was so insignificant to be nothing.

The site stayed up for months and Joe forgot about it but then when more things popped up, including an email Joe had sent to all his writers, Joe knew two things at once. One was that he had been betrayed by one of his writers, a writer he had given the opportunity to be published, and two, that the creator of the hate blog was still going strong.

Once more Joe wondered who it could be. See, he couldn't imagine who would be so petty, so cowardly as to make this site; for they did so anonymously.

Joe wondered why, if someone was so upset with him, why they wouldn't email him and state their complaint. See, the creator of the blog knew Joe's personal email and that of the small press he was growing. But how could Joe make it right if the person was a mystery? Hell, Joe didn't even know what he'd done to offend this person so badly. What could he have possibly done to upset someone so badly that they would spend so much time on him, only wanting to hurt him.

And then someone wrote in to the blog and left a comment and the creator of the blog was foolish enough to reply back. See, whenever Joe had argued with Jake, Jake had a clever way of twisting everything, of never answering a direct question, but would always skew the issue.

And that was what the creator of the blog did.

Joe began to put the pieces together. By the way creator had fabricated the blog and the way certain sentences were worded, it was quite easy to see that the creator had inside knowledge of many of the items now posted. And Joe realized Jake had that knowledge for Joe had spoken with him many times as writer to a publisher; information that should have been private between the two of them, no matter what might happen later.

Joe wrote back privately and attacked the creator of the blog, demanding him to come clean and say who he was and why he was making a hate blog.

To his surprise, the creator replied back, though the name on the email was anonymous.

Joe was accused of being unprofessional and unethical and the creator of the blog wanted the world to know so no one would do business with him, and by the content of the sentence, short and clipped, Joe knew it was Jake, for Jake would always reply to Joe in the same way whenever Joe attacked Jake in their emails and arguments online.

So Joe had his answer. Jake was so petty, such a sore loser, that he created a hate blog to discredit Joe. Plus, he must have been upset over the lost funds Joe's books would have made him, now all gone.

So what did Joe do now that he knew the truth?

Well, that's easy. He ignored it all for good. For to Joe, it was better to have a hate blog up on the internet and to own all his books outright, then to bow down and be a sucker to someone who lied to him and tried to take advantage of a naïve writer.

Joe may have made some mistakes along the way, and will probably make more in the future, but that's okay, we all make mistakes; only the internet isn't so forgiving of mistakes, as it has a long memory.

But Joe is in control of his destiny and is slowly making a horror press to rival Jake's, and he will keep working hard, treating people right, and writing himself till the day he dies. And right or wrong, he knows he was honest to the only person that really matters in this and any other life—himself.

And to anyone who tries to tell him how to lead his life, to dictate what he can and cannot do, he will tell them what he told Jake.

Fuck You

IT'S FOR YOU

Walter Whitaker walked up the pathway to his two-family home in Quincy, Massachusetts.

He had lived in his home for almost forty years, and always found himself chuckling at the length of time it now took him to cross the distance from the street to his front door.

He was in his late eighties, his bones tired and weak from carrying him around for such a long time. Still, he was a happy man, glad for every day he had lived on God's green Earth, and hopefully, for the many more days to come.

Just before he reached the front door, it opened and out popped his tenant. She was a pretty thing in her early twenties, and Walter sighed as she smiled at him.

In her smile was compassion for a sweet old man, and Walter still felt like he was twenty-five in his head, despite the arthritis and back pain that plagued his fragile form every day of his existence.

He remembered a time when he was young and healthy and sweet things like her gazed at him with a different look in their eyes.

"Good morning, Walter, how are you doing today?" Susan asked as she opened the door for him. It was well past eight at night and the sun had set hours ago.

"Fine, fine, dear, thank you for asking. A little sore, but I won't bore you with my troubles."

She smiled wider. "Oh, it's no trouble. You know that. How's Evelyn doing?"

"My wife? Oh, she's fine. She should be waiting for me upstairs. I stayed out a little late tonight, having a good time with the fellas at the VFW."

She stepped to the side to let him pass and he entered the small foyer of his house. To the right was Susan's door, which led to her first floor apartment and to the left was his door, which opened on a set of stairs that would bring him to his own place of residence, the top two floors of the house.

Every day it became harder to climb those stairs, but he had managed so far and figured he'd end up dying on those stairs of a heart attack one day.

His wife, Evelyn had been having trouble with the stairs also, as of late, the seventeen steps that led to the kitchen causing her more and more problems each day. She had been pestering him as of late about selling their house and finding something smaller. Something that was easier to clean and navigate.

He had laughed at her, telling her he would die in this house before he ever sold it. Years of his sweat and tears had been poured into the walls and floors of his house. Countless items had been changed or added to so he could live in a house that was beautiful as well as functional.

No, he would prefer to die than to give up his house.

Susan was stepping out of the foyer now and heading down to the street, where her parked car was waiting for her.

"Oh, I see. Well, please give her my best when you get upstairs. I haven't heard a peep out of her all day. No walking around, not even the television was on, which was kind of weird." She checked her watch. "Oh, I'm late. I'm going out with a few girlfriends tonight. I'll see you later, Walter."

Walter used his cane as a way of saying goodbye, waving it in the air in front of him. As Susan moved off into the night, he turned and slid his key into the lock of his door. Opening it, he stepped into the stairway, and after flicking on the light, began his trek up the stairs.

When he was halfway up them, and pausing for a much needed rest, he called up to Evelyn, hoping she would hear him.

"Evelyn, I'm home!" he hollered, but when he received no reply, his lips creased into a frown. "Evelyn? Are you there?"

That was odd, he thought. He knew she didn't go out today and even if she had, she would have been home well before dark. Evelyn didn't have the same vision she once had and found it difficult to see in the dark, especially outside where there were conflicting lights, such as headlights and flashing signs.

Not knowing why, his heart skipped a beat and he began climbing the stairs once again. His knees protested and his breath grew short, but he persevered, wanting to reach the main floor and see where his wife was.

With a final lifting of his right leg—minutes later—he stepped onto the landing of his home. Above him were the bedrooms, on the third floor, and he made a silent prayer that he wouldn't have to climb them in his inspection of the house.

While he slowly pushed his aging frame down the hallway to the kitchen, he thought back to a discussion he had shared with Evelyn a few days ago. She had wanted him to entertain the idea of getting one of those chairs that attached to the wall so he could ride up the stairs every day instead of climbing them. But stubborn till the end, he denied her petition, stating when he couldn't walk up the stairs on his own two feet, that it would be time for the grave.

She had crossed her arms over her chest and pouted at him in such a way that she reminded him of the young, twenty-something beauty he fell in love with all those years ago. Not wanting to upset her, he had deftly changed the subject, causing her to forget about the electric chair.

Now, as he walked down the hallway, the kitchen only a few feet away, he absently gazed at the pictures on the wall. There was their trip to the White Mountains from twenty years ago. Evelyn had been wearing a yellow sundress that made her legs look absolutely fabulous, the dress complimenting her bosom to the point he could barely wait to get her back to their hotel room. He smiled to himself, remembering the night they had spent in that hotel room, making love for hours on end.

The sexual part of their marriage had ended years ago, but not their love for one another. In fact, he loved her more now than he ever had all those years ago when they both had smooth skin and taut muscles.

Upon reaching the kitchen, he noticed steam in the air, and began wondering if perhaps she was in the bathroom and had forgotten to turn off a pot of water. As he turned the corner from the hallway and stepped fully into the kitchen, he realized that wasn't the case.

Evelyn was lying on the kitchen floor, her arms curled into her body like she had been in pain. Her eyes were open, gazing up at the ceiling, as if she was counting all the cracks that had appeared over the years, Walter now to frail to fix them.

"Evelyn! Oh my God, no!" he screamed, and on arthritic knees, leaned down and picked her up, cradling her to his chest. Her eyes stared up and past him and he knew without a doubt she was dead. That was when the tears came, the racking sobs of grief following soon after.

His vision grew clouded as he sobbed with the love of his life in his arms, and when he settled her to the floor, his foot kicked a bottle of pills. With a shaking hand he reached out and picked them up, seeing it was Evelyn's heart medication.

Evidently, something had happened so fast she never had the chance to open the bottle. The pan of hot water still roiled and bubbled on the stove, the steam collecting on the ceiling to become water droplets primed to fall. It must have been boiling for hours and the water was all but gone.

Turning off the stove, he pulled his wife to him, squeezing so hard his arms ached as he cried tears of loss and grief.

Above him, the ceiling dripped tears as well, as if the structure itself was mourning the loss of his one and only.

* * *

The funeral was three days later.

There were many people there to say their goodbyes to his wife, but he barely saw them, too lost in his grief to think straight, let alone play the host.

The priest droned on about her immortal soul finally being at rest and how they could all look forward to the eternal rest Evelyn now enjoyed.

He thought it was all horseshit. His wife was gone and he knew damn well she wasn't resting. If she was up in Heaven right now, she would be filled with an angst all her own, filled with guilt at how she deserted him without so much as a goodbye.

Now he was alone in the world. He had no children to help him get through his sorrow or keep him company, and most of the people he called his friends were two-faced bastards that were only really his friends when they needed something from him.

No, he was alone now; in a quiet world of one.

After the funeral, he informed the priest to send everyone to the VFW. He had rented the hall in the back of the building. It was there so the mourners could get their reward for having to sit through a sermon and drive to the cemetery. At the VFW, they could eat their fill and tell themselves at least they got a free meal out of the deal, then they would say their platitudes and go home.

At least until it was his turn.

Vultures, all of them, Walter thought as he turned and left the hall, letting the guests do as they liked.

Climbing into the limousine waiting for him, he had told the driver to take him home, where he planned on getting good and drunk, despite his doctor's repeated warnings of consuming alcohol. He figured he had the right today of all days.

And that was what he did. After climbing the stairs to his home, knees aching the entire time, he had pulled out a bottle of bourbon and had gotten good and drunk, finally passing out in his easy chair with his wedding picture in his lap. As he drifted off into an alcohol-induced sleep, he could have sworn the eyes of his wife in the wedding picture were crying for him.

Or perhaps it was just his own tears splashing onto the glass covering the picture, the tears then running over her smiling face and washing away what was left of his future.

*   *   *

It was on the one year anniversary of Evelyn's death when the ringing first began.

It was a little past three in the morning and he had just drifted off into a restless sleep. He didn't sleep well anymore, not since Evelyn had left him.

Now, when he went to bed, the mattress felt like a massive island where he was the only occupant. He missed the smell of her hair, the peach aroma of her shampoo, and the smell of the baby powder she would often douse herself with after a shower.

As he lay sleeping, his hands twitched spasmodically, his mind already falling into a tumultuous dream where he was the only man alive in the world and he had to live the remainder of his life devoid of human contact.

At the moment, the recurring dream had him walking down a lonely street, the tall buildings reaching up to the sky, the shadows covering everything like a carpet of darkness, always creeping closer as the sun crawled toward the horizon.

When he walked by a pay phone, he was startled when it began to ring. He stood perfectly still, staring at the phone, wondering who could be on the opposite end in the dead world he now inhabited, when the phone stopped ringing.

That was when he went into action, lunging for the phone and picking up the receiver. "Hello, hello, is anyone there?" he panted into the phone, desperate for a voice to be waiting to talk to him on the other end.

But there was nothing. Dead silence. No dial tone, no voice, nothing but dead air.

He placed the receiver back on its hook out of habit, and as he did this, he saw the strong young hand that held the receiver. Only inside his dreams was he no longer a man in his eighties, weak and frail. In his dreams, he was young and strong, a man in his thirties, or perhaps maybe twenties.

In his dreams his arthritis was gone and he could run for miles without shortness of breath, where the simplistic act such as picking up the phone was not an experiment in arthritic pain.

With the phone forgotten, he stepped away from it and wandered back into the lonely street, searching for someone, anyone, who might still be with him in the city, perhaps hiding somewhere in one of the shadow-filled buildings that stared at him accusingly as he passed them by.

He wandered and wandered until the city was behind him, the buildings looking like modern caricatures of mountains. With nothing but trees and grass surrounding him now, he was startled again when a phone began ringing. Looking around frantically for its source, he could not find one.

Still, the ringing persisted and he spun in circles, hoping to spot the origin of the sound.

"Where are you, dammit, where are you coming from?" he yelled to the trees, disturbing birds from their perches in the tree limbs overhead.

But the ringing didn't stop, but grew in intensity until he fell to his knees and covered his ears, trying to smother the annoying sound.

Stirring in his bed, he snapped awake, his eyes gazing up at the dark ceiling. Before he realized what he was doing, he reached out to feel for Evelyn, and for just the fraction of a second, he was surprised not to find her next to him.

Then reality flooded back and he remembered he was alone in his bed and would be until the day he died.

He opened his eyes wider when he realized he could still hear the ringing echoing inside his head, despite the fleeting memories of his dream already drifting back from whence they came.

In the darkness of the room, he reached out and picked up the phone on the bedside table. It was over twenty years old, an old Bell telephone, with a rotary dial.

Computers, cell phones, microchips, bah! He was not one to embrace technology, in fact, he rebelled against it. Things were better when he was a child, simpler, back when people had to see one another if they had information to pass on, not like the world now with their impersonal e-mails and text messaging.

His hand fumbled for a minute, searching in the darkness until it rested on the phone. Picking up the receiver, he placed it to his ear, the cold plastic giving him a chill.

"Hello?" he said hoarsely from sleep.

No one answered, and that was when he heard the dial tone, signifying there had never been anyone on the line to begin with. But if no one had called, then why was the ringing still in his head?

With a fumbling hand he hung up the phone and sat up in the darkness of his bedroom.

Ring, ring, ring!

It had only been a few minutes, but he was already becoming aggravated.

Ring, ring, ring!

He squeezed his eyes closed so tightly that he saw spots, and buried his head into the pillow, trying to stop the infernal ringing, but it continued.

Ring, ring, ring!

"Stop it, for God's sake! For the love of all that's holy, stop it!" he screamed to the empty room, and all at once, silence descended on him.

He looked around as he sat in the bed, his eyes wide.

Heavy breathing filled his ears, and at first he thought he was imagining it, but as the seconds crawled by and silence reigned once more, he slowly regained his composure.

Sliding out of bed, Walter slowly crept across the carpet and into the bathroom, splashing water on his face to make sure he was awake. In the glow of the small nightlight in the hallway, he stared at his gaunt face. It was times like this when he was most shocked to see himself. In his mind's eye, he always thought of himself as young, perhaps in his thirties or forties like in his dreams, but the face staring back at him was of an old man. Wrinkles, loss of hair, and a drawn face, all gazing back at him without apology or condemnation.

This was who he was now. He was an old man, all alone with his dead wife, who was now interred in the ground for exactly one year tonight.

His bladder was always one of weakness, so he peed and had himself a drink of water. Though not too much or he would be up in another hour, draining it off.

When he was feeling slightly better, he walked back into the bedroom and lay back down on the bed. His eyes were wide open as he stared at the darkness circling overhead. A car drove by outside the window, the dagger-like lines of its headlights cutting through the thin curtains of the room to play across the wall until they vanished into the night.

As the minutes slowly ticked by, his breathing calmed and his mind slowly came to rest. Sleep followed soon after, and though he sobbed out once or twice for his late wife, missing her more each day, he otherwise slept well that night.

* * *

The day passed uneventfully, the ringing of the previous night forgotten. He racked it up to a crazy dream, his subconscious running wild on the anniversary of his wife's death no doubt.

He spent a few minutes with Susan on the front porch and the two chatted about the weather and other mildly interesting things. She was a good woman, a caring woman, and would always ask him how he was.

She knew he was hurting at the loss of his wife, even after a full year, and she always had her hand out to help him if he needed it. She was most helpful when she would give him a ride down the street to the VFW or the grocery store. He had stopped driving a few years ago, his eyes not up to the task anymore.

She was a good woman and Walter had already decided, as he had no other heirs, to leave his house and money to, that he would leave everything he had to Susan. Besides, better her than the damn state, who would auction his possessions out piecemeal, with no regard to the late owner's attachments to the items. At least this way, he knew his beloved home would be in good hands, hopefully for many years to come.

He spent the day walking and chatting with a few neighbors, and before he realized it, the day was over and it was time for bed.

When he walked into his bedroom, gazing forlornly at the bed, something deep inside him wished his beloved Evelyn was there, waiting for him.

But, alas, the bed was empty, as it had been for a year now.

Climbing into bed, his back flaring with twinges of pain, he pulled the covers up to his neck and tried to get comfortable. When he found his desired position, he reached out his hand to where Evelyn once laid beside him. Times like this was when he wondered if it was time to die himself. His soul-mate was gone and he was an old man with only idle days filled with nonsense to pass the time until his own day of judgment finally arrived.

He caressed the sheet, thinking back to better times, and as he reminisced, his hand resting by his side, he drifted off into a restless sleep.

* * *

Ring, ring, ring!

The inside of his head was echoing like a church bell, the infernal ringing returning yet again.

Doing the same as the previous night, he reached out to the telephone on the nightstand and picked it up, placing the cold plastic receiver to his ear.

"Hello? Who the hell is this?" he demanded into the receiver. Once more his eyes went to the small clock on the nightstand and he saw it was almost four a.m. But there was no voice on the other end of the line, only a dial tone.

Then the ringing began anew, filling his head with its echo.

Dropping the phone onto the floor, he sat up in bed. He placed both hands to his ears, and as he did so, the ringing became muted, but still continued its chiming rhythm. He could feel the vibration inside his mind, as if the bell was bolted to the inside of his skull.

Throwing the blankets off the bed, he charged out of the bedroom, ignoring his arthritis and bad back. Stumbling into the bathroom, he turned on the light, becoming momentarily blinded by the glare.

Drawn and tired eyes filled with sleep and terror gazed back at him from the bathroom mirror, and for a second he stared back, lost in the emptiness of his forlorn eyes. But then the ringing snapped him out of it, and he threw open the medicine cabinet, the shelving hiding behind it now exposed. His wrinkled, frail hands reached out, brushing aside the floss, aspirin and cold medicine sitting within.

On the third shelf, in a small box, was what he needed.

Sleeping pills.

He sat on the toilet and tried to get the small foil packaging of individually packed pills open but failed miserably. He howled up at the ceiling in his frustration, eventually having to rip at the packaging with his teeth, like he was an animal fending in the garbage for sustenance. He destroyed three pills before he succeeded in opening four more. Though the side of the box recommended taking only two at a time, he ignored this and washed four down with a glass of water taken from the sink.

With the ringing still inside his head, making it hard to think, let alone study his situation, he stumbled back to bed. Falling into the mattress, he covered his face with the pillow. Though his ears were covered, the ringing persisted, and he lay sobbing into the pillow, the surface becoming wet with his tears.

He lay still for almost an hour, until the sleeping pills began to work and he eventually passed out, falling into a drug-induced slumber.

When he finally fell out of consciousness, drifting into sleep, he could still hear the dreaded ringing, as if his entire world was filled with nothing but chiming bells.

*   *   *

The next morning, Walter woke up feeling drowsy and tired, thanks to the sleeping pills suffusing his system. True, it had been a rough night, and despite the disruption in his sleep schedule, his body still had a bad habit of rousing him at five a.m. on the dot, sleeping pills or not.

He idly played with the thought of trying to sleep longer, but knew the futility of it, so he decided to get up and get dressed. Feeling groggy, like he was sleepwalking, his body fought off the rest of the drugs still floating in his system.

At seven he would go downtown to the Dunkin Donuts on the corner of Main Street and Dearborn Street and grab a cup of coffee. If he was there precisely at seven, his friend, Fred Prescott, would be there.

Fred was a general practitioner in the field of family medicine, and though he should have retired years ago, the man still carried on a steady practice, though he had cut down in the last two years.

Fred would always get a cup of coffee in the morning and relax with the newspaper, not needing to be in the office until nine. Though Walter could make an appointment, he knew if he was at the donut shop at seven, he could talk to Fred...and he had something serious to talk to the man about.

At five minutes to seven, Walter entered the donut shop, and of course, Fred was in his corner booth, a small coffee and a muffin sitting unobtrusively on the table in front of him. His head was buried in a newspaper, the man oblivious to the other customers moving in and out of the shop around him.

Walter stepped over to him and slid into the same booth, but on the opposite side so that he was now sitting across from the good doctor.

Fred lowered his newspaper and looked over the top of it at Walter's haggard face. "Walter, how good to see you. I didn't expect you here this morning." Fred then took a better look at Walter and frowned. "My word, you look awful. You feeling all right? You got the bug? I hear it's going around."

Walter shook his head back and forth, the gesture causing him pain in his neck. "No I don't have the bug. I just haven't been sleeping well these past few nights."

Fred put the paper down, now fully engaged. "I see. Do you want to come in for a check-up today? Maybe we can see what's wrong with you. Check under the hood, so to speak."

Walter looked down at his hands, once again still surprised at how wrinkled and frail they looked. It seemed like it was just yesterday that his hands were like iron, strong and sure.

"I'd rather talk to you here, if it's all right," Walter said.

Fred shook his head. "No, I'm so sorry, Walter, but I can't." He checked his watch. "Actually, I have to be going in a minute or so. I have a patient coming in at eight today."

Walter's eyebrows went up. "Oh, really, since when do you see someone before nine?"

Fred chuckled. "I do when it's my wife. She needs me to go over some travel packages for our trip to Italy next month for our fortieth anniversary. She's getting them this morning from the travel agency and she's so excited that she can't wait for me to get home. So I told her to meet me at the office."

Walter only nodded. "I see, well, congratulations on your trip."

Fred only smiled in reply. "Look, if you still want me to check you out, why don't you come in around one o' clock? I'll fit you in during my lunch hour. Shouldn't take longer than fifteen or twenty minutes."

Walter sighed, realizing Fred was offering him a favor. He nodded and said, "Okay, fine, at one. I'll be there."

Fred stood up and slid the paper on the table toward Walter. "Good, I'll see you at one. Here, take this and read it, will you? Relax a little bit, you look like you need to. And we'll see what's wrong with you later, all right?"

Walter only nodded, Fred patted his shoulder, and with a wave, was out the door of the donut shop and walking to his car.

Walter watched Fred leave, gazing through the glass wall of the donut shop to the street. He sat for a full two minutes, watching people walk by on their way to work before he stood up. He had better things to do today than sit in a donut shop sipping coffee and reading the paper. He had a little less than six hours before he would meet with Fred for his appointment, so he decided to try to put the previous night out of his head and focus on the here and now.

He had a few things he could do around the house to pass the time and there was always a walk around the block. And if there was still time, he might try to sneak in a nap.

Stepping out of the donut shop, the bright sun filling the morning sky with hope and beauty, he began the trek back to his house.

*   *   *

Walter sat in the exam room, wearing nothing but a paper gown, while he waited anxiously for Dr. Fred Prescott to return.

It was well past four and Fred had sent him to the nearby hospital where they had poked and prodded him until he felt like a test patient in some bizarre lab experiment. So much for fifteen to twenty minutes and he was done.

Now he was waiting for the test results, which the doctor had rushed, thanks to his connections with some of the staff on duty today at the hospital.

Walter sat quietly, swinging his wrinkled legs as they hung off the table. The wax paper lining the table was sticking to his butt cheeks, and despite the wool socks on his feet, they were growing cold, another present from the old age fairy.

When he told Fred about the ringing in his ears, the man had frowned in curiosity. Fred had done a fair share of poking and prodding Walter himself, trying to find the reason for the odd occurrence, before sending him off to the hospital for tests.

Walter thought back to the only standout part of the exam. It was after Fred had checked his ears, blood pressure and the like. As they talked quietly, Walter trying to fill him in on everything he could think of, Fred had slid on a white latex glove.

Walter stared at the glove for a heartbeat before he pointed to it and asked, "And just what do you think you're going to do with that?"

Fred looked perplexed. "Why, I'm going to check your prostate."

Walter shook his head back and forth vehemently. "Oh, no, you're not." He slapped his forehead with his left hand, signifying his head. "I told you the ringing is in my head, not my ass. Besides, I was just in here two months ago and you checked my prostate then. Thank you, but having you stick your finger in my ass once a year is more than enough for me."

Fred frowned slightly, but when he saw the look of determination on Walter's face, he gave in. "All right, fine. You're probably right. I'm just trying to be thorough."

"Well, fine, let's just say we did that test and leave it at that."

Fred agreed and had then handed him the forms for blood work at the hospital, then he sent Walter on his way.

Now Walter was back, and for the life of him, he didn't understand why he had to take his clothes off again and put on another ridiculous paper gown.

The door opened and Fred Prescott walked in. He saw Walter in the gown and gestured to his clothes. "Oh, sorry about that, Walter. My nurse didn't realize why you were here. You can get dressed if you want."

Walter slid off the table, his ass cheeks pulling the wax paper along with him. In frustration, he pulled it away from him, wrinkled it up, and tossed it into the corner angrily.

Fred watched it all impassively at first and then Walter realized the man was staring, so he calmed down.

"Sorry, Fred, it's just that I've been waiting here for what seems like forever and you don't know the things going through my mind."

Sitting down in the only chair in the room, Fred nodded. "It's quite all right, Walter, really. I have your test results right here."

Walter began dressing while Fred worked his way through the sheaf of paper, reading the results to himself.

"Well, and?" Walter asked as he slid his right leg into his pants, his knee joint protesting the action.

"Well, at first I thought it might be tinnitus, but there doesn't seem to be any sign of a middle-ear infection. And you said you're not suffering from symptoms such as a fever or an earache or an unusual amount of pressure in your ears, correct?"

Walter nodded.

"And you said you don't hear the ringing all the time?"

Walter nodded again, now a look of concern crossing his face. He didn't like where the questions were going.

"Hmm, then it's not tinnitus. If it was, the ringing would be constant. And you just said that isn't the case."

"That's right. It only seems to happen at night when I'm asleep. It keeps waking me up and it only happens around three or four in the morning."

"Well, according to these results everything else is fine. There are no fractures or signs of a concussion. There doesn't seem to be anything wrong with your spine. No tumors or any other foreign bodies."

"Other foreign bodies? Like what?" Walter asked.

"Hmm, let me see," Fred said, thinking on it while tapping his lips with his pen. "I'll give you an example. There was this fella last year that came in to see me. He had a bullet lodged in his skull. Evidently, some idiot shot his gun into the air like those rednecks do when they're celebrating something. Well, what goes up must come down and this poor guy was sleeping in his hammock in his yard when the bullet entered the top of his head just a little above the ear. At the time, the guy thought he had gotten hit with a stick or a rock or something. There was a miniscule amount of blood and just a small entry wound no larger than the tip of a pencil. Well, after that he started to get headaches, and when they did an MRI, do you know what they found?"

"The bullet," Walter replied flatly.

Fred nodded. "Yup. Went in just enough to give the guy headaches, but that's all. "They operated and took it out and the guy's fine to this day."

"Huh, imagine that. Okay, what else could it be if it's not a bullet or a foreign object?"

"Well, let's see. Your cholesterol is a little high and I don't like the look of your sodium count, not to mention your heart sounds a little rough, it's possible you may have a heart murmur. We'll have to do some more tests on that, but you are in your eighties, after all. Other than that, you appear to be in fairly good health."

"Then what the hell am I supposed to do? Am I going crazy?"

Fred moved closer to his friend and patted him on the shoulder. "No, of course not. I'm sure there's a rational enough reason for this to be happening. We just need to find out what it is."

Fred began thinking, chewing his lip idly, and then his eyes lit up with an idea.

"Listen, don't tell anybody I told you to do this, but why don't you try going to a chiropractor? I knew someone who thought they were suffering from tinnitus, and after they had their neck adjusted, the ringing went away."

Walter pondered the suggestion and then shrugged. "Okay, fine, if I don't get a good night's sleep tonight, that's what I'll do tomorrow." He moved a little closer to Fred. "So, do you have anyone you can recommend?"

Fred frowned, but stood up and walked to the door. "I'll have to check my referral book, I'll be right back."

Walter waved him away and finished dressing.

Maybe he would be fine tonight. Maybe there would be no ringing.

He would just have to wait and see.

* * *

It was exactly three-thirty in the morning when he was pulled from his slumber.

The ringing was back, filling his head like a parade of bells.

He lay in the lonely bed, staring up at the darkened ceiling. His hands were at his sides, both balled into fists of rage. Though the arthritis in his knuckles screamed at him, he ignored it, the rage he felt more than enough to override the pain.

On a whim, he sat up, reached over, and picked up the telephone receiver.

"Hello, is anyone there?"

But of course there was nothing but a dial tone.

"Goddammit," he screamed into his pillow. "Tomorrow, bright and early, I'm going to the chiropractor!"

He lay back down and stared at the ceiling in frustrated agony as the ringing of a mystical telephone continued in his head all through the rest of the night.

* * *

He arrived at the chiropractor at two-thirty in the afternoon, after calling that morning for an appointment.

Dr. Valmont had been able to squeeze him in after someone had called in a cancellation at the last minute. The doctor had especially wanted to help him after Walter shared his difficulty with him.

It didn't hurt that Walter's insurance would cover the entire visit with no questions asked.

Walter sat in the waiting room, waiting to be called in to see the doctor. As he waited, his eyes kept wandering to the secretary seated at her desk, typing away. She was a pretty thing in her twenties, with flowing blonde hair and a bosom that would stop traffic. Every now and then she would look up and see him watching her. She would smile at him and then go back to her typing.

He chuckled softly at that. Though in his eighties, Walter still couldn't help but admire the young ladies. He found it odd that no matter how old he became, he was still attracted to the same women and age group as when he was in his twenties.

Though sex was a thing of the past, he still couldn't help but admire the curves of a woman or the way her buttocks swayed when she walked. Not that he would have ever contemplated cheating on his late wife. No, he had loved her far too much. But what was wrong with admiring other women for their beauty?

Even if the pretty secretary had somehow been attracted to him and not thought of him as a dirty old man for admiring her in a sexual way, he would have posed her no harm.

The only way he was going to get his penis hard was with a bottle of Viagra, and if he did that, he would probably end up killing himself from a heart attack.

No, his sexual days were most definitely over, but still, the way she moved in her small dress couldn't help but make his stomach flutter like he was a teenager.

Finally, the doctor called him, opening the door that led deeper into the building, smiling at his secretary as he waited for Walter to cross the waiting room.

From the smile Dr. Valmont flashed his secretary, he couldn't help but wonder if the doctor was banging her on the side. That would surely explain why he had such a pretty young thing for a secretary. But then again, maybe she was just an excellent receptionist.

Walter and the doctor chatted lightly while they walked down the small hallway with doors lining each side. Once he was escorted into one of the rooms, he was told to take off his shirt and lie face down on the table centered in the middle of the room. There was a padded opening for his face so he wouldn't suffocate as the doctor worked on him.

When he was good and comfortable, Dr. Valmont began working, poking, prodding and rubbing.

"So you say you have a ringing in your ears?" the doctor asked as he pulled back on Walter's arm.

Wincing slightly in pain, Walter nodded an affirmative, and then realizing the futility of the gesture, he grunted a yes.

"I see, well it does seem your spine is a little off alignment, let me see if I can realign it for you, hmm?"

Dr. Valmont placed one hand on Walter's neck, another on his shoulder, and began pushing. Walter grunted on the table and finally could stand the discomfort no more.

"Enough, Doctor, I'm, not a goddamn chicken wing. What the hell are you trying to do, make a wish?"

Dr. Valmont backed off and Walter rolled off the table, standing up now, bare-chested in the cold room.

"I'm very sorry, Mr. Whitaker, but I'm only doing what I have to if you want me to realign your spine."

Walter leaned over, picked up his shirt, and began dressing. "Look, I think this was a bad idea. Forget it. My damn spine is fine."

"But, Mr. Whitaker, I'm sure I can help you," Dr. Valmont pleaded.

"Bah, whatever is happening to me, it's in my head, not my spine. I'll thank you to leave me be." Finished dressing, and with his coat and cane in hand, he opened the door to leave.

"Look, thanks for trying, Doctor, but I'm an old man. I'm truly afraid you'll snap me like a dry piece of toast. Thank you anyway." With a curt smile, he began walking to the exit.

Dr. Valmont followed. "I'm truly sorry I couldn't be of more help, Mr. Whitaker, but I have to tell you there will still be a bill for today's session."

Walter waved to the man. "Fine, just send me the difference from whatever the insurance doesn't pay for. Good day." He smiled briefly to the secretary as he exited the office.

Oh well, at least he gave it a try, he thought. And who knows, maybe the poking and prodding the doctor had done to him had already done the job and finally silenced the infernal ringing.

He guessed he would just have to wait for tonight to find out.

* * *

When Walter went to bed that night, he found he couldn't sleep. He didn't want to, he was far too restless. For the past few days, every time he closed his eyes, he found himself being thrown awake again by the constant ringing.

As he lay alone in his bed, he wondered if the ringing would come tonight. Though he prayed it didn't, there was another part of him that almost hoped it did. In the past year, his life had been without meaning. Since the loss of his wife, Evelyn, everything had seemed so washed out to him.

Food had become tasteless and the sky seemed a little more faded than it used to look. The truth was that he was wondering if he really wanted to continue going on anymore.

But he would never kill himself, oh no, that would be ridiculous, he would just have to wait for nature to take its course and finish him off the old fashioned way.

The only thing was, with his luck, he would end up living until he was ninety.

A truck rumbled by outside on the street and he was pulled from his reverie. The ceiling hovered over him, and he gazed up at it for the hundred-thousandth time since he had moved into this house all those years ago.

He knew every crack and crevice, every nuance of the ceiling. He had repainted it many years ago and now, as he studied the paint job intently, he saw every brushstroke and curve he had done all those years ago. The light fixture in the middle of the ceiling had some paint on the brass base bolted to the ceiling. Evidently, he hadn't done as good a job of taping up the fixture as he thought.

He almost wanted to stand up on the bed and try to scratch the paint off the fixture with his fingernail, but knew he would probably lose his balance and kill himself in the process.

So he stared at the paint on the light, a memory of his sloppiness from all those years ago. The minutes ticked by, soon turning into hours, and before he knew it, the clock was changing to three a.m.

He stared at it, lying on his side, waiting for the inevitable to happen. When the clock had reached three fifty a.m., he was actually beginning to hope his ordeal was over. Perhaps whatever was happening to him had finally stopped for good. But when the clock changed to three fifty-one a.m., the first ring sounded in his head.

"Nooo!" he screamed at the top of his lungs, throwing his pillow at the clock, as if the inanimate object could somehow accept the blame for what was happening to him.

The pillow struck the top of the nightstand, the clock and phone falling to the floor in a clatter. The small lamp teetered on the edge for a moment, as if it was deciding if it should join its friends, and then it fell off the night stand to land on top of the clock and phone.

He sat up in bed, the ringing continuing in his mind, and he squeezed his hands on each side of his ears to try and stop it. Of course this did nothing but muffle the noise. On the floor, the phone, now off the hook, began beeping.

At first he thought it was in his head, but soon realized this noise was external. Reaching down with a twinge of pain in his back, he picked up the phone and placed the receiver back on its base.

There, at least one annoying noise was silenced.

With a weary sigh, he picked up the lamp and pillow, but the clock he left on the floor, and lay back down. With his eyes once again staring at the ceiling, a few frustrated tears falling down his cheeks, he lay quietly while the ringing continued.

The right corner of his lip twitched slightly, and deep in his mind, something cracked. He knew, at that precise moment, that if he couldn't stop the ringing soon, he would end up doing something drastic.

But there would be a bright side to this action. At least he would get to Heaven quicker and join his beloved Evelyn.

* * *

The next morning, Walter stumbled into the Dunkin Donuts, hoping to find Dr. Fred Prescott at his usual table as he enjoyed his morning coffee.

He was in luck and Fred was where he always was, a creature of habit if there ever was one. Walter moved up to the table and plopped down without an invitation.

Fred lowered his newspaper and his jaw dropped slightly when he saw how his old friend looked.

"My God, Walter, you look terrible," he said in mild shock.

It was true, Walter had looked better. His eyes were drawn and he had large bags below his eyes. His face seemed to sag more than usual and his hair was a mess, a tangled hive of string on his head—what was left of it, anyway.

But it was the eyes that were the worst. The eyes which were usually bright and friendly were now glossy and unfocused.

"No, shit, Fred. Is that an expert opinion? Am I going to get a bill for that diagnosis?"

Fred took his friend's roughness and lack of health into consideration, took a guess to the reason, and leaned over the table so he could speak quietly. "Is it that ringing in your head? Is it still happening?"

Walter slapped his right hand on the table, causing Fred's coffee cup to jump a half inch, but not spilling. With all the sleep he had lost in the past few days, he was becoming irritable and grouchy. The classic stereotype of the crotchety old man.

"Of course it's that damn ringing. I tell you, Fred, if it doesn't stop, I'm going to have to do something crazy. I can't take it anymore. It's driving me mad!" His voice went up in pitch, causing some of the other patrons in the donut shop to glance at him curiously. Fred merely nodded at them with a polite smile and the patrons decided it was nothing.

Fred reached out a hand and placed it on Walter's right wrist. "Look, old friend, there has to be something we can do about this." His forehead creased as he thought about the situation. "Okay, tell you what. We've been looking at this like it's a medical problem, right?"

Walter only grunted.

"Okay then, what about if we look at it like it's psychological. Maybe it has to do with stress or something in that category."

"I'm not crazy, Fred, and I'm not going to see a damn headshrinker, if that's what you're suggesting."

Fred waved his hand in the air, dismissing the idea before it could take root in Walter's mind. "No, of course not, that's not what I meant. Now, please, tell me exactly how the ringing sounds. Is it like a church bell or maybe a car horn?"

Walter shook his head. "No dammit, I told you before that it's exactly like a telephone. Exactly."

Fred creased his lips as he concentrated on the idea of the ringing.

"A telephone you say. Okay, then I have only one piece of advice to give you," he said as he leaned back in the booth, his face looking like a man who had solved a great mystery.

Walter stared at Fred, his face contorted with aggravation. "Yes, well, out with it then, what's your advice?"

Fred said each word carefully, almost as if he didn't believe his own advice. "Well, if it truly is a telephone ringing in you head, perhaps it's your subconscious or something trying to contact you in some bizarre way. If there truly is something trying to get in touch with you, then did you ever think to just answer it?"

* * *

For the rest of the day, Walter walked around in a daze. He couldn't stop thinking about Fred's suggestion.

Just answer it.

If it was the ringing of a telephone inside his mind, then could he just answer it and find out if there was actually anything on the other end of the mystical line?

But what if there wasn't? What if there was no caller in his head and the ringing just went on and on and on until he finally went mad. Questions such as these filled his mind the entire day, but eventually the day ended and night fell across the land.

A little past eight p.m., he proceeded to get ready for bed. Though anxious about what might come later that night, he also felt a sense of calm as if he was finally in control of the situation.

Crawling into bed, he reached over to Evelyn's side of the bed, wishing for the millionth time that she was still with him. As he laid his head down on his pillow, he let out a long, weary sigh.

God he was so tired.

He closed his eyes.

Sleep wouldn't come at first. It was like a stray piece of paper blowing in the midst of a heavy wind, always out of reach, yet always in sight. But as he slowed his breathing and relaxed a little more each hour, eventually he fell into a restless slumber.

Dreams of his wife filled his mind; times when they had been young and so very happy.

Just as the dreams were getting good, a ringing fractured the tableaux of happiness and he found himself falling back to reality. Opening his eyes in the darkness, he saw nothing unusual, but the ringing had most definitely returned.

It was like an old friend visiting after months away, Walter thought and smiled.

Thinking back to what Fred Prescott had said, he decided to give it a try. He visualized a phone sitting on a table. The phone was ringing, the same chiming filling his mind now. He pictured himself walking over to the phone, and ever so carefully, picking up the receiver. When he did this, the ringing stopped, and silence descended once more.

In the real world, his body lay stretched out on the bed, perfectly still, his chest rising and falling in cadence to his steady breathing. Deep inside his mind, he placed the receiver to his ear, and with a dry mouth, he swallowed slightly, cleared his throat, and asked, "Uhm, hello? Is anyone there?"

There were a few clicks and beeps on the other end that lasted two heartbeats, but then a woman's voice came on the line. Her voice was nasally, reminding him of operators from the 1950's

"Ah yes, finally. Is this Mr. Walter Whitaker?" the voice asked in a formal voice. There was no inflection in the voice, only a business attitude. Walter swallowed again, his throat moving with the motion, and he nodded his head. Then, realizing he was talking on a phone, he said, "Uhm, yes. Yes, this is Walter Whitaker. Can I ask who you are?"

"That is unimportant, Mr. Whitaker. All you need to know is we have been trying to get in touch with you for almost a week. You've been causing quite a problem in scheduling in your refusal to answer the line."

Not knowing how to react, Walter fell back on his manners. "Uhm, I'm sorry? I didn't know what the ringing was."

"Irregardless, Mr. Whitaker, at least you've finally answered. Now, I have a person to person call for you, do you accept the call?"

Though not quite understanding why, Walter knew he wanted to accept this phone call. In fact, he knew he had wanted to receive this call for almost a year, but had no way of understanding when it would come or how it would finally show itself.

In his mind, he nodded and said, "Yes, operator, yes, I'll accept the call."

"Excellent, Mr. Whitaker, excellent, and before I transfer you, I have a message for you. Your wife told me to tell you that she's waiting for you and she'll see you soon."

With his real body still lying on the bed, tears of sadness mixed with joy seeped out of his closed eyes, and deep inside his mind, Walter smiled. "Thank you for that operator, thank you."

"You're welcome, Mr. Whitaker. Now please hold, I'm transferring the call now."

Walter stood by the phone in his mind, patiently waiting for the call to be transferred.

Three heartbeats later, and there was another click, followed by the sound of someone breathing softly. "Hello, Walter, it's good to finally talk to you," a deep voice said, the voice filled with sympathy and love. "I've been trying to contact you for quite a while now."

Walter grinned happily in his mind. "I know that now, I'm sorry, I didn't understand. I've wanted to talk with you, too."

Lying on the bed, Walter's lips creased into a slight smile and his breathing began to slow, his chest rising and falling with less speed.

In the darkness, his chest rose one final time, and was still.

The ringing would not be back again. It was finally silenced, for the call had been answered.

Now and forever.

DEAD RAGE
by Anthony Giangregorio
Book 2 in the Rage virus series!

An unknown virus spreads across the globe, turning ordinary people into bloodthirsty, ravenous killers.

Only a small percentage of the population is immune and soon become prey to the infected.

Amongst the infected comes a man, stricken by the virus, yet still retaining his grasp on reality. His need to destroy the *normals* becomes an obsession and he raises an army of killers to seek out and kill all who aren't *changed* like himself. A few survivors gather together on the outskirts of Chicago and find themselves running for their lives as the specter of death looms over all.

The Dead Rage virus will find you, no matter where you hide.

CHRISTMAS IS DEAD: A ZOMBIE ANTHOLOGY
Edited by Anthony Giangregorio

Twas the night before Christmas and all through the house, not a creature was stirring, not even a. . . zombie?

That's right; this anthology explores what would happen at Christmas time if there was a full blown zombie outbreak. Reanimated turkeys, zombie Santas, and demon reindeers that turn people into flesh-eating ghouls are just some of the tales you will find in this merry undead book. So curl up under the Christmas tree with a cup of hot chocolate, and as the fireplace crackles with warmth, get ready to have your heart filled with holiday cheer. But of course, then it will be ripped from your heaving chest and fed upon by blood-thirsty elves with a craving for human flesh! For you see, Christmas is Dead!

And you will never look at the holiday season the same way again.

BLOOD RAGE
(The Prequel to DEAD RAGE)
by Anthony Giangregorio

The madness descended before anyone knew what was happening. Perfectly normal people suddenly became rage-fueled killers, tearing and slicing their way across the city. Within hours, Chicago was a battlefield, the dead strewn in the streets like trash.

Stacy, Chad and a few others are just a few of the immune, unaffected by the virus but not to the violence surrounding them. The *changed* are ravenous, sweeping across Chicago and perhaps the world, destroying any *normals* they come across. Fire, slaughter, and blood rule the land, and the few survivors are now an endangered species.

This is the story of the first days of the Dead Rage virus and the brave souls who struggle to live just one more day.

When the smoke clears, and the *changed* have maimed and killed all who stand in their way, only the strong will remain.

The rest will be left to rot in the sun.

THE BOOK OF CANNIBALS
Edited by Anthony Giangregorio

Human meat . . . the ultimate taboo.

Deep down, in the dark recesses of your mind, can you honestly say you never wondered how it might taste?

Honestly, never wondered if a chunk of thigh tasted like chicken or pork?

Or if a hunk of an arm was similar to steak? And what kind of wine would be served with it, red or white?

Would a human liver be no different than one from a cow, or a pig?

For all we know, human flesh is as tender as veal, better than the finest tenderloin. And that is what the stories in this book are about, eating each other. But be warned, after reading these tales of mastication, you may just become a vegetarian, or at the very least, think twice before taking your first bite of that juicy steak at your local restaurant.

DEADFREEZE
by Anthony Giangregorio
THIS IS WHAT HELL WOULD BE LIKE IF IT FROZE OVER!

When an experimental serum for hypothermia goes horribly wrong, a small research station in the middle of Antarctica becomes overrun with an army of the frozen dead.

Now a small group of survivors must battle the arctic weather and a horde of frozen zombies as they make their way across the frozen plains of Antarctica to a neighboring research station.

What they don't realize is that they are being hunted by an entity whose sole reason for existing is vengeance; and it will find them wherever they run.

VISIONS OF THE DEAD
A ZOMBIE STORY
by Anthony & Joseph Giangregorio

Jake Roberts felt like he was the luckiest man alive.

He had a great family, a beautiful girlfriend, who was soon to be his wife, and a job, that might not have been the best, but it paid the bills.

At least until the dead began to walk.

Now Jake is fighting to survive in a dead world while searching for his lost love, Melissa, knowing she's out there somewhere.

But the past isn't dead, and as he struggles for an uncertain future, the past threatens to consume him. With the present a constant battle between the living and the dead, Jake finds himself slipping in and out of the past, the visions of how it all happened haunting him. But Jake knows Melissa is out there somewhere and he'll find her or die trying.

In a world of the living dead, you can never escape your past.

DEAD MOURNING: A ZOMBIE HORROR STORY
by Anthony Giangregorio

Carl Jenkins was having a run of bad luck. Fresh out of jail, his probation tenuous, he'd lost every job he'd taken since being released. So now was his last chance, only one more job to prevent him from going back to prison. Assigned to work in a funeral home, he accidentally loses a shipment of embalming fluid. With nothing to lose, he substitutes it with a batch of chemicals from a nearby factory.

The results don't go as planned, though. While his screw-up goes unnoticed, his machinations revive the cadavers in the funeral home, unleashing an evil on the world that it has not seen before. Not wanting to become a snack for the rampaging dead, he flees the city, joining up with other survivors. An old, dilapidated zoo becomes their haven, while the dead wait outside the walls, hungry and patient.

But Carl is optimistic, after all, he's still alive, right? Perhaps his luck has changed and help will arrive to save them all?

Unfortunately, unknown to him and the other survivors, a serial killer has fallen into their group, trapped inside the zoo with them.

With the undead army clamoring outside the walls and a murderer within, it'll be a miracle if any of them live to see the next sunrise.

On second thought, maybe Carl would've been better off if he'd just gone back to jail.

ROAD KILL: A ZOMBIE TALE
by Anthony Giangregorio
ORDER UP!

In the summer of 2008, a rogue comet entered earth's orbit for 72 hours. During this time, a strange amber glow suffused the sky.

But something else happened; something in the comet's tail had an adverse affect on dead tissue and the result was the reanimation of every dead animal carcass on the planet.

A handful of survivors hole up in a diner in the backwoods of New Hampshire while the undead creatures of the night hunt for human prey.

There's a new blue plate special at DJ's Diner and Truck Stop, and it's you!

DEAD THINGS
by Anthony Giangregorio

Beneath the veil of reality we all know as truth, there is another world, one where creatures only seen in nightmares exist.

But what if these creatures do actually exist, and it is us that are only fleeting images, mere visions conjured up by some unknown being.

Werewolves, zombies, vampires, and other lost things that go bump in the night, inhabit the world of imagination and myth, but all will be found in this collection of tales.   But in this world, fiction becomes fact, and what lurks in the shadows is real. Beware the next time you sense you are being watched or catch movement in the corner of your eye, for though it may be nothing, it might just be your doom.

INCLUDES THE EXCLUSIVE DEADWATER STORY: DEAD GRAVE

THE DARK
by Anthony Giangregorio
DARKNESS FALLS

The darkness came without warning.

First New York, then the rest of United States, and then the world became enveloped in a perpetual night without end.

With no sunlight, eventually the planet will wither and die, bringing on a new Ice Age. But that isn't problem for the human race, for humanity will be dead long before that happens.

There is something in the dark, creatures only seen in nightmares, and they are on the prowl. Evolution has changed and man is no longer the dominant species. When we are children, we're told not to fear the dark, that what we believe to exist in the shadows is false.

Unfortunately, that is no longer true.

SOULEATER
by Anthony Giangregorio

Twenty years ago, Jason Lawson witnessed the brutal death of his father by something only seen in nightmares, something so horrible he'd blocked it from his mind.

Now twenty years later the creature is back, this time for his son.

Jason won't let that happen.

He'll travel to the demon's world, struggling every second to rescue his son from its clutches.

But what he doesn't know is that the portal will only be open for a finite time and if he doesn't return with his son before it closes, then he'll be trapped in the demon's dimension forever.

SEE HOW IT ALL BEGAN IN THE NEW DOUBLE-SIZED 460 PAGE SPECIAL EDITION!

DEADWATER: EXPANDED EDITION
by Anthony Giangregorio

Through a series of tragic mishaps, a small town's water supply is contaminated with a deadly bacterium that transforms the town's population into flesh eating ghouls.

Without warning, Henry Watson finds himself thrown into a living hell where the living dead walk and want nothing more than to feed on the living.

Now Henry's trying to escape the undead town before he becomes the next victim.

With the military on one side, shooting civilians on sight, and a horde of bloodthirsty zombies on the other, Henry must try to battle his way to freedom.

With a small group of survivors, including a beautiful secretary and a wise-cracking janitor to aid him, the ragtag group will do their best to stay alive and escape the city codenamed: **Deadwater**.

DEAD END: A ZOMBIE NOVEL
by Anthony Giangregorio
THE DEAD WALK!

Newspapers everywhere proclaim the dead have returned to feast on the living!

A small group of survivors hole up in a cellar, afraid to brave the masses of animated corpses, but when food runs out, they have no choice but to venture out into a world gone mad.

What they will discover, however, is that the fall of civilization has brought out the worst in their fellow man.

Cannibals, psychotic preachers and rapists are just some of the atrocities they must face.

In a world turned upside down, it is life that has hit a Dead End.

BOOK OF THE DEAD 2: NOT DEAD YET
A ZOMBIE ANTHOLOGY
Edited by Anthony Giangregorio

Out of the ashes of death and decay, comes the second volume filled with the walking dead.

In this tomb, there are only slow, shambling monstrosities that were once human.

No one knows why the dead walk; only that they do, and that they are hungry for human flesh.

But these aren't your neighbors, your co-workers, or your family.
Now they are the living dead, and they will tear your throat out at a moment's notice.

So be warned as you delve into the pages of this book; the dead will find you, no matter where you hide.

ANOTHER EXCITING ADVENTURE IN THE DEADWATER SERIES!
DEAD SALVATION
BOOK 9
by Anthony Giangregorio
HANGMAN'S NOOSE!

After one of the group is hurt, the need for transportation is solved by a roving cannie convoy. Attacking the camp, the companions save a man who invites them back to his home.

Cement City it's called and at first the group is welcomed with thanks for saving one of their own. But when a bar fight goes wrong, the companions find themselves awaiting the hangman's noose.

Their only salvation is a suicide mission into a raider camp to save captured townspeople.

Though the odds are long, it's a chance, and Henry knows in the land of the walking dead, sometimes a chance is all you can hope for.

In the world of the dead, life is a struggle, where the only victor is death.

INSIDE THE PERIMETER: SCAVENGERS OF THE DEAD
by Alan Spencer

In the middle of nowhere, the vestiges of an abandoned town are surrounded by inescapably high concrete barriers, permitting no trespass or escape. The town is dormant of human life, but rampant with the living dead, who choose not to eat flesh, but to instead continue their survival by cruder means.

Boyd Broman, a detective arrested and falsely imprisoned, has been transferred into the secret town. He is given an ultimatum: recapture Hayden Grubaugh, the cannibal serial killer, who has been banished to the town, in exchange for his freedom.

During Boyd's search, he discovers why the psychotic cannibal must really be captured and the sinister secrets the dead town holds.

With no chance of escape, Broman finds himself trapped among the ravenous, violent dead.

With the cannibal feeding on the animated cadavers and the undead searching for Boyd, he must fulfill his end of the deal before the rotting corpses turn him into an unwilling organ donor.

But Boyd wasn't told that no one gets out alive, that the town is a death sentence.

For there is no escape from *Inside the Perimeter*.

DEADFALL
by Anthony Giangregorio

It's Halloween in the small suburban town of Wakefield, Mass.

While parents take their children trick or treating and others throw costume parties, a swarm of meteorites enter the earth's atmosphere and crash to earth.

Inside are small parasitic worms, no larger than maggots.

The worms quickly infect the corpses at a local cemetery and so begins the rise of the undead.

The walking dead soon get the upper hand, with no one believing the truth. That the dead now walk.

Will a small group of survivors live through the zombie apocalypse?

Or will they, too, succumb to the Deadfall.

LOVE IS DEAD: A ZOMBIE ANTHOLOGY
Edited by Anthony Giangregorio

THE DEATH OF LOVE

Valentine's Day is a day when young love is fulfilled.

Where hopeful young men bring candy and flowers to their sweethearts, in hopes of a kiss...or perhaps more. But not in this anthology.

For you see, LOVE IS DEAD, and in this tome, the dead walk, wanting to feed on those same hearts that once pumped in chests, bursting with love.

So toss aside that heart-shaped box of candy and throw away those red roses, you won't need them any longer. Instead, strap on a handgun, or pick up a shotgun and defend yourself from the ravenous undead.

Because in a world where the dead walk, even love isn't safe.

ETERNAL NIGHT: A VAMPIRE ANTHOLOGY

Edited by Anthony Giangregorio

Blood, fangs, darkness and terror...these are the calling cards of the vampire mythos.

Inside this tome are stories that embrace vampire history but seek to introduce a new literary spin on this longstanding fictional monster. Follow a dark journey through cigarette-smoking creatures hunted by rogue angels, vampires that feed off of thoughts instead of blood, immortals presenting the fantastic in a local rock band, to a legendary monster on the far reaches of town.

Forget what you know about vampires; this anthology will destroy historical mythos and embrace incredible new twists on this celebrated, fictional character.

Welcome to a world of the undead, welcome to the world of Eternal Night.

BOOK OF THE DEAD
A ZOMBIE ANTHOLOGY VOL 1
ISBN 978-1-935458-25-8

Edited by Anthony Giangregorio

This is the most faithful, truest zombie anthology ever written, and we invite you along for the ride. Every single story in this book is filled with slack-jawed, eyes glazed, slow moving, shambling zombies set in a world where the dead have risen and only want to eat the flesh of the living. In these pages, the rules are sacrosanct. There is no deviation from what a zombie should be or how they came about. The Dead Walk.

There is no reason, though rumors and suppositions fill the radio and television stations. But the only thing that is fact is that the walking dead are here and they will not go away. So prepare yourself for the ultimate homage to the master of zombie legend. And remember... Aim for the head!

REVOLUTION OF THE DEAD
by Anthony Giangregorio
THE DEAD SHALL RISE AGAIN!

Five years ago, a deadly plague wiped out 97% of the world's population, America suffering tragically. Bodies were everywhere, far too many to bury or burn. But then, through a miracle of medical science, a way is found to reanimate the dead.

With the manpower of the United States depleted, and the remaining survivors not wanting to give up their internet and fast food restaurants, the undead are conscripted as slave labor.

Now they cut the grass, pick up the trash, and walk the dogs of the surviving humans.

But whether alive or dead, no race wants to be controlled, and sooner or later the dead will fight back, wanting the freedom they enjoyed in life.

The revolution has begun!

And when it's over, the dead will rule the land, and the remaining humans will become the slaves...or worse.

KINGDOM OF THE DEAD
by Anthony Giangregorio
THE DEAD HAVE RISEN!

In the dead city of Pittsburgh, two small enclaves struggle to survive, eking out an existence of hand to mouth.

But instead of working together, both groups battle for the last remaining fuel and supplies of a city filled with the living dead.

Six months after the initial outbreak, a lone helicopter arrives bearing two more survivors and a newborn baby. One enclave welcomes them, while the other schemes to steal their helicopter and escape the decaying city.

With no police, fire, or social services existing, the two will battle for dominance in the steel city of the walking dead. But when the dust settles, the question is: will the remaining humans be the winners, or the losers?

When the dead walk, the line between Heaven and Hell is so twisted and bent there is no line at all.

RISE OF THE DEAD
by Anthony Giangregorio
DEATH IS ONLY THE BEGINNING!

In less than forty-eight hours, more than half the globe was infected.

In another forty-eight, the rest would be enveloped.

The reason?

A science experiment gone horribly wrong which enabled the dead to walk, their flesh rotting on their bones even as they seek human prey.

Jeremy was an ordinary nineteen year old slacker. He partied too much and had done poorly in high school. After a night of drinking and drugs, he awoke to find the world a very different place from the one he'd left the night before.

The dead were walking and feeding on the living, and as Jeremy stepped out into a world gone mad, the dead spotting him alone and unarmed in the middle of the street, he had to wonder if he would live long enough to see his twentieth birthday.

THE CHRONICLES OF JACK PRIMUS
BOOK ONE
by Michael D. Griffiths

Beneath the world of normalcy we all live in lies another world, one where supernatural beings exist.

These creatures of the night hunt us; want to feed on our very souls, though only a few know of their existence.

One such man is Jack Primus, who accidentally pierces the veil between this world and the next. With no other choice if he wants to live, he finds himself on the run, hunted by beings called the Xemmoni, an ancient race that sees humans as nothing but cattle.   They want his soul, to feed on his very essence, and they will kill all who stand in their way.   But if they thought Jack would just lie down and accept his fate, they were sorely mistaken.

He didn't ask for this battle, but he knew he would fight them with everything at his disposal, for to lose is a fate worse than death.

He would win this war, and he would take down anyone who got in his way.

THE WAR AGAINST THEM: A ZOMBIE NOVEL
by Jose Alfredo Vazquez

Mankind wasn't prepared for the onslaught.

An ancient organism is reanimating the dead bodies of its victims, creating worldwide chaos and panic as the disease spreads to every corner of the globe. As governments struggle to contain the disease, courageous individuals across the planet learn what it truly means to make choices as they struggle to survive.

Geopolitics meet technology in a race to save mankind from the worst threat it has ever faced. Doctors, military and soldiers from all walks of life battle to find a cure. For the dead walk, and if not stopped, they will wipe out all life on Earth. Humanity is fighting a war they cannot win, for who can overcome Death itself? Man versus the walking dead with the winner ruling the planet. Welcome to *The War Against Them*.

DEADTOWN: A DEADWATER STORY
B OOK 8
by Anthony Giangregorio

The world is a very different place now. The dead walk the land and humans hide in small towns with walls of stone and debris for protection, constantly keeping the living dead at bay.

Social law is gone and right and wrong is defined by the size of your gun.

UNWELCOME VISITORS

Henry Watson and his band of warrior survivalists become guests in a fortified town in Michigan. But when the kidnapping of one of the companions goes bad and men die, the group finds themselves on the wrong side of the law, and a town out for blood.

Trapped in a hotel, surrounded on all sides, it will be up to Henry to save the day with a gamble that may not only take his life, but that of his friends as well.

In a dead world, when justice is not enough, there is always vengeance.

END OF DAYS: AN APOCALYPTIC ANTHOLOGY
VOLUMES 1 & 2
Edited by Anthony Giangregorio

Our world is a fragile place.

Meteors, famine, floods, nuclear war, solar flares, and hundreds of other calamities can plunge our small blue planet into turmoil in an instant.

What would you do if tomorrow the sun went super nova or the world was swallowed by water, submerging the world into the cold darkness of the ocean? This anthology explores some of those scenarios and plunges you into total annihilation.

But remember, it's only a book, and tomorrow will come as it always does. Or will it?

Eternal Night

A Vampire Anthology

Edited By

Anthony Giangregorio

THE BOOK OF CANNIBALS

ISBN 13: 978-1-935458-52-4   ISBN 10: 1-935458-52-3

ARE YOU HUNGRY YET?

Blood of the Dead
A.P. Fuchs

Bits of the Dead
edited by
Keith Gouveia

Axiom-man
The Dead Land
A.P. Fuchs

$15.99
(Trade Paperback)
ISBN: 9780984261017

$15.99
(Trade Paperback)
ISBN: 9780984261024

$15.99
(Trade Paperback)
ISBN: 9780984261055
(Also Available in Hardcover)

Visit www.pillhillpress.com
For the best in speculative fiction!

www.ingramcontent.com/pod-product-compliance
Lightning Source LLC
Chambersburg PA
CBHW070633170726
48291CB00003B/994